Fight Or Flight

A MAPLETON NOVEL

DIANA DEEHAN

For Will—

the Johnny to my Moira,
the Roland to my Jocelyn,
the Patrick to my David.

I love you.

CHAPTER BY CHAPTER SOUNDTRACK

1. Hot Child In The City • Nick Gilder

2. She Ain't Pretty • The Northern Pikes

3. The Weight • The Band

4. Something Big • Shawn Mendes

5. Steal My Sunshine • LEN

6. Heart Of Gold • Neil Young

7. Here Among The Cats • Max Webster, Kim Mitchell

8. It's A Beautiful Day • Michael Bublé

9. 1234 • Feist

ONE

Natalie Alvarez sprinted down the busy London sidewalk through opaque sheets of cold rain, dragging her suitcase through the puddles behind her. It was only three blocks from where the coach bus had parked to the tour office where she worked, but in a thin blue dress and slippery gold sandals, she might as well have had to run to Singapore.

She cursed Jess, her boss, yet again, for asking her to stop by the office after her tour. She'd spent the last thirty-six days on her nineteenth once-in-a-lifetime trip around Europe and wanted nothing more than to check her bone-tired body into a hostel and sleep for the next five days before embarking on number twenty.

She only stopped once along the way to hand a five-pound note to a poor soul sheltered under a tattered tarp on the sidewalk, but by the time she made it to the overhang of the building and pushed her way through the door, she was freezing cold and soaked through like a sewer rat. Her long, dark brown hair had fallen over her face like a curtain, dripping from the ends and splashing onto her hot-pink toenails. She reached up and pulled it from her eyes, then came face to face with a crowd, staring at her, waiting.

"What—"

"Congratulations!" they shouted, drowning out her voice.

She stumbled back slightly and scanned the crowd, taking in the faces of roughly twenty colleagues: fellow tour guides, bus drivers she'd worked with over the years, and pressing through the bodies, Jess, who came forward holding a tea towel from the staff kitchen.

"She still hasn't bought a coat or wellies," she said with a laugh, causing a chorus of laughter to ring out behind her. Everyone she worked with knew Natalie travelled light.

None of them knew why.

Natalie took the towel and squeezed the drenched ends of her hair with it, wringing out as much rain-water as she could. "What are you all doing—"

The rest of the sentence died in her throat as Alira Keete appeared behind Jess. She stood a foot taller than most, with raven black coiled hair and tilted hazel eyes.

"Not to worry, Natalie," Alira said in a thick Australian accent with a grin tugging at her full lips. "You won't need a jacket or wellies where you're going."

Natalie gasped. "Alira, hi. I didn't know you were in London."

Natalie had only spoken to Alira twice during interviews through video chat. She wasn't prepared to see her in real life.

"I wanted to meet with you in person. I spoke with Jess about your Instagram following and your travel goals. It's quite remarkable, what you've been able to accomplish."

Alira held out her hand, and Natalie shook it, trying to grasp for words. For the past ten years, Natalie had been on a mission to visit one hundred countries and all seven continents before she turned thirty. She'd documented her journey on Instagram, which had built her a huge following. Currently, she was one country and one continent short of her goal.

Guess which one.

"Thanks."

"You must already know why we're all here."

Natalie smiled. "I hope so. You have good news for me?"

Alira nodded. "I came to offer you the tour guide position in Australia. It's an East Coast tour: twenty days, Sydney to Cairns. Six days off in between."

Natalie's jaw dropped. She had to lock her knees in place to stop herself from falling over. Everything she'd worked toward was finally happening, and a twenty-day tour with six days off was about as good as it got.

She'd set Australia as her last destination, partly because it had been her top pick when she first made her list of countries to visit, and partly because she knew it would be oh so satisfying to tick off both columns at the same time and finally say she'd accomplished it.

"Say something," Jess said, nudging her in the arm.

Natalie cleared her throat. "This is incredible. I've been applying for this position for so long now."

Alira nodded. "It's our most requested tour, but I know you will be perfect for it. Jess speaks highly of you. And truth be told, I once dreamed of travelling to a hundred countries and every continent, too. But life and family, and mostly love, got in the way. You're going to be the first person I've ever met to accomplish it."

"You still haven't said yes," Jess said out of the corner of her mouth. "You better not turn it down. I've already booked myself on your first tour."

"Yes, sorry. Of course I accept," Natalie said. "This is a dream come true."

"Excellent. Training starts in six weeks," Alira said.

"That means," Jess added, "your next Europe tour will be your last. You'll never see the world's sexiest Venetian gelato maker again."

Natalie rolled her eyes as her smile split across her face. "No problem. Arrivederci, Marco."

Jess and Alira laughed, then went to the kitchen together. They popped open a bottle of champagne and sliced into a sheet cake. Natalie spent the next half hour making her way around the room and hugging her friends before it finally started sinking in. She'd moved all over the world with this goal in mind, and now, it was finally happening.

She wanted to jump in the air, dance, and celebrate. But a teeny voice deep in the recesses of her brain asked, Then what?

She shook off the discomfort as people began saying goodbye and filing out of the office.

The last person to leave, other than Jess, was Alira. "I gotta get going. But I'll see you in Sydney."

"Thank you so much for coming," Natalie said.

Alira smiled and nodded, then left the room.

"Oh my God," Jess said as soon as the door closed behind Alira. "How cool is she?"

"Impossibly cool." Natalie walked around the room with Jess, cleaning up the plates and cups sitting on the desks. "I can't believe this is happening! It's going to be so amazing."

"I know," Jess held out the garbage bin for Natalie.

"Are you really coming on my first tour?"

"Absolutely. As soon as Alira told me the news, I booked it. I've always wanted to go. Plus . . ." She paused, looking down at her perfect white sneakers. "I'm going to miss you."

Natalie smiled and hugged her. She'd met Jess a year and a half ago, and it was impossible to avoid becoming friends with her. Of all the countries and all the people she'd met along her journey, Jess was the only person she was a little sad to say goodbye to.

"I'm going to miss you, too."

"You know," Jess said, pulling back and sliding a hand over her glossy black bob, "when I first met you, I never would have imagined we'd become friends."

Natalie threw back her head and laughed. "I know. You hated me."

"I didn't hate you. I was terrified of you."

"What?" Natalie asked. "You never told me that."

"Oh yeah. Remember Todd, the South African?"

Natalie barked out a laugh. Todd had been an arrogant recruit who Natalie lost her patience with after two disgusting minutes of being relentlessly hit on.

"He deserved that. You know how much I hate smarmy douchebags."

Jess laughed. "But did you have to call him that in front of everyone?"

Natalie shrugged. "It worked, didn't it?"

"All the guys were scared of you after that. I think I saw one or two protectively cover their balls. Maybe that's why it's been so long since you dated."

"I don't date because I'm always travelling. I'm down for one-night stands, but I can't stand slimy men. And guess what type of man is always into one-night stands?"

"A slimy slimeball?"

"Exactly."

"What about Marco?"

"Not slimy at all. He just likes casual sex. And he's very good at it."

"He won't be sad when you tell him you're moving to Australia?"

Natalie laughed and shook her head. "I probably won't even tell him. We barely speak to each other. His English and my Italian are way too spotty."

Natalie moved around the room, collecting the last pieces of garbage and throwing them into the bin. Then she gave Jess another hug.

"Thank you so much for the party and for everything with Alira."

"I only told her the truth. You're the best we have."

"I hope you find a replacement that's more patient than me."

"That won't be difficult. Not sure I'll find someone who chooses better day songs, though."

"It's a skill," Natalie said with a smile. In fact, choosing a song to play at the beginning of each day on tour was one of the best parts of her job. She would hear songs from years ago and remember travellers.

"You must be exhausted," Jess said. "Go get some rest. I'll lock up."

Natalie nodded, then walked toward the door and grabbed her still-soaked suitcase by the handle. She'd just swung open the heavy glass door when Jess's voice stopped her.

"Wait," she said. She came from around the desk, holding out a business card. "I almost forgot with the party and Alira and everything."

"What's this?" Natalie took the w hite card with bold black lettering and read it. "Private investigator?" she asked.

"Yeah, he came in here looking for a Natalie, but not your last name. He insisted I give this to you."

Natalie's heart ceased. "What . . . what last name did he ask about?"

Jess's eyebrows shot up. "Monroe. He was looking for a Natalie Monroe."

The sound of that name coming out of Jess's mouth was more shocking than if she'd come out of the tube at Piccadilly Circus and seen the Taj Mahal. She never thought she would ever hear that name again.

Ever.

"What did you tell him?"

Jess's dark eyebrows rose up past the tops of her eyeglass frames. "What the bloody hell is this all about? You're Natalie Alvarez. I've seen your passport."

"Jess," Natalie said, taking a calming breath. "What did you tell him?"

"I told him that no one by that name works here."

Natalie drew in a long breath, forced her tense shoulders to drop. "Good." She crumpled the card in her fist. "See ya."

She walked out of the door, leaving Jess speechless and gawking behind her. Jess was the closest thing she had to a friend, but she never spoke about her past, and she wasn't about to start now.

She turned right on the sidewalk toward her pre-ferred hostel two blocks away before realizing that, if this private investigator knew where she worked, maybe he'd know where she stayed when she was in town.

The thought made her skin crawl, so she doubled back past the office and jogged six blocks in the rain to a smaller hostel in a dodgy neighbourhood that she rarely stayed at. With any luck, she could sleep there for five days and be back on the coach bus before this guy ever knew he'd missed her.

· · ● ● ●● ● ●● ● · ·

The moment Natalie stepped into the hostel from the street, she knew she was in trouble. It had been almost a year since she'd been there. And the place was a ghost town.

Completely empty.

The other hostel would be packed with travellers from all over the world, shoulder to shoulder in the lobby, sitting on big cushions at low tables, drinking beer and playing board games. She could blend into the crowd there.

Here, she stuck out like a sore thumb.

She made her way to the front desk, then stood for thirty seconds, waiting for the attendant to look up. When he didn't, she rapped her knuckles hard on the counter. Finally, he pulled his attention away from his phone and coated Natalie with it. He looked her up and down. As he took in her thin, wet clothes, a gross smile came over his face.

"Hiya, need a bed?"

His tone of voice made her want to puke all over his desk and leave, but she knew how to handle men like that. A private investigator who knew her last name, and whose intentions were unknown, was much worse.

"I need four nights."

"Private?" he asked, staring at her boobs. The soaked fabric wasn't leaving much to the imagination.

"No."

He let out a huff, then turned to his screen and clicked away. A minute ticked by before he finally spoke. "We have a room ready to go. A twelve, but you'll probably have the place to yourself."

"Fine, I'll take—"

"Or . . ." He cut her off and leaned toward her over the desk, causing a waft of noxious body spray to assault her. "You can come home with me. For free."

She took a step away from him, her nose scrunching up in her face. "Ew," she said, pausing and letting that sink in. Hopefully, he'd understand where he stood with her. "No."

She pulled her credit card from her small purse and dropped it on the counter. She didn't want to risk him trying to touch her hand if she passed it to him.

"Rude," he said, picking up the card and clicking away at his keyboard. "I shouldn't be surprised, bloody American."

Natalie rolled her eyes and silently pointed out all of his rude behaviour and the fact that she wasn't American, but she didn't vocalize it. The last thing she wanted was more conversation with him.

He took his time processing the payment before finally dropping a key card and her credit card back onto the counter. She snatched it up and turned away, marching down the hall until the door to her room came into view.

Behind her, the front door of the lobby chimed, and the rushing sound of rain filled the room. She looked over her shoulder. A man in a black jacket and hat walked through the lobby to the front counter. For a split second, their eyes connected before Natalie looked away. She moved faster toward her door, but the suitcase and her slippery sandals slowed her down.

"Ms. Monroe?" he called.

She broke into a run for her door as the attendant came from behind the desk to stop the man from coming down the hall.

"Paying customers only past this point," he said.

She inserted the key, pushed into the room, and closed the door behind her. She only had a few minutes to celebrate her victory when she heard the mechanical whirl of a key card entering the lock, then watched in horror as the door swung open and the man in the black jacket and hat walked through.

"Ms. Monroe?" he asked.

"It's Alvarez," she said. "You've gone through a lot of trouble for the wrong person."

He took a few more strides to close the distance and peered into her eyes. He looked to be in his forties and in good shape. Tall and broad, with two permanent vertical lines between his eyebrows. "I'm certain I have the right person."

He reached into a cross-body bag and pulled out a photo. He held it out to Natalie. It was a photo taken many years ago. The picture showed her as a sullen seventeen-year-old, wedged between an elegant old lady and a pretty blond girl a few years younger than her.

Her brain flooded with unwanted memories.

"What do you want?"

"A Mr. Speeler hired me."

"Don't know him," she said, then turned to leave.

"He was Elizabeth Monroe's attorney."

Natalie stopped, looked up into his murky, light eyes. "Was?"

"Yes. I'm sorry to inform you that your grandmother died."

Natalie squeezed her eyes shut. Sadness and guilt churned through her gut. When she'd first heard Jess say the name Monroe, she wondered whether it was Elizabeth who was looking for her, but she knew it was best to leave her past in the past. When she'd last seen Elizabeth ten years ago, she figured that would be the last time she'd ever see her. Now she knew.

She forced a breath in, and then back out, trying to squash the rising dread. "When?"

"Three weeks ago."

She nodded. "Thank you for letting me know."

"There's more." He pulled a large white envelope out of his bag, slipped the photo inside, and handed it to her.

"What's this?"

"Instructions."

Confused, Natalie peeked inside the envelope and saw two pages. "Instructions for what?"

"Your grandmother's last wish was for you to spread her ashes. Everything is waiting for you in . . . What's the name of that town?"

Natalie could barely squeak the word out. "Mapleton."

"That's it. Everything you need to know is in there."

Natalie pulled the papers from the envelope. Along with the photo were two letters: One, a typed, step-by-step list of instructions from Mr. Speeler. The other, a handwritten letter from Elizabeth.

She shoved the papers back into the envelope. "Elizabeth had lots of family. I can't go back there."

The private investigator's eyebrows drew together in annoyance, deepening the lines. "I'm not here to be your therapist. My job was to find you, tell you about Elizabeth Monroe, and hand you that envelope. It took me longer than I care to admit, given that you legally changed your name and are basically a nomad."

Natalie's jaw clenched. She wanted to bare her teeth and hiss. She passed the envelope back to him. "You can tell Mr. Speeler that I'm not going back there. He can ask Chelsea to do it."

The PI ignored her offering, zipped up his bag, and fixed his collar. "If you've got something to say to Mr. Speeler, tell him yourself. His contact information is in there."

"I'm really hating this Speeler person," Natalie muttered.

The PI stopped and looked her in the eye, evaluating her. "Look, Speeler is an adamant man. He hired five PIs on three different continents to hunt you down. If he wants to find you, he will. I've been doing this job for a while. I've seen many people running for many reasons. And you know what?"

He paused for effect, but Natalie refused to speak.

"Eventually, they all realized the same thing. You can't run forever."

With that, the PI turned and walked away, leaving Natalie alone in the room, standing halfway between the door and her temporary bed.

Her shoulders dropped, and her head started pounding. It was all becoming too much, the lack of sleep, the hunger, and now the news of Elizabeth's death.

Her back felt heavy. She backed up to the green-and-brown papered wall, then slid down it until she was sitting on the dirty floor. A few moments passed with her wallowing deeper and deeper into guilt and frustration. She squeezed the envelope in her hand. The weight of it was far heavier than a few sheets of paper.

It was crushing.

Finally, she summoned the courage to open the envelope and slip Elizabeth's letter out. She took in the tilted cursive handwriting and remembered the first time she'd seen it. It was on a note Elizabeth had handed her to give to the principal on the day she transferred to Mapleton High. She remembered the chilly November day so clearly.

Natalie moved past the beautifully written date at the top of the page, down to the start of the correspondence.

Dear Natalie,

I would like you to spread my ashes by the willow tree at the edge of the waterfall. My Edward planted that tree as a child. It holds an important place in my heart.

I know this is hard for you, but please find it in your heart to do me this favour.

I dearly love you. Always have and always will.

Grandma

Natalie's throat closed. She carefully returned the page to the envelope, then pulled out Speeler's instructions. The urn was at Monroe Manor, in the parlour on the coffee table. She was to retrieve the urn, spread the ashes at the waterfall on the Monroe property, then inform him 'at once.'

Natalie would have rolled her eyes at Speeler's audacity, but she feared the tears welling up would fall. So she put the instructions into the envelope and slid it into the front pocket of her suitcase.

Unsure what to do, she sat on the floor for a few more minutes. She'd sworn to herself that she'd never return to Mapleton. The place held too many memories—and people—that she wished to avoid. But Elizabeth had asked specifically for this. There was a time when Natalie had needed someone, and Elizabeth had been the only person on earth who was there for her.

She was certain that, despite the private investigator's warning, she could run forever. But she wasn't so sure she could live with the guilt of denying Elizabeth her last wish.

She looked at the bed, then at the door. She was so tired. Her eyelids so heavy. Maybe she could just lie down, sleep for a few hours, and figure out how to get out of this without the guilt later. Maybe she could get a hold of Chelsea and ask her to do it. She was probably still in Canada.

Then a thought occurred to her.

It was only an eight-hour flight from Heathrow to Pearson, another hour's cab ride to the Monroe property in Mapleton. The Monroes had built the manor on a sprawling piece of private land, tucked away from town. She could stay there, and no one would be the wiser. Plus, it had twelve bedrooms. If she left right then, she could spread Elizabeth's ashes, catch up on her sleep, and still be back before her tour left in five days.

It would be tight, but she'd travelled more hours than that in fewer days before. She could do it again.

She picked herself up off the floor, grabbed her suitcase, and walked back through the lobby, barely stopping at the front desk as she slapped the key down.

"Give me a refund. I'm not staying."

Without waiting for a response, she walked out the door.

TWO

A great sense of relief washed over Ethan Pierce as he pulled through his hometown of Mapleton, Ontario. He loved everything about the town, from his favourite café on Main Street to the sandy beach where he and his friends spent their summers growing up. But the best thing about Mapleton was his family.

He smiled, thrilled to be back. He'd left three weeks ago on a research trip to a remote area in the Hudson Bay lowlands. It was a trip he made every year with a group of thirty scientists from all over Canada. Most of them were researchers and professors, like him. They went every spring as soon as their semesters ended and the worst of the ice had melted.

Some of them were experts on climate change or studied patterns of migratory birds. He was there collecting data on the health markers of the overall ecosystem. Besides the scientists, a team of guides accompanied them, armed with machine guns and keeping watch for polar bears.

He was happy to be home, where the threat of being eaten alive was almost nonexistent.

Ethan smiled as he turned down his street. It was in a pleasant neighbourhood, with friendly people. He'd moved there two years ago, into a small home he bought off of his parents' friends' mother. It was small, but it was only him living there, so he liked it well enough. He'd been working with Adam, his best friend since childhood, to renovate it. It still had old lady vibes, but it was coming along well. He especially appreciated the little house after roughing it in the woods with no electricity or running water.

He couldn't wait to take a shower.

He passed by an older lady who lived two doors down from him and waved, but she looked away and sped up. He'd been optimistic that the drama he'd left behind would have blown over by the time he returned. Maybe he'd been too hopeful.

Or maybe he was overthinking it. She probably didn't recognize him. He reached up to his face and scratched through his thick, dark beard.

He turned the corner, expecting his little old house to come into view, but instead of the red brick walls and black shutters, all he could see were trees. Several dozen trees, in fact, packed onto his postage-stamp front lawn.

"What the . . . ?"

He drove along slowly, in a daze, staring at the trees instead of the road. As he got closer, he remembered he'd put in an order for trees and native bushes right before he left. They were for a project he was working on over the summer, but he'd specifically scheduled them to be delivered after this weekend.

When he pulled into the driveway, the trees gave way to a view of his front porch. Standing there were his sister, Amy, and Adam in the throes of an argument.

They stopped as soon as he hopped out of his truck. Amy gasped as her jaw dropped.

Adam laughed. "Guess you've never been here when your brother gets back from his research trips, eh?"

"Ethan!" Amy shouted. "You look like a sasquatch."

He looked down at his grimy clothes and dirt-caked nails. Then reached a hand up to feel the ends of his out-of-control hair. "What did you expect?"

"I expect my brother, my man of honour, to look civilized! I'm getting married in three days, Ethan!"

He closed the driver door, then opened the back door and pulled out a case of beer he'd brought back, holding it out for Adam. "For your services."

Adam's smile broke out as he reached for the case. "Tipped Canoe, Churchill Manitoba," he read on the side of the case. "This is the best beer in Canada?"

"Without a doubt."

"It better be. Filling in as best man for the last three weeks has been rough."

"It's man of honour," Amy corrected, then turned her death stare at Ethan. "You bribed him to help me?"

"Compensated."

"You didn't get what you paid for." She shot a look at Adam. "All he did was tell me I need therapy and flirt with all my vendors."

"Hey, I asked Ethan to bring the beer for research. Max and I are buying a pub." Adam said. "I didn't expect you'd be so difficult and drive me to drink."

Ethan laughed and shook his head. He imagined Adam did a lot to help Amy. He was a great friend, almost like a brother to them both. But he couldn't turn down attention from women, and patience wasn't his strong suit. That said, he probably wasn't far off with the suggestion that Amy seek therapy. This wedding was really taking a toll.

"You're going to go to the barber, right?" Amy asked.

"I have an appointment Friday afternoon."

"For a shave, too?"

Ethan raised a brow at her. She was puffed up like a cornered raccoon. "Yes, Amy."

Adam took a few steps toward the front door. "I'm gonna put a couple of these in your fridge. You're going to need them." As soon as he'd passed Amy, he turned and looked over her head at Ethan and mouthed, "She's out of control."

Amy's head snapped back toward him, but he'd wisely taken off.

"He's on my last nerve. Do you know who he's bringing to my wedding? Mrs. P."

"Mrs. P.?" Ethan tried to place the name but couldn't.

"Grade twelve English."

It finally dawned on him. Mrs. P. was the pretty, young teacher that everyone had a crush on in high school. Ethan laughed.

"It's not funny. He thinks it's totally okay because he's thirty and she left her husband. He keeps saying, 'It's Ms. P.'"

Ethan turned his smile away from her toward the back seat, though his bushy beard probably covered his smile, anyway. He wasn't sure why Amy was surprised. Adam always lived without worrying about any consequences.

Whenever Ethan tried that, it blew up in his face.

He shook away the image of his ex-girlfriend that the thought brought to his mind and grabbed his suitcase from the back seat. After spending four hours of the day before in waist-deep, ice-cold water, he wanted nothing more than to walk into his house and take a hot shower. When he fell asleep last night on his hard cot, he literally dreamed that his hand was turning a tap and hot water was coming out.

Unfortunately, that would now have to wait.

He walked through the trees, counting how many there were. Some trees were looking wilted. "When did the trees get here?"

"About a day after you left," Amy said.

Ethan let out an annoyed sound. "Have you been watering them?"

"Uh . . . no. But it rained twice. Sorry, Ethan, I've been too busy. Adam's useless. My mind is everywhere."

Ethan waved her off. It wasn't her fault. "I'm going to be too busy this weekend to deal with these trees."

"Yes, you are. We have the rehearsal Friday night, and the ceremony is at three on Saturday. I sent all the details in an email, but I don't think you got it."

"No," he said. "There was no connection, and I haven't checked my email since I left."

He bent down to an oak tree and felt the dirt. It was bone dry. He moved to a few more, and they were all the same. There was no way they'd last any longer baking in the hot sun in their nursery cans. He'd have to get them planted right away. If he left now, he could borrow his dad's trailer and get them all off his lawn and to the pond before dark. He might even plant some of them . . .

"Ethan."

His thoughts stopped at his sister's hesitant voice. He looked up at her. Her annoyance had given way to worry. "What is it?"

"I came to see you for a reason. Some things happened after you left."

Ethan's mind immediately went back to Lindsay. He'd broken up with her a few days before he left, and although he knew without a doubt that he'd made the right decision, he couldn't help but wonder what had become of it.

"Mom wanted to come to tell you, but she was busy with the seamstress, and Dad couldn't come because I sent him to the caterer, and I just got all the succulents delivered for the wedding favours, and I have to plant them all in these tiny copper pots Jaclyn picked out, and no one trusted Adam to tell you—"

"No one trusted me to what?" Adam asked, coming back across the lawn.

Amy waved a hand at him as if she were swatting away a fly, then took a deep breath.

"Elizabeth Monroe died."

It took a minute for the gears in Ethan's head to change directions, from his ex to the old lady whose land he'd been restoring. When it finally sank in, he was in shock. He made his way over to the front porch and sat down on the hot concrete step.

Amy and Adam followed.

"When?"

"Same day the trees got here," Amy said.

Ethan closed his eyes and bent over, resting his dirty head in his dirty hands. Elizabeth Monroe, or Liz, as he came to refer to her, had become his friend. Three years ago, when he moved back home after completing his PhD, he'd been interested in taking on the ecological challenges of Mapleton to improve his hometown. He'd done an in-depth analysis of the entire Niagara region where Mapleton sat and found that the Monroe property was the crux of the area's problems.

"I can't believe this. How?"

"The obituary said she passed peacefully in her sleep. She was old."

She had been in her eighties, but it was easy to forget it. She was sharp, funny, an avid gardener, and loved the idea of restoring the wetlands. It had taken very little effort to convince her to convert the barren area back to a pond. And he'd worked tirelessly to see the plan through. He fundraised, applied for government grants, and even bribed his students with extra credit if they'd help. The pond was finally dug early that spring. He and his students had already planted over two hundred native grasses around it. The trees that were scattered across his lawn would go in next. After that, the wildflowers.

He planned to spend the summer at the pond, planting and tending to the trees and grasses. As an added benefit, he could avoid Lindsay.

But now . . .

"I'm so sorry, Ethan," Amy said, moving beside him. She put an arm around him and bent her head toward his shoulder before gagging and standing back up. "Sorry, you stink."

Ethan rolled his eyes and turned to Adam. He was, without a doubt, Mapleton's biggest gossip. "Have you heard anything about the property?"

Adam shook his head. "No. The town is abuzz about it, though. The Monroe property is just so big. There's a good chance it'll get developed into a million cookie-cutter houses."

Ethan bared his teeth. Adam's family owned a contracting company that built custom mansions for filthy rich people. "You're not touching it, right?"

He held his hands out in defence. "Easy. You know that's not our style. Besides, no one knows anything for sure yet. I heard that Anne Monroe will probably inherit it."

Ethan thought for a moment. Anne was Liz's daughter-in-law and the mayor of Mapleton. Liz never mentioned her, so he assumed they weren't close. Maybe they'd been closer when Robert, Liz's son, had been alive. That was before Ethan's time. But he knew Anne was running for re-election on the campaign promise of "Keeping the charm of Mapleton intact." It was her campaign slogan last election, too. If she felt that strongly about preserving Mapleton, then maybe she wouldn't sell to developers and his project would be safe.

"If Liz died three weeks ago, shouldn't we know by now?"

"Well, I heard from Karen, who said she heard Warren telling Jacob that Elizabeth decided not to be buried in the Monroe cemetery. She was cremated and wanted her ashes spread on the property instead. Once that's done, they'll proceed with the will."

"What's the holdup?"

"They're waiting for some distant relative to come and do it."

"Hmm." There was no point in worrying about it now. All he could do was carry on as normal with his project. The trees and the pond needed him. And it would be a nice way to honour Liz. She loved watching the project come together and was especially interested in the critters that came back to life.

Speaking of which . . .

"Can you find out how Anne feels about snakes?"

Amy let out a snort. "Probably the same way everyone feels. Terror. Disgust. Hatred."

Adam laughed. "I'll put out some feelers."

"Thanks." Ethan stood from the porch, grabbed his suitcase, threw it inside the door, then locked up.

"What are you doing?" Amy asked.

"I'm going to pick up Dad's trailer and get these trees off my lawn."

Amy stood in place, looking uncomfortable.

"It's okay, Ames. I can get this done and take on all the best man of honour stuff, too. I'll even drop by your place on the way and help you with the succulents."

Amy's head dropped.

"Hey," he said, tapping her arm. "I will."

"Yeah. I know you will. You've never let me down before."

"Come on," Adam told her, throwing a brotherly arm around her shoulders. "I'll give you a ride home."

But Amy refused to move. Her eyebrows drew together, and the knuckles on her clasped hands turned white. "There's something else."

He and Adam both stared her down. Amy would eventually say what was bothering her, so he crossed his arms and waited. Adam wasn't capable of waiting.

"Spit it out, you!" he shouted.

"Lindsay called," she said with a small voice.

"When? I told you not to answer the phone if she calls!" Adam said.

"This morning, when you were off flirting with the florist," Amy said.

"Oh." Adam backed down, looking sheepish.

Ethan rolled his eyes. "And?"

Amy began pacing back and forth. This didn't look good.

"Well, I didn't think she'd still come to the wedding. I only invited her as a plus one for you. But I guess I wrote her name on the invitation instead of 'plus one,' and she assumed her invitation stood."

"And you relieved her of that ridiculous assumption, right?!" Adam demanded.

"Well . . . I tried, but she's very forceful."

Adam let out a string of curses that made Amy recoil, then looked over at Ethan. A thousand words passed silently in his look. Ethan was sure that, if Adam could have, he would've screamed, "This is what you get for trying to be nice!"

Ethan ignored him. "So she's still coming?"

"Yes, but there's more."

Adam swore again. "What else could there possibly be?"

"She, uh, asked if she could bring someone."

"Who?" Ethan and Adam asked in unison.

Amy looked up with worried eyes.

"Derek."

THREE

Natalie tensed as the cab rounded the gradual bend where the country highway gave way to North Shore Drive and led into Mapleton. She wasn't sure whether it was curiosity or adrenalin fuelling her discomfort. She tried to distract herself by brainstorming what day song she'd choose for this trip.

Day songs were always positive and upbeat, something that would stick with people forever. But this trip wouldn't have a cheerful song. It called for something far more sinister that gave the listener a deep sense of impending doom.

She glanced out the window, and her eye snagged on a sign stuck in the grass on the side of the road. She sat up straighter and stuck her head halfway out of the window like a dog to get a closer look.

Lining each side of the street for at least a hundred metres were huge navy-blue campaign signs, one after the other. Framed in the centre of each sign was a pixie-like face with an elegant smile, surrounded by platinum-blond hair.

Natalie's stomach plummeted down to her toes.

She'd hoped she'd never come face to face with Anne Monroe again—once was more than enough. But this was worse. It was as if the woman were waiting for her at the edge of town, begging her to turn back.

She sank down in her seat and dropped her sunglasses down over her eyes.

"Is there an election coming up?" she asked the cab driver.

"Yuuuup," he drew out, peering at her through the rear-view mirror. "For town council. You know Anne?"

"No," she said, looking away from his inquisitive stare. She cursed herself for giving Elizabeth's address. It would have been better to be dropped off at some anonymous corner somewhere and walk.

He shrugged and turned his attention back to the road. "She'll probably get re-elected for Mayor. She's got my vote."

Natalie hummed a polite agreement and turned to look out the window. She'd taken the same road a decade ago when she moved to Mapleton. Only instead of a cab, she'd been in the passenger seat of Elizabeth's silver Lincoln, and instead of a suitcase, she'd had a duffle bag at her feet holding her mother's prized possessions and a few boxes of clothes in the trunk.

She shook off the thought and reminded herself that she wasn't a trapped seventeen-year-old with no options anymore. She was an independent twenty-seven-year-old who'd travelled the world and didn't need anyone's help. Thank you very much.

And she'd only be here for three days.

The cab meandered along North Shore Drive, past more campaign signs, making its way to the centre of town. It was as picture perfect as it had been a decade ago. The town had lined the street with decorative lamps. Each held a hanging basket, dripping with purple and red flowers. Benches sat along the sidewalks that families of the town had donated in their loved ones' memories. Past the sidewalks were storefronts with flower boxes and small patios where people sat, sipping their late afternoon coffee.

They stopped at the only street light in town, where North Shore Drive intersected with Main Street. Main Street started at the beach and climbed all the way up the escarpment back to the highway.

Natalie looked right, toward the lake from the cab window, and became lost in the calm blue water sparkling in the sunlight.

She blinked and turned her head away from it, rolling her eyes. As a naive outsider, Mapleton had seemed idyllic. But Natalie knew better now. Mapleton would never be perfect because it was lacking something crucial to a person's happiness.

Anonymity.

The light turned green, and the cab driver turned left, away from the lake toward the escarpment. They passed more perfect little stores coated in perfect little flowers until the landscape became more and more green. Finally, the wrought-iron gates that separated the Monroes from the rest of the world appeared, just at the base of the escarpment.

The driver turned left and pulled the car into the small section of driveway in front of the gates.

"You got a code or something?"

"Here's fine." She handed him some Canadian bills she got at the airport and hopped out of the car.

He followed her to the trunk and pulled her suitcase out, then squinted at her as he passed it over. "I was real sorry to hear about Liz. She was a great lady."

"I know."

"So you knew Liz, but not Anne?"

Natalie looked away, not liking where this line of questioning was going. "Thank you for the ride."

She grabbed the handle of her suitcase and dragged it behind her through the deep gravel toward the gate. She couldn't remember the code for the gate, so she pushed through the bushes and weeds around it until she got back to the gravel, then followed the winding driveway uphill toward the manor.

She was out of breath and sweating through her thin yellow dress by the time the manor came into view. The house itself was an enormous Victorian mansion, built in 1889 by Clarence Monroe, the first son of a wealthy businessman who had immigrated to Canada from England.

The front facade had about forty windows, an upper balcony in the centre, and a turret at the corner going up the three stories. The entire house was wrapped in a huge front porch.

Natalie assumed the door would be locked, but she climbed the five front steps, crossed the wide porch, and jiggled the door handle, anyway.

It was locked.

She remembered Elizabeth had hidden a key for her when she moved in. It was under a rock in her prized rose bushes that lined the porch. The rose bushes were a wild, rambling brush now, but the rock was still there, and when Natalie lifted it up, the tarnished key was still there, half-buried in the mud.

Maybe Elizabeth had forgotten about it. Natalie hoped she hadn't left it there, waiting for Natalie to return someday.

She brushed the rush of guilt aside, shoved the key into the handle, and pushed the door open. The entryway was just as she remembered it.

Huge.

A floating, hand-carved oak staircase dominated the centre of the room. To the left was the parlour; to the right was the formal dining room. Both rooms were closed off from the foyer by twenty-foot-high solid oak pocket doors.

Natalie pulled the key from the knob and slipped it in her pocket. Pulling the front door closed behind her, she eyed the parlour door but walked past it to the staircase. She climbed the winding stairs, then turned at the top, and headed down a long hall to her old bedroom.

And found it exactly as she'd left it.

Directly ahead, the large window was still draped in lace curtains. A small metal, unmade bed rested along one wall, and an ornate wood dresser with a large mirror sat against the other.

She went to the dresser and found her white sheets trimmed in lace, carefully folded in the top drawer and topped with a lavender sachet.

She took them out and made the bed. The temptation to fall face first into the pillows and sleep the rest of the day away was strong, but she'd come all this way and was determined to do her assigned task. Sleep would have to wait.

She put her suitcase flat on the floor and unzipped it. Inside was nestled a large wooden jewellery box that was closed with a gold fastener and had her mother's name carved on top. She placed it on the dresser, then pulled out three small photo albums and did the same.

Once her clothing was more accessible, she stripped out of the dirty, sweaty dress she had on and searched for something appropriate to wear into the woods. Of course, she only had thin clothing and sandals, so she grabbed a plain white cotton dress with three buttons down the front and thin straps and put it on. Trudging through the woods probably called for more clothing, but she owned nothing suitable, so she'd just have to wing it.

Downstairs, she slid open the parlour doors. The room was as it had been. Elegantly appointed, with bay windows that looked out over the vast gardens. An antique tea cart was off to the side of the window.

Opposite sat a large buffet that held several generations of Monroes' tea sets. In the centre of the room was a formal sitting area, with two dainty floral loveseats and two sets of matching chairs situated around an ornate wood coffee table.

On the coffee table sat the urn.

Natalie walked to the loveseat and plopped down. She closed her eyes and took in the room's silence. When she heard a faint scratching noise in the distance, she opened her eyes. The old house always had a problem with mice. She turned behind her and looked at the stone fireplace, remembering the first time she'd seen a mouse in the house. It had been a few months after she moved in. The little grey mouse had scurried out of the fireplace and rushed across the floor at her. She'd shrieked and jumped on a chair to avoid it.

After that, Elizabeth had promised to set some traps and see about getting a cat.

She walked closer to the fireplace and peered inside. The hearth was big enough to fit a whole family inside. On top of the mantel was a collection of knick-knacks and picture frames. The largest picture in the centre was the same one the private investigator had given her.

Natalie looked away until her eyes rested on a clunky brown leather chair that looked too modern

and out of place in the room's corner. She remembered that chair vividly. The last time she'd seen it,
Robert was sitting in it.

A foul taste rose in her throat, and she swallowed
it down. But no matter how hard she tried, she
couldn't keep the memories of Robert in that chair
from coming back. It was likely because that was the
day she decided on her future . . .

*It had been a school day in the early spring. Natalie
had been living in Mapleton for about six months. She
hated everything about the town and the school. She
was still grieving and had only made one friend, a
kind, shy girl who was the target of a bully and hadn't
realized it yet but was way too good for that town.*

*That day had started like any other chilly spring
day, but by the time school let out, the weather had
turned, and a snowstorm passed through. Natalie had
taken the back way home, the way she always did,
passing through part of the forest to avoid seeing
people in town. She walked through the back kitchen
door, then heard shouting.*

*She tiptoed through the house toward the sound
until she heard that it was coming from the parlour.
She grabbed hold of the big door and slid it open.
From the doorway, she saw Elizabeth standing in the
middle of the room, hands on her hips. The other
woman, also on her feet, was crying into a balled-up*

tissue. They both stopped immediately when Natalie walked in. The other woman's bloodshot eyes lifted to Natalie's, then popped out of her face.

A slight movement in the room's corner caught Natalie's eye. She looked over and found Robert, lounging in the brown leather chair, one ankle rested on the opposite knee, a cigar between two fingers dropping ash onto the antique rug.

He barely moved when she entered, didn't bother looking at her. Frankly, he looked bored with the entire exchange.

"What's going on?" she asked.

Elizabeth turned toward her, squared her shoulders, and brushed her hands across the wrinkles on the front of her dress. "We need some privacy, dear. Why don't you go for a walk to the waterfall."

Natalie looked out the bay window at the thick snowflakes falling, then back at Elizabeth. "But—"

"Please," Elizabeth said.

"Okay."

After a beat, she backed out of the room and closed the doors behind her, but didn't leave. She was way too curious. She recognized Robert right away, even though he'd never spoken a single word to her in her life. He'd visited her mother enough over the years for her to piece together who he was. When she was thirteen, she asked her mother whether he was, in *fact, her biological father and got confirmation. When she had found out from the Mapleton High gossip mill that Robert was not only married to someone else, but that he also had a daughter with her and another daughter from a different mistress, Natalie became furious with her mother. She never imagined her mother would knowingly sleep with a married man, and continue to do so for years and years. As much as she tried to stop it from tainting her memories of her mother, it had.*

Natalie pressed her ear against the door and listened. She could only make out Elizabeth's voice.

"That's enough!" Elizabeth shouted.

Natalie could hear a high-pitched, garbled voice reply.

"No, Anne, I'm not asking her to leave."

Natalie had backed away from the door at that point.

Anne was Robert's wife, and from what Natalie could tell, she was a very sweet woman. She cringed at what Anne was going through. Natalie knew she didn't belong in Mapleton, but she hadn't considered that her presence there would harm anyone. Especially the innocent person who Natalie's mother had victimized by not ending things with Robert when she found out he was married.

Not only that, but she hated that she was putting Elizabeth in an awkward situation after the kindness she had shown.

At that point, Natalie did what Elizabeth suggested and set off toward the waterfall. She'd walked out the front door and down the front steps when she saw Anne's car. Anne had rolled the back window down, and a small strawberry-blond head with two curly pigtails and two giant eyes peered out just over the edge of the frame.

That had to be Emily, her half sister.

Well, one of them at least.

Natalie left then, ran around the side of the house, past the rose bushes, and through the gardens. She spent several hours at the waterfall in the freezing cold and thought about what she was going to do. She didn't want to cause trouble for anyone and didn't want to stay in Mapleton anyway, so she decided she would leave town as soon as she finished the semester. Several universities had offered her acceptances, but she knew then that she wouldn't accept any of them.

What she wanted, more than anything else in the world, was to just be free.

Another scratching noise snapped her attention back. She walked toward the coffee table to get the urn while watching the fireplace, just in case a mouse darted out at her. When she picked it up, a small notecard dropped from behind it that read: "My office. Friday, 10 a.m."

Natalie dropped the card on the coffee table and walked out of the parlour, sliding the doors closed to trap all the memories inside. She'd leave in a couple of days and try to never think about Robert or Anne or Emily ever again.

She hefted the stone urn up onto her hip and wrapped an arm around it.

"Come on, Elizabeth. Let's get you where you want to be."

· · · ● · ● ● · · ·

Natalie walked through the terraced gardens that covered the sloped grounds from the house on the hill to the edge of the woods. Ten years ago, the gardens were Elizabeth's pride and joy. She'd had a crew come in every week to maintain them. A prominent garden design magazine had even once featured them as a cover story.

Now, they were a weedy, crumbling mess.

To the right of the gardens was an orchard, filled with apple, peach, and cherry trees, and in need of a good mowing. To the left was a large victory garden that sat barren. Beyond that were fields. In front of her was an entrance to the woods that Mother Nature had entirely reclaimed.

Natalie pushed her way through, stepping carefully so the bare sides of her sandalled feet wouldn't get stabbed by twigs and branches. Weeds, grass, and bushes had grown over the once well-trodden path. Natalie knew the general direction of the waterfall, but without the path, it would be tricky. She forged ahead, listening through the sounds of birds chirping and leaves rustling for the sound of rushing water to guide her.

After about four minutes of walking, she finally made it to the river. Once there, she knew to turn right and follow it along to where it started at the base of Monroe Falls. A hundred metres later, the enormous old willow tree came into sight. Its long, wispy fronds swayed from the branches and dipped into the pool of frothy water below.

She walked around the tree, then stopped and took in the view of the only good thing about Mapleton: her waterfall.

The spring melt from the escarpment made the water flow fast. It rushed down a twenty-metre drop, with three tiers of rock impeding its fall. Behind the waterfall was a backdrop of rock, bushes, flowers, and enormous trees.

She took a deep breath, then let it out. There was something so secluded and magical about the place, it was almost a meditative experience. She could breathe deeply here, away from the rest of the world.

She'd first seen the waterfall in the winter, when the water was frozen solid in place, instead of flowing. Elizabeth had guided her there a few weeks after she'd moved in. It was there, sitting on a blanket and sipping hot chocolate, that Elizabeth had confirmed that the rumours she heard at school were true. Natalie had two half sisters, Emily and Chelsea.

Natalie went back to the waterfall every week thereafter to see how it would melt and transform. Over time, she went more and more often, whenever she felt the world was asking too much. She'd even bring her mother's photo albums with her, as if she could share the magical place with her.

She walked to the edge of the riverbank and watched the clear water crashing over the rocks at the bottom. It almost entranced her. It was so peaceful. She could see why Elizabeth had chosen this place to rest for all of eternity. You could certainly do much worse.

Natalie took the urn to the gnarled base of the tree's trunk, removed the lid, and gently tipped the urn, dropping the ashes in a ring around the tree. She replaced the lid and stared at the circle.

It seemed too fast, and suddenly, everything felt so real.

The thought of leaving Elizabeth there all alone made her skin crawl. How many times had Elizabeth been alone over the years? How many birthdays and Christmases? She knew Chelsea would visit from time to time but doubted that Robert had cared enough to bother. She should have made more of an effort. Shouldn't have griped so much about doing this for her.

It all became too much. Setting the urn down, she lay on the ground next to the tree and stared up at the sky through full eyes. The canopy of fluttering leaves shielded the blue sky like a green stained-glass window. She'd done this often as a teen, especially in the winter, when the trees were bare and the snow made a nice pillow.

She reached behind her, gathered some dried leaves, and pulled them under her head into a makeshift pillow, then stopped when she heard a strange, shaking noise. It was a noise she'd never heard before. Her heart rate sped up. God, was it another mouse?

She let out a shudder and slowly turned her head to the waterfall.

Nothing.

Then she turned to look at the overgrown path.

And came eye to eye with a snake. Only a few feet from her face.

She stared at it in disbelief for a moment, then shook her head, as if she could make some other creature appear instead. There weren't any snakes living in this wood. Maybe she was seeing things?

She forced herself to blink. When she opened her eyes, the snake was still there. It reared up, slimy tongue slipping out of its mouth toward her. Behind it, its tail appeared in the air with a rattle shaking at the end.

Natalie jumped to her feet. She looked around, panicked. That was when she saw a million snakes covering the ground all around her. One slithered toward her, then over her leaf pillow.

She screamed.

FOUR

E than placed his pencil and graph paper on the
tailgate of his truck, then hopped off.

He'd drawn a map of the new pond and metic-
ulously planned where to plant all fifty trees and
countless shrubs to make the area natural and beautiful. Hopefully, whoever saw the pond would like it
. . . and decide to keep it.

He eyed his design one more time while pulling his
work gloves from his bag. It had taken about a billion
edits to get the plan just right so that the tallest
growing trees would be in the background, and the
shorter bushes in the foreground. He grabbed his
work gloves and put them on, cringing as the rough
fabric grazed all the new cuts on his hands.

He'd just left Amy's house after planting nine-
ty-four greenish-blue succulents into tiny copper
pots. Amy had been little help. She just sat across the

table from him, wringing her hands and occasionally tossing a bit of moss on to cover the soil. She was worried about her wedding day, but at least she wasn't questioning getting married. She and Jaclyn were very much in love. It was all the other stuff that came along with it.

And especially his outspoken and, frankly, unstable ex-girlfriend inserting herself into his life.

Part of him wished his sister was more forceful and told Lindsay no. But it wasn't her fault. He suspected there was a fair amount of bullying involved. Besides, if there was anyone to blame, it was himself. He knew from the beginning he shouldn't have got involved with Lindsay.

He slid his shovel out of the bed along with a bag of compost, then walked to the first tree. As he walked through the grass, he noticed an unusual number of snakes out, so he had to be careful where he stepped and dropped the bag.

The first tree was in rough shape. It was a young birch, with wilted, spotted leaves. "I got you," he said to it.

He'd just dug the tip of the blade into the ground when he heard a blood-curdling scream.

He started at the sound. It was so loud, the birds in the tree canopy took flight. He turned in the direction and squinted, but the distance was too great, and the forest too thick, to see anything.

After a few seconds and no additional screams, he rolled his eyes and began digging.

It had been a while since he'd noticed trespassers at the waterfall, but it wasn't uncommon to find them there. When the snake population around the river increased, he'd fundraised for a fence to go around the property, along with No Trespassing signs. He also spread the word around town that there were rattlesnakes in the area. It worked well enough to deter the local kids from jumping the fence.

The problem now was the ridiculous TikTokers and Instagrammers from out of town who were willing to jump the fence and risk their life for a photo in the waterfall.

He stabbed his shovel into the ground and dug, but he only got a few shovelfuls deep when he saw another snake. Then another.

Then he started worrying about them. They had become an endangered species because people were afraid of them and killed them en masse. He didn't want to stop his task, but he also couldn't stand the thought of someone trespassing and killing the innocent animals.

Annoyed, Ethan dropped his shovel and walked upstream from the pond to the waterfall. He'd just make sure they left, then he could concentrate on planting without having to worry. It wasn't that far, only a few hundred metres.

As he got closer, he finally glimpsed a person, and sure enough, it was exactly what he thought. Some woman was standing under the willow, with her long, dark hair flowing, wearing a white dress and shiny sandals.

She couldn't have chosen a less suitable thing to wear in the woods if she tried. He imagined she chose this outfit because it would make her look like some damn forest fairy in the photo, and people would just gush over how magical it was.

What they wouldn't see was the trip to the ER for a shot of antivenom.

"Excuse me!"

He yelled pretty loud, but she didn't hear. She looked to be in a panic. Her back was to him; her head jerked from side to side. He went a little closer, and that's when he saw she was holding a large stick, about the same size as her. She lifted it overhead with both hands.

"Hey!"

She stopped midair, then jerked her face at him. A second passed. He braced himself for another scream, but none came.

"Stop right there!" she said.

He didn't want to scare her, and he didn't want to get hit by the stick, so he did as the ridiculous woman said. He even slightly lifted his hands, as if the stick were a gun. "You can't bludgeon innocent animals with a stick."

"Innocent? They're snakes!"

"Irrelevant. Go home."

She pulled herself to her full height, then narrowed a set of striking dark eyes at him. "You are on private property."

"I have permission."

"I find that difficult to believe. Are you living in here?"

He reared back from the question. Living in here? Then he remembered the state he was in, unshaven and dirty, only made worse by hauling all the trees around the pond. "No."

"Lot of hesitation there, buddy." She looked around at the ground, then pulled the stick back and swiped at a snake.

"Stop that now!"

"Look, I'm not judging you. I'm no stranger to being homeless myself. If you show me the quickest way out of here, I'll get you a meal and some help, okay?"

"Good, whatever."

He didn't care what she thought anymore. He just wanted her out of there. He walked toward her and grabbed the opposite end of her stick. The shortest distance was past the waterfall, where the edge of the property ended at Main Street. That's probably where she parked, anyway. These city folk get two feet inside a forest, and they're lost.

He walked a few minutes in silence, dragging her behind him at the other end of the stick, as she yelped and squealed passing the few visible snakes, until the fence appeared. It was short enough to climb over with little effort, but after he'd hopped over, he helped her over, too. He looked up and down the road but didn't see a car.

"Thank y—" She stopped midsentence and slapped a hand over her forehead. "The urn."

Urn?

"Did you say urn?"

"Ugh, I can't believe this." She paced back and forth for a moment, eyed the forest, then closed her eyes and seemed to take deep breaths.

"Wait a minute. Who are you?"

"I'm Natalie. Will you go back and get it? It's small, stone, under the willow tree."

"Natalie . . . who?"

"Alvarez."

Alvarez. Ethan's mind whirled. "Are you the distant relative everyone's been waiting on?"

She stopped, assessed him in an instant. Then lifted her stick and pointed it at him. "Who the hell are you?"

"Ethan."

She pointed her stick at the woods. "I'm going to ask you one more time. Do you live in there?"

He rolled his eyes. "No."

"Why do you look like you do?"

He pretended he didn't hear her. "I've been working on this property for three years, restoring the river and wetlands. I have— I had permission from Elizabeth Monroe to be here."

"So you're responsible for putting all the snakes in there?"

"What?"

"There were never any snakes before."

"Well, that can't be true. There had to have been at least two."

She snarled at him, baring her teeth like a wolverine.

"They're usually very shy creatures. They're just out right now because it's hot. Most of the time, you don't even see them."

"Is that supposed to make me feel better? That they're lurking around, unseen?"

"I don't care how you feel. But I will not let you hit them with a stick just because you're scared of them. Would you hit a puppy with a stick?"

She looked down at the stick, and for a split second, almost looked ashamed.

But it passed quickly.

"I hope you know, Ethan, that this waterfall was the only redeemable thing about this godawful town. And you've ruined it."

"That seems a bit dramatic. There are a lot of good things about this town. And, besides, the snakes only have a small amount of venom. Enough to kill a rabbit or a mouse."

Her face became a mask of horror, and a visible shudder worked through her body. "Those things are venomous?!"

"Well, yes. But they have very small teeth. There are only a handful of people who have ever died from a Massasauga rattlesnake bite."

"Died?!"

"You just have to wear boots and thick pants."

Her face turned livid, and she leaned in toward him, speaking through a clenched jaw. "I don't own anything thick."

With that, she turned on her heel and stomped off down the road, stick still in hand. Ethan stood on the side of the road, staring at her back in complete and utter confusion.

"What the hell does that mean?"

FIVE

Natalie called a cab to take her to Mr. Speel-er's office on Friday morning. She would have walked; she enjoyed walking. But she wanted the cab ready and waiting to take her to the airport. As soon as this meeting was over, she wanted to make a quick escape.

The cab pulled through town and stopped just down the street from the office. Natalie stepped out but left her suitcase in the car.

"Will you wait for me? I shouldn't be long. Just keep the meter running."

"Sure." The driver sat back in his seat, pulled out a magazine.

"Good."

She hurried up the sidewalk toward the office. There weren't many people milling about, but she still put on her sunglasses and kept her head low.

She was nearly at the front door when something caught her attention. It was a young blond woman stepping out of a rusty red car parked in the river of luxury vehicles lining the street. She was wearing a sunflower printed dress over a yellow T shirt with white socks and black combat boots. She seemed far too artsy and way too interesting to fit into an oppressively perfect place like Mapleton.

As she walked closer, she looked more and more familiar. Then Natalie finally recognized her. The last time she'd seen her younger half sister, Chelsea was only twelve.

"Chelsea?"

Chelsea's head snapped over, her bright-blue eyes stabbing at Natalie. She squinted through the sunlight before recognition came. "Oh my god, Natalie?"

Chelsea closed the three steps between them in record time and grabbed Natalie in a viselike grip. "I haven't seen you since I was, like, twelve."

Natalie returned the hug, adding a little pat to her back before pulling away. She didn't know whether Chelsea would be happy to see her. She'd thought about her over the years, wondered what she was up to. But she always stopped short of actually reaching out. "I know. It's been a while. What are you doing here?"

Chelsea let her go but kept staring at her with those innocent blue eyes. "I got a message from Mr. Speeler asking me to come today. He told me that Grandma wanted you to spread her ashes."

"Yeah. It's done."

"Did it go okay?"

Natalie nodded. Spreading the ashes hadn't been as difficult as she thought. It actually felt good to carry out Elizabeth's wishes for her.

Getting attacked and fleeing the woods without the urn was another story. The homeless forest dweller and his band of venomous snakes had been on her mind ever since. She had to admit, she was grateful that he got her out alive. But she was equally annoyed that he lectured her on her clothing choices. She may have been able to forgive him for that—it was a ridiculous outfit for the woods, after all. But then he tried to take her stick.

Unacceptable.

Besides, who the hell was that comfortable around such vicious creatures? A weirdo, that's who.

Natalie looked at Chelsea, who was studying her with hard eyes that Natalie thought looked too old for a twenty-two-year-old.

"You still don't talk too much, eh?"

Natalie shrugged her shoulder and let the corner of her mouth form a half smile. "What have you been up to?" Natalie asked.

"Oh . . . uh . . ." Chelsea looked up and down the street. "I'm in film school."

"Wow."

"Yeah, it's fun. But it's been challenging. I've had some setbacks. But I'm finally in my last semester. I'll be finished soon. What about you?"

"I've been working as a tour guide in Europe. But I'm moving to Australia next month."

"That's incredible. I haven't been able to travel anywhere."

"I'm sure you'll have more opportunity after you graduate."

"Yeah . . ."

"Maybe you could come on one of my tours? It's eighteen-to-thirty-five-year-olds, so you'd be with people your age. And you'd get to meet people from all over the world."

Chelsea took a breath as if she was going to say something, but didn't. The conversation stalled out and became awkward. What did you say to a half sibling you abandoned a decade ago and barely knew?

Natalie walked a few steps and reached for one of the huge black door handles. She swung the door open and let Chelsea in, then followed her.

As soon as she walked in, she saw him.

The homeless guy.

He was sitting in the waiting room wearing a dark-grey jacket over a pale-blue dress shirt. His way-too-long hair was falling forward into his eyes as he typed away on a phone, and he had a leather bag on the floor at his feet.

"You."

His head snapped up from the screen of his phone, and his deep-blue eyes stared at her through round, wire-rimmed glasses. "Uh . . . hi. Natalie. Did you find the urn?"

She was frosted over, ready for another fight, but despite her best efforts, she thawed a little. He had gone back for the urn, after all, and left it on the front porch for her.

"Yes," she said, then added, "thank you."

She told herself to let it go and forget about him, the snakes, and the woods. No point in holding a grudge when she had a cab waiting to whisk her away.

He stood and came closer, and Natalie tipped her head up to keep eye contact with him. She hadn't realized how tall he was in the woods. Or how note-worthy his eyes were. She'd been too busy running for her life.

He slid his phone into his pocket and extended a hand toward Chelsea. "I'm Ethan."

"Chelsea Davenport. Did you get a call last night, too?"

"Yes."

"Welcome," came a gravelly voice from down the hall.

All three of them turned at once to find an older man with grey hair in a baggy suit coming down the hall.

"I'm Reginald Speeler. Thank you all for coming. Please, follow me to the conference room."

Ethan stepped aside to allow her and Chelsea to go through, but she stood where she was. "Sorry, I can't stay. I have a cab waiting."

Mr. Speeler clasped his hands together in front of him. "Ms. Monroe, this will take a while. Why don't you send him off."

"It's Alvarez, and no. I have a flight at three."

"Reschedule," he said in a cold voice, all trace of politeness gone. "We have a rather large will to get through."

Natalie stared at him. "Will?"

"Yes. This way."

Speeler took off down the hall. Ethan and Chelsea followed behind. Natalie stood there for a few minutes before Speeler beckoned her. "Ms. Alvarez, join us."

There was no way she was calling off her cab. Or rescheduling her flight. It would take a hurricane to keep her on land in Mapleton. But she couldn't very well turn and flee.

He would find her.

She knew he would.

Resigned, she followed the group down the hall, then turned into a large conference room where Ethan and Chelsea were sitting. Speeler pointed to a chair across from them, issuing her a silent command to sit. She figured it would be quicker to comply than fight, so she sat.

"Now, then, Ms. Alvarez, did you follow the instructions I sent for the ashes?"

Natalie chanced a look at Ethan. The corners of his mouth turned up in a pleasant way, barely visible through the beard covering his face. "Yes."

"Excellent. Elizabeth had said she wanted to be resting peacefully before I read the will."

Natalie cocked her head to the side. "Why?"

He ignored her. "Let's start with Dr. Pierce."

Ethan turned in his seat toward Speeler, waiting patiently.

"Doctor?"

He glanced at her and nodded, then turned his attention back to Speeler.

"Elizabeth loved the work you're doing on the property. She wanted to be sure you would see it through. So she left the pond in your trust. These are the coordinates. It's all the land east of the manor grounds."

Ethan sat up straighter, surprised. He took the paper and stared at it. "Wow."

"The rest of the property," Speeler continued, "including the house and its surrounding property, river and waterfall, has been left to Natalie Alvarez and Chelsea Davenport."

Chelsea let out a gasp. Her blue eyes lit up. "Oh my God! Really?!"

Natalie sat in shock for a moment, taking in her sister's and Ethan's gleeful faces, before shaking her head.

"Why would you let her do this?" she asked.

"Elizabeth decided how she wanted her property divided. Not me. I simply wrote the will."

"This isn't fair."

"Fair? You just inherited fifty percent of a property worth twelve million dollars."

Natalie shook her head. "I mean, it isn't fair to lead these two on like this," she said, gesturing to Ethan and Chelsea. "Elizabeth shouldn't have done this."

Her head wouldn't stop shaking back and forth now. "We shouldn't have to deal with this."

"Deal with what?" Ethan asked.

He turned an intense deep stare at her, waiting. When he said nothing else, she wondered whether he would wait forever or eventually blow up.

Something told her he had a very long fuse.

"Deal with the Monroes," she said. "Elizabeth told me that when her husband died, he didn't have a will, and his brothers wanted the house to go to them, but Elizabeth took them to court."

"Yes. That is exactly what happened," Speeler said. "I represented her myself. She won, and the property was legally hers. Now it's yours."

Natalie dropped her head into her hand and rubbed at her temples. She knew this would never happen. The Monroes were extremely wealthy. And old school. They would never allow their family home to be given to Robert's illegitimate children.

That cab was looking superb right about now.

When she looked across the table, Ethan was staring at her again.

"I guess you're not a distant relative?" he asked.

She shook her head.

He looked at Chelsea, then back at her. "Robert's daughters?"

She nodded.

He looked to Speeler. "Is this going to be a problem?"

"Potentially, yes. Elizabeth left the shares she owned in Monroe Corp. to Edward's remaining brothers. Victor is the eldest and acts as President and CEO. She left most of the antiques and family heirlooms in the home to all the other family members. I met with them last night."

"And they are satisfied with that?"

Speeler paused for a deep breath. "No. But they are never satisfied with anything. The shares are a small amount compared to the fortune they've already amassed. The property has deep sentimental value to them."

Chelsea's small voice broke in, resigned. "So, we aren't actually going to get it?"

"You are going to get it." Speeler was more adamant now. He stabbed a stubby finger at the folder on the table. "This will is ironclad. Elizabeth and I wrote it together ten years ago. The only amendment was when she severed off the pond property. It's legally binding. My only fear is that if you give them reason to believe they can win, they might contest. And they have the means for a lengthy court battle."

"Wait," Natalie said, sitting up in her seat. "Did you say ten years ago? She wrote this will before Robert died?"

"That's right. It was just after you left."

Natalie sank back into her chair, letting that sink in. "What about Anne? And . . . Emily?"

Speeler's bushy brows rose. "She left them out."

"Completely?" Natalie asked.

"Yes."

The room fell silent as Natalie processed what she was hearing, trying to come to terms with Elizabeth cutting her third granddaughter from her will. She looked over at Ethan and Chelsea, and they seemed to be doing the same.

Then she remembered her cab, and her suitcase, and her flight. She stood up from the table. "All right. I gotta go."

"Wait. There's still the matter of Mi and Mi."

"Meeanmee?" Natalie asked, racking her brain to figure out what he was talking about. "What the hell is meeanmee?"

"Mi and Mi," he annunciated slowly. "And it's not what. It's who."

Natalie leaned forward and raised her voice to a yell. "Start making sense, or I'm gone."

"Mi and Mi are Elizabeth's cats. She wanted one cat named Mimi, but ended up with two, so she named them Mi and Mi. She left them to you."

"Cats?"

"Yes. Cats."

Natalie fell back into her chair, astonished. Then a laugh bubbled up. "Is this some kind of joke?"

"Of course not."

"Okay, sure," she said, the laughter coming stronger now. "I'll just toss them in my suitcase."

"I figured you wouldn't need a suitcase anymore."

"Did you think I was going to stay? In that house? Is that what Elizabeth thought?"

"Well, she hoped you would, yes."

Natalie stared at the man for a moment, telling herself to calm down. She was about to yell at him and storm off when Ethan cleared his throat.

"Why don't you just take the cats home with you?"

"I don't have a home."

He blinked. Then again. "Wait, are you homeless?"

She tipped her chin up. "I'm currently without a permanent address."

Ethan's eyes scrunched up, as if he was looking at the most clueless person he'd ever seen. "Is that different?"

Natalie rolled her eyes. The last thing she needed was judgment from this guy, with his sparking eyes and doctorate degree. Ugh. She stepped behind her chair and pushed it in. "Send the cats to a shelter or something," she said. "And give my share of the property to Chelsea. Good luck with the Monroes. You're going to need it."

She started walking toward the door.

"Ms. Alvarez," Speeler spoke.

She stopped and turned. "What now?"

"I'm afraid that the Monroes will contest the will if you dispute it like this. If they do, it will probably go to court and get thrown out. Elizabeth had a previous will to this one. The judge may fall back to it."

"What are you saying?"

"By not accepting this inheritance, you may force Chelsea and Ethan to forfeit theirs."

Natalie looked over at Ethan. His face was utterly unreadable other than one judgy eyebrow slightly cocked. Chelsea's face was wide open, like a book. She was on the verge of crying.

"Natalie," she said, then swallowed.

Then swallowed again.

Natalie closed her eyes. She wished she were in the cab instead of a lawyer's office being stabbed with a thousand guilt knives. She didn't want to be the reason anyone was hurting. But there was no way she could stay in that town.

She just couldn't.

Chelsea looked as if she was struggling to get by. Inheriting a property would probably be a huge game changer for her. Natalie knew Chelsea had grown up rough, just like her.

Chelsea's soft plea broke in. "Please, Natalie."

Natalie looked at her half sister's welled-up blue eyes, then let out a deep exhale.

"Fuck."

· · · ●·●· · ·

"Okay, here's how this is gonna go down."

Natalie was pacing the sidewalk in front of the empty parking space where her cab once sat. On the curb sat her suitcase. Chelsea sat on a bench, watching, waiting.

"First, we are going to donate the damn cats."

"You mean put them up for adoption?"

"Right. Unless you want them?"

Chelsea shook her head. "I wish I could, but I don't have room in my apartment for two cats."

"Fine. We'll take them to . . ."

"The Humane Society?"

"Yes. Then, we'll get a real estate agent and put the property up for sale."

Chelsea leaped up from her seat. "What?! You want to sell it?"

"Of course. What other options are there?"

"Why don't we just keep it? It seems wrong to get rid of something that's been in our family for over a century."

"Our family?"

Chelsea paused for a few breaths, then sat back down. "I know you don't like our family. But you can't just run away and pretend they don't exist. I always felt like I belonged with Elizabeth."

"Yeah, well, your circumstances were very different from mine, weren't they?"

Chelsea's eyes softened for a moment before hardening once more. She crossed her arms over her chest and tipped her chin into the air. "I don't want to sell the property."

Natalie closed her eyes and took a deep, calming breath, then reached her fingers up to dig into her temples. "Look, it seems pretty obvious that you could use some financial help right now. Selling the property would allow you some freedom. You could travel, get yourself a decent car." She gestured at the dilapidated vehicle down the street. "You said your apartment is small? You could buy a house somewhere, put a film studio or whatever the hell you need in it."

"A film studio?" she asked with a snort and an eye roll.

"Whatever, I don't know. The point is, we can both benefit from this and move on with our lives."

"It just feels wrong." She looked out across the street, staring away from Natalie.

"It's an enormous house, Chelsea. I can't stay. You can't afford it. It's just bad timing."

Chelsea said nothing, just continued staring over Natalie's shoulder.

Natalie went in for the kill. "I'm sure Elizabeth's intention was to help us out, the way Robert hadn't. As long as you're happy and taken care of, that's all that would matter to her."

"Natalie," Chelsea said.

"What?"

"There's someone staring at you."

Natalie turned to look over her shoulder, and sure enough, a young woman was standing across the street, staring at her. She had short brown hair and an armload of binders. Natalie looked away, unsure who it was and not wanting a run-in with anyone. She was about to say something else to Chelsea when she cut her off.

"She's coming over here."

"Oh, for the love of—"

Natalie turned, ready for a fight. As the woman got closer, a prick of recognition stabbed into Natalie's brain.

"Natalie?" the girl asked. "Natalie Monroe?"

Natalie took in the girl. Small stature, shy, a little mousy.

"Amy?"

"Yes! It's me! Amy ! I can't believe you're actually here."

"Me either. It's good to see you." Once the words were out, Natalie actually felt how true they were. Amy had been Natalie's only friend when she lived in Mapleton. For about six months, when Natalie was at her lowest point in life, they'd been inseparable.

"Do you still live here?"

"Yeah, I went to U of T for school, but I moved back a couple of years ago. What are you . . ." She stopped and blinked her eyes closed for a moment. "Of course. Elizabeth. My mind is in a thousand places right now. I'm so sorry for your loss."

"Thank you. This is Chelsea. I don't think you two have met."

Chelsea gave a little wave. "Hi."

Amy returned it with her fingertips, but the movement caused her enormous shoulder bag to slip down. "Sorry, I wish I could stay, but I'm already late for an appointment. Are you staying in town for a while? Maybe we can get together and catch up?"

"I think I'll only be here for a few days. I have some things to iron out before I leave. Maybe we could get together on Saturday?"

"Oh, actually, I'm getting married on Saturday."

"Whoa, really?"

"Yes. I'm . . . marrying a woman named Jaclyn."

Natalie felt her whole face split into a smile. "That's amazing, Amy. I'm thrilled for you."

"Thanks." Amy tapped her foot for a moment, looked up the street, then down at the binders, then back at Natalie. "Do you want to come?"

"To your appointment?"

"No. I mean, do you want to come to my wedding? On Saturday."

"Umm . . ."

"I know this is a little weird, but I would love for you to meet my fiancée. I actually told her about you a long time ago," she said with a laugh.

Natalie wondered how she could get out of this. It was super weird to get invited to a wedding the day before. She couldn't say she was busy—she'd already suggested Saturday. She glanced at Chelsea, who was watching the exchange with a grin.

"Are you sure? Don't these things get planned out months ahead of time?"

"We've had some people cancel last minute, so there's room."

Natalie wavered for a moment. "Um, okay," she said. "Why don't I drop by in the evening for a drink?"

"Perfect!" Amy said. "Here."

She handed the stack of binders over to Natalie, then opened one and pulled out a scrap of paper and a pen.

"The reception is at Cherry Hill Estate Winery. It's just outside of town." She jotted the address down and handed the paper over, then took the binders back. "This is going to be great!"

Natalie smiled. "I'll see you Saturday."

Amy hurried off down the sidewalk, then crossed the street and disappeared.

"Wow," Chelsea said. "Such an *awful* place, eh? People here are so horrible."

"That," Natalie said, pointing a finger in Amy's direction, "is the only nice person in this town. Maybe her parents, too. But I can assure you, everyone else is awful."

Chelsea crossed her arms again but kept a smug, disbelieving look on her face.

"Whatever. I'm not staying."

Chelsea dropped her arms. "Fine. I can't make you stay, and I obviously can't buy you out. Even if you gave it all to me, I wouldn't be able to afford the upkeep on a house that size, and I can't fight the Monroes on my own. Not to mention, where would I even work? So I have no choice."

Natalie breathed a sigh of relief. "Good."

"There's only one problem."

"What?"

"I can't help you with this." Chelsea handed Natalie a yellow legal pad.

"What is this?"

"Speeler handed it to me as I was chasing you out the door. It's the list Grandma made of all the heirlooms the Monroes are inheriting."

Natalie panic-flipped through the top three pages. Speeler had covered them front and back with at least thirty names, the item that corresponded with the name, and date and time when they were to be picked up. She flipped through to the backside of the last page. "What . . . This goes on for two weeks?!"

Chelsea nodded. "Apparently a lot of them can't be in the same room together, so they came up with a schedule."

"Can't I just throw all the shit on the lawn and let them have at it?"

Chelsea snorted a laugh. "No. Anyway, I'm in school, and I have . . . other obligations. I can come next weekend to help you, but that's the best I can do."

Natalie closed her eyes and rubbed around her eye sockets. What a nightmare. She wanted to be in and out of Mapleton as fast as possible, not interacting with every fucking Monroe in town. At least it didn't conflict with when she had to be in Sydney. She'd have to call Jess, tell her she was in Canada and see whether someone could cover her for the first two weeks of her last tour. She could still salvage this.

"Fine. I can handle this. I'll get all the damn Monroes their shit and get the cats to the humane society. But after that, I'm leaving. You'll have to hire the real estate agent and sell it on your own."

"It'll have to wait until I finish school."

"Yeah, I don't really care how long it takes."

Chelsea gave a resigned nod. "Fine. Deal."

Six

"Guinness, please."

Ethan stood patiently, waiting for the bartender to pour his drink. He stretched his neck from side to side and rolled his shoulders back. Who knew getting married would be like running a marathon?

The planning of the event for months and months had been bad enough. But the last two days had felt like a wedding tornado barrelling down on him. He'd been pulled in a hundred different directions every hour. He'd had to make a spreadsheet just to get through it.

The positive takeaway was that it left no time to worry about the future of the Monroe estate.

"Guinness," the bartender mimicked as he passed the pint glass over the polished wood bar.

"Thank you."

Ethan took a deep drink as he looked out over the wedding. He had to admit, Jaclyn's "vision" was beautiful. Rows of wood tables were adorned with tall centrepieces overflowing with white and green flowers. Tapered navy-blue candles in different height copper candlesticks sat in clusters between the centrepieces and lent a soft glow to the room. Overhead, the wood ceiling beams were wrapped in a million twinkling lights.

The five-course dinner had been devoured; the three-tiered cake had been cut, and Ethan's best man of honour speech had been delivered. It had all gone according to plan. And now, Amy and Jaclyn were on the dance floor, swaying together to the sound of the band, with ear-to-ear smiles on their faces.

And since his mind was no longer on all the pressing concerns, it roamed back to the pond and the snakes. And to the homeless girls warning about what he was getting himself into.

"That's a pretty picture," Adam said, coming up to stand next to Ethan. He silently gestured to the bartender, who nodded and went about getting Adam's drink ready.

"You know what's not pretty? That." Adam jerked his thumb over his shoulder.

Ethan followed its direction. In the corner of the room was Lindsay in a low-cut, skin-tight red dress, the exact same colour as her fake dyed hair. She was sitting in Derek's lap at a table with Jaclyn's friends. Amy had stuck them there in the seating plan, hoping the family wouldn't notice her and ask Ethan questions all night. The last time most of his family had seen her was when he brought her to their family's annual Easter brunch. Most of them probably didn't even know about the breakup, and now she was here with someone else.

Lindsay let out a shrill laugh, and Ethan looked away, taking a large swig of his stout. "It's fine."

"It's not." Adam took the drink from the bartender with a smile and a thank you before turning back. "Anyway, you've been MIA for a few days, hiding out, and I have news."

"What is it?"

"Eileen said that Norm, the cab driver, told Betty that he dropped off a 'beautiful young lady' at Monroe Manor. Must be the distant relative Speeler's waiting on."

"Yeah . . . I met her, actually."

"You did?"

Ethan nodded and filled Adam in on the details from the first meeting at the waterfall, to Speeler's news at the office, and the realization that she was Robert's first-born child.

"Man," Adam said, taking a drink. "Homeless?"

Ethan nodded.

"So do you think she'll live there?"

"God, I wish. It would be ideal if someone lived there instead of selling it. But I highly doubt it. She already had a flight booked to go back to wherever she came from, and she laughed in Speeler's face when he suggested she live there. I asked him what I can do to stop the land from being sold or developed, but he said it's private property and up to the new owners."

Adam took a sip of dark liquid from his glass, scratched his chin. "Weird, eh? That she can afford flights, but she's homeless? How does that work?"

"Don't know."

"Well, was Norm a reliable source? Is she beautiful?"

Objectively gorgeous.

His brain immediately pulled up the image of her rich brown hair, cool stare, and full soft lips, then he shook it off. "Yes. She's beautiful. But she's also heartless, short-tempered, impatient, sarcastic—"

The heavy door entering the ballroom slammed shut, breaking Ethan from his thoughts. His gaze snapped to the door, along with the other hundred people in the room, and there she was, standing in front of the gigantic double doors. She had pulled her long hair back behind one ear, and she was wearing a short black dress that was fitted at the top and flared out at her waist. When she noticed people looking at her, she looked down and started moving.

Ethan elbowed Adam. "That's her," he whispered. "Natalie Alvarez."

She scanned the room, then her eyes zeroed in on a target, and she marched with precision forward, her black dress swishing around the middle of her thighs with each click of her heels on the wood floor. When she passed by them and turned, Ethan saw that her dress was almost completely backless, save for the two impossibly thin, criss-crossing straps that formed an X across her naked back.

"Good God," Adam muttered. "She doesn't look homeless. Is she married?"

Ethan hadn't even considered that. Maybe that's why she wanted to leave town so badly. Did she have a Mr. Alvarez to be homeless with? He didn't even know how that worked. "I don't know."

"What's she doing here?"

"No clue."

"Argh . . . I need answers."

Ethan rolled his eyes. "Where's Mrs. P.?"

Adam gave him an annoyed look. "It's Ms. P. And she saw a student she wanted to say hi to."

Ethan snorted a laugh and shook his head. He kept watching as Natalie walked across the dance floor, directly to Amy and Jaclyn. She tapped on Amy's shoulder, and when Amy turned around, she clapped a little, then pulled Natalie into a tight hug. He watched with his jaw nearly to the floor, but the real shocker came when Natalie warmly returned the hug.

After a few seconds, Amy seemed to introduce Natalie to Jaclyn before turning and heading directly toward him. Presumably, to the bar behind him. Before they could pass by, Adam cleared his throat. It was a noise loud enough to stop traffic.

"Hey, Amy!"

She stopped, and her eyebrows drew together. "What?"

"Introduce us."

Natalie's eyes narrowed at Adam. Amy took Natalie by the arm and walked to them. When Natalie's eyes met Ethan's, her step slowed, but she said nothing. He was expecting to be skewered by her, as he was at Speeler's.

"Natalie," Amy said, drawing her attention away. "This is Adam. He's ridiculous."

Adam shot Amy a look. "Thank you for that," he said under his breath, then extended a hand. "It's nice to meet you, Natalie."

Natalie took his hand but only nodded. Then her sharp gaze snapped from Adam back to Ethan, and she stared directly into his eyes.

"And this," Amy said, gesturing to him, "is my brother, Ethan."

Ethan knew the exact moment the recognition came. Natalie's eyes widened before narrowing once more. She let her gaze slowly scan down his body and back up to his eyes. He resisted the urge to turn and run.

"Snake charmer. This is a good look for you."

Ethan couldn't help the smile. He looked down at the slim navy suit Jaclyn had chosen, completed with a crisp white shirt and silver-sage tie. "Thanks."

"Snake charmer?" Adam said.

"You two know each other?" Amy asked.

Natalie turned to Amy. "We met at the waterfall. He tried to take my stick."

"She was using the stick to beat the snakes."

Natalie nodded, as if this were an admirable thing to do. Quick thinking on her part.

Ethan's smile dropped, replaced by a scowl.

He had just opened his mouth to lecture her on the importance of the snakes to the overall ecological balance of the land when, out of the corner of his eye, he saw a flash of red moving across the floor toward him.

He pulled his gaze from Natalie and looked over to find Lindsay staring at him with a Joker-like, bright red smile slashed across her face. Following her was Derek, wearing a messy black suit with a matching red tie.

Amy followed Ethan's gaze. A sick look took over her face, prompting Adam to look as well. His eyes dropped closed for a second in exasperation.

"Fuck," he muttered.

Yes, thought Ethan. Fuck, indeed.

· · • • • • • • · ·

"Ethan!"

Ethan dropped his face into neutral, and nodded.

"I've been meaning to come say hi. How are you?" she asked, leaning in close, nearly pressing her chest against his arm.

"Fine," he said without elaborating. He took a side-step away from her, bringing him closer to Natalie.

"Natalie Monroe?" Derek chimed in with a greasy smile. "Is that you?"

Natalie looked at him, then bared her teeth slightly. "Derek?"

"Yeah! It's me, Derek."

She looked over at Lindsay. "Lindsay Carlisle?" she asked incredulously.

Lindsay nodded. "Wow. You haven't changed at all," she said. "Still that same horrible expression on your face." Lindsay mimicked Natalie's annoyed face, then laughed.

It made his skin crawl.

Natalie stared at Lindsay until she stopped laughing. Seconds ticked by. Lindsay started fidgeting and finally looked away. Natalie glanced over at Amy, who had shrunk with nervousness, then back at Lindsay. "What the hell are you doing here?"

Adam choked on his drink with a laugh.

Ethan remained, in his view, stoically neutral.

Derek leaned in closer to Natalie, probably to diffuse the situation. "Do you want to dance?" he asked, placing a hand on her forearm.

"No," she said, then seemed to remember her manners and added, "thank you."

"Oh, come on," he pressed. He gripped her forearm, attempting to pull her toward the dance floor.

Natalie wrenched her arm away, then squared her shoulders, bringing herself up to her full height. "I said no." She stared at Derek, unflinching, until he shrivelled. Then she twisted the knife. "Go. Away."

Derek's face turned the exact red of his tie. "What the fuck?"

"What are you confused about?" she asked.

His tomato face turned vicious in a second. "You were always such a bitch. Come on, Lindsay," he said, then stomped off to their table without waiting for her.

Lindsay looked from Amy's uncomfortable face to Adam's smile and finally Natalie's pissed-off stare. As if to save face, she mumbled, "Whatever," then turned and left.

The group collectively watched them retreat.

Adam broke the silence first. "That was spectacular. He'll hate you forever."

Natalie tilted her chin up. "Good. The feeling is mutual. Deplorable Derek and Lamentable Lindsay can sod the fuck off."

Adam laughed. "Brilliant. She has nicknames."

Natalie unleashed a smile that transformed her face and made Ethan's heart lodge in his throat. "I wish I could take credit, but it was all Amy."

Ethan summoned all his strength to pull his gaze from Natalie's smile and look at Amy. She'd shrunk back like a week-old flower. She hated confrontation. "You used to call her Lamentable Lindsay?"

She shrugged, then said to no one, or everyone, "Long story."

Ethan worried there was more history between Amy and Lindsay than he'd known. They were in the same grade through school, and Amy was always a victim of bullies. But he hadn't considered that he might have invited one of them into their family circle.

The thought made him sick.

"Let's go get that drink," Natalie said, breaking Amy's discomfort. She looped her arm through Amy's and brushed past Ethan and Adam to get to the bar.

Adam watched over his shoulder as they passed, and as soon as they were out of earshot, leaned toward Ethan. "I like her."

"Go find Mrs. P."

"Ms. And I don't mean it like that. Look . . ." He jerked his chin toward the door just as Derek and Lindsay walked out. "All we had to do was sic the hot homeless girl on them."

Ethan smiled. "She doesn't really hold back, eh?"

"She's fucking terrifying," he said with a grin. "I heard Robert was like that. Shot straight from the hip, you know." He stopped, assessed Ethan. "She seemed pretty into you."

Ethan turned to his friend's grinning face. He meant well, but was clearly way off base.

Adam rolled his eyes. "They're coming back. I'm gonna go find Ms. P."

He left just as they came back. A second later, Jaclyn came over.

"Ames, I need you," she said, taking Amy's hand.

Amy looked at Ethan and Natalie. "Please be nice to each other," she said, then took off arm in arm with Jaclyn.

Suddenly, Ethan and Natalie were alone.

Good.

He had about a thousand questions. Where to begin? Lindsay or the inheritance?

"Would you like to dance?" she asked.

Ethan's brain stopped working. Just went completely blank. He looked at her as she watched him with her terrifying, albeit kinder, stare, waiting for an answer.

"Uh," he said, silently screaming at himself for being such a clod.

"Careful. Amy asked you to be nice," she said in a softer voice than he thought she was capable of.

Ethan didn't really want to dance with her—she was too . . . something. He couldn't quite put his finger on it. But he wanted to sort out this Lindsay and Amy thing, and she seemed to have answers. He also wanted to find out what she and Chelsea were doing with the property.

"Okay."

The band had switched to a slow dance. Ethan led Natalie to the centre of the dance floor, under the lights. He clasped her hand in his, then rested his other hand on the small of her back, where her soft bare skin reached fabric. She moved closer and started moving with him to the slow beat of the song. From the corner of his eye, he could see more couples joining them on the dance floor, but he couldn't move his eyes off of her face or stop his brain from wondering what the smell of her perfume was.

Vanilla? Coconut? Some kind of sweet-smelling fruit?

"Who is that dancing with Adam?" she asked, her voice a whisper. "She looks familiar."

Ethan looked over at his friend. When he located him, Adam wagged his eyebrows at him.

"That's Mrs. P."

Natalie squinted at her. "I think she was my English teacher."

"She was Adams English teacher, too."

Natalie's sharp little nose scrunched up. He looked closer and noticed how warm and glowing her tan skin was. And she had the tiniest sprinkling of freckles just over the tops of her cheeks.

He cleared his throat. "How long did you live in Mapleton?"

"I moved here in November of grade twelve."

"And you became friends with Amy?"

"Mm-hmm," she said.

"Why were you surprised to see Lindsay at Amy's wedding?"

Natalie's head tilted up, causing her long hair to slide down and tickle the back of Ethan's hand. "Amy is one of the sweetest people I've ever met. And Lindsay was horrible to her." Natalie looked over at Amy, then back at him. "It doesn't surprise me that Amy would forgive her, but I still hate it. I don't enjoy seeing good people taken advantage of."

"But bad people?"

Natalie's smile flashed. "Fuck 'em."

Well, at least there was a moral code, no matter how grey, buried under all the animal abuse. Maybe he could work with that. Ethan cleared his throat. "Actually, she didn't forgive Lindsay, I don't think. Lindsay's here because of me."

She tilted her head to the side, like a confused puppy, waiting.

"I, uh, dated Lindsay."

"Okay . . .that actually raises more questions than it answers."

"I broke up with her after Amy invited her as my plus one. She brought Derek last minute."

"Wow. That is some audacity."

Ethan let himself laugh. "Yes, well, she's always been rather—"

Natalie stopped dancing abruptly and stiffened, cutting his thought short. Her eyes popped open, and she looked down. He followed her gaze down and saw the top of her dress slipping down her chest.

"Shit!" she whispered, then jolted forward, latching her warm body onto his. "My dress just broke."

Ethan looked down at her neck. Sure enough, one of the tiny straps had broken off and was dangling down her back amongst her hair.

"Can you fix it?" she asked, panic leaking through her voice.

"Uh . . ."

He leaned over her shoulder and brought his arms around her back. There was too much hair to see anything, so he gently gathered up the soft strands and laid them over her opposite shoulder. She tilted her head to the side, and he followed the string down her incredibly smooth, bare back to where it broke off right at the edge of the dress. He had to remind himself to breathe.

"It broke away from the dress. I can't reattach it."

"Bloody fucking— Can you tie it to the other strap?"

He took the strings, trying to ignore the soft warmth radiating off her, and crossed them over twice before pulling tight. It only took a second, thank God.

"Done."

She tentatively pulled back, looking down. "Oh, that's not too bad."

Ethan's throat went dry. He was staring. He knew it. But he couldn't look away. "Mmm . . . actually, it's sort of pulling to the side."

She twisted around to look. The motion pulled the dress even more, revealing the whole side of her boob.

"It's a good look," he breathed.

The second the words came out, he regretted it. But it didn't stop the smirk that formed on his face.

When he finally forced his eyes to her face, she looked as if she was going to slap him. Her breath was coming at a frenzied pace. He wasn't sure whether she was angry, scared, annoyed, or on the cusp of a panic attack. Probably all the above.

"I have to get out of here," she said, eyes darting around the room to see whether anyone was looking.

Taking pity on her, he shrugged off his jacket and swung it over her shoulders. His brain returned once she was covered again. "Come on."

He led her across the ballroom, through the door, and into the foyer. It was empty of people, but there was a round table in the centre of the room with all the succulents he'd planted lined up in rows on it. He paused at the table and picked up one of the spiky little plants. "Here."

She stared down at it, then looked up at his eyes. "That looks like a plant."

He rolled his eyes. "It is a plant. They're the favours. Take it home."

She reached out, took the plant, and set it back down on the table with a clunk. "I don't think you've completely grasped how being homeless works. I only own what fits in my suitcase."

He stared at the rejected little plant on the table. "So you're not staying in Mapleton?"

"Of course not."

"Is Chelsea?"

"No. We're selling."

Ethan's eyelids dropped closed for a moment. This was his worst fear come to life. The property she now owned had serious effects on his project. Not to mention, most of the snakes were on it. "Why?"

She narrowed her eyes. "Why do you care? You have the pond. We would never try to take it from you."

"I care because if the land were to go to developers, it would be detrimental to my project. The watershed in the area has to be protected. Plus, the snakes have a bit of a PR problem. If there are people around . . ."

She straightened herself, then glanced at the door before her cool stare landed on him. "Look, I have already sacrificed my sanity coming here for Elizabeth. I've sacrificed my job to stay here for Chelsea. I will not sacrifice my future and my goals for some Godawful snakes. I have a job lined up in Australia starting next month."

"Could you just keep the house? Maybe one day you won't want to live out of a suitcase anymore."

"I will never live in this town again."

Ethan stared at her, trying to figure her out. In all likelihood, she was single, and she obviously moved around a lot for her job. But that was a separate and almost unrelated issue. The real issue was that she hated Mapleton. He didn't know why, but he wasn't about to do a deep dive into her reasons.

"Fine. Then could you at least sell it to a family?"

"I can't imagine there are many families interested in a ramshackle twelve-bedroom mansion sitting on snake-infested land, so . . ."

"So . . . you'll wait until one comes along?"

"No," she said. "We'll sell it to the first person to make us a decent offer."

Ethan huffed out a breath. He figured this would be the case, but now he had confirmation. He was incredibly annoyed that he'd spent the last half hour dazzled by her smile and mesmerized by her soft skin and forgot how selfish and cruel she was. He'd sworn up and down after leaving Lindsay that he'd never let a pretty face drive how he felt about someone again, yet here he was.

She took a few steps toward the door, then paused. "I realize this is a bad timing, but is it okay if I take your jacket? I'll get it back to you."

Ethan gave her a half-lidded look of annoyance before realizing this would actually be good. He would have to see her again, and in the meantime, he could pull himself together and figure out how to talk her into protecting the land.

"Sure," he said, straightening his back and plastering on a smile. "Not a problem. You have a good night."

She eyed him suspiciously for a moment. "Thanks."

He watched her leave, even gave her a wave when she looked back. Then he stood there for a moment, brainstorming how was he going to convince her to care about two things she clearly despised: the snakes and Mapleton.

SEVEN

Natalie was not a patient person.

She had to make a conscious effort to achieve an air of calm when in the company of a dawdler, but she could usually manage if she took deep breaths and counted backwards from a hundred by sevens.

Even now, as she slammed the back screen door behind her and marched toward the barn in search of Elizabeth's old bike, she had to go to her happy place. Dealing with the first of the inherited relatives, the patriarch of the family, Mr. Victor Monroe, had taken a toll.

He was in his late seventies, still tall and unbent, as if he refused to let gravity get the upper hand. His once dark hair, same as all the Monroes, had completely greyed, and his impeccable suit gave off an entitled air that reminded her of Robert.

It was hard to be in the same room as him.

But the worst of it was when he strutted around, taking his time looking at every sight as if walking through a museum. He ran his hand along the furniture, peered into the fireplace, took in photographs. When he stopped at the china cabinet in the dining room and stared at the dishes for an eternity, she reminded him that the grandfather clock he inherited was on the second floor, near the balcony doors.

He stopped in his tracks, looked down his aristocratic nose at her, and spat, "I know where my clock is. It's been sitting in that spot since before I was born. I'll take my time in my family home, Natalie."

The entitled remark had made her temper flare, just as it had as a teen when Robert would visit her mother and make comments about their small, broken-down apartment. The apartment that her mother worked so hard to pay the rent for, all by herself.

She had volleyed back, "I believe this is my home now, Victor," then she sat down at the head of the dining table and crossed her legs.

It had done the trick. He bared his teeth but made no further comment. Then he clapped his hands three times like gunshots at the hired help he'd brought along. They leaped into action, and within five minutes, they were history.

She had felt a rush of satisfaction, but now she berated herself for it. Giving off an air of indifference was far more effective than fighting. Fighting meant you cared. And she didn't. When the next relative, Harold Monroe, came to collect his grandfather's gun collection, she would breathe deeper, count longer.

She checked her phone just as she got to the barn. She had about forty minutes before he came. It was just enough time to find the bike, get to the grocery store, and buy some much-needed groceries.

The only grocery store in town was a family run business that didn't even have a website, so her plan to place an online delivery order was out. The last thing she wanted to do was make an appearance in town, but she was desperate for proper food. She'd eaten a can of creamed corn for breakfast, and the only thing left in the house was a jar of pickled beets that had expired two years ago.

Hopefully, this time when she stepped out, she wouldn't have another wardrobe malfunction and nearly flash everyone. Thank God the shockingly attractive nerdy snake lover was there with a jacket to save her a lot of embarrassment. She would never have guessed that Ethan was Amy's brother, but to be fair, she couldn't see half his face until the wedding. Once Amy introduced them, she could see the similarities. He had a demeanour and a general goodness about him that was just like Amy and his parents. She knew she shouldn't have asked him to dance, but there was something comforting, maybe even protective, about him when she was feeling so out of place.

The words were out before she could stop them, and when he pulled her into his deliciously male smelling wall of chest, she thought it was the best impulse she'd ever had.

Then her stupid dress broke, and the feeling of his rough hands on her skin and his warm breath fluttering down her neck and shoulders made her want to both sink into him and run away.

She shook the thoughts out of her head and grabbed hold of the handle on the huge barn door. The second the door was open a crack, a black bat swooped down from above the door and flew deeper into the barn.

Natalie watched in horror, a shudder working its way through the hollows of her spine.

She peered around the corner and caught sight of the old baby-blue bike with a basket on the back that Elizabeth used to ride around town. It was only a few feet in. There was a good chance the old barn was home to many bloodthirsty creatures hiding amongst the rusting farm equipment, but she had no choice. She'd never make it back in time for Harold if she went on foot. Taking a cab only increased the interaction with the townspeople. So she counted to three, darted into the barn, grabbed the bike, and bolted out of there.

Five minutes later, she arrived at the store.

The grocery store, opened eighty years ago, was built into an old building on a corner lot, giving it an awkward V shaped layout. The entrance to the store was on one street, and the exit led to another street.

Natalie propped the old bike against the far side of the building near the entrance and walked in. She grabbed some fruit and veggies, then went to the bakery section and stopped in her tracks at the towering display of butter tarts.

It had been a decade since she last had the deliciously gooey treat. Her mouth watered, and she grabbed a box, then hesitated and picked up three more. It was going to be a long two weeks. She might as well have something to enjoy. In fact, there were probably a ton of long-forgotten Canadian delicacies she hadn't had in years. She went on a hunt through the rest of the store for all her favourite childhood treats.

By the time she made it to the checkout lanes, her arms were bursting with boxes of Kraft Dinner, all dressed chips, Nanaimo bars, and some local beer and two bottles of icewine. She dumped it all on the belt with a nostalgic smile and happily watched as the cashier scanned the items.

She paid, hefted her bags toward the door, and nearly tripped over her own feet.

In front of her, blocking the exit, was a long, white table with a navy-blue banner pinned to the front that read ANNE MONROE FOR MAYOR. On either side of the table were bunches of blue and white balloons, and behind the table stood Anne Monroe herself, wearing a pressed white suit with an intricate sapphire pin on the lapel, high heels, and petal-pink lipstick outlining a soft, genuine smile.

Natalie felt all the blood drain from her face. She forced her step to steady, not wanting to draw attention. Luckily, a mother with a little girl in a pretty pink dress stopped at the table and drew Anne's attention. She bent down to the little one and handed her a perfectly decorated sugar cookie in the shape of the letter A, wrapped in cellophane and tied with a little blue bow.

Watching the interaction made Natalie's stomach drop. She looked around, hoping to make an escape, but the only other way out was the entrance, and there was no way she could get over there without causing a scene.

She would have to get past the table unnoticed.

Natalie tipped her face away from Anne and picked up speed, but just as she neared the table, the mom beckoned the girl, and they took off.

Natalie chanced a glance and found Anne staring directly at her.

"Hi there. Would you like a cookie?"

Her smile faltered as Natalie shook her head, broke eye contact, and kept walking. It was hard to tell whether it was because her rudeness appalled Anne, or whether she realized she'd just offered her late husband's love child, who ruined her marriage, a cookie.

Natalie sped up and bolted for the automatic doors, but they were old and rickety and took forever to open. When the crack was large enough for her and her bags to fit, she turned sideways and slipped through.

"Natalie!"

Across the street, Ethan was jogging toward her, hand waving and shouting her name. Dammit.

"Natalie! Hold up!"

She wanted to lift a finger to her nose to silence him, but the bags were too heavy. She chanced a look back to the door, hoping that they had closed or that Anne was distracted with another potential voter, but no such luck. Anne stood staring out the open door, stiff as a board, with a sad look where her smile had been. She looked as if she was going to cry. Her worried eyes darted from Natalie to Ethan and back.

Natalie turned, trying to block the image, and speed-walked to her bike.

"Natalie!"

She kept ignoring him, silently praying for him to stop screaming her name. Unfortunately, he wasn't giving up. And he was fast. He caught up with her in a few strides.

"Hey! Why are you brushing me off?" he asked, jogging in front of her so she had no choice but to look at him. He stood in her way and stared down at her, eyes flicking between hers from behind his lenses, analyzing as he patiently waited for her answer.

She found herself lost and forced a blink. "I'm not. I'm brushing someone else off."

He made a show of looking up and down the completely empty street. "Oooookayyyy . . ." he said.

She rolled her eyes at him. "I'm not delusional."

He raised his eyebrows in an irritatingly unreadable way. "Who was it?" he asked.

She couldn't tell whether he was genuinely curious or thought she was insane. And for some reason, she actually wanted to explain herself to him. "Anne."

He glanced back. "Ah, I see."

The thought of Anne standing there sadly made her skin crawl. She had to get out of there. The last thing on earth she wanted was for Anne to come out and try to talk to her. She brushed past Ethan and reached for her rusty old bike.

"Do you want a ride?" he asked. "I've got a truck. I can take you home and get my jacket."

He tilted his head behind him toward a big, black truck parked on the side of the street, away from the grocery store exit doors.

Part of her wanted to just get his address and drop the damn jacket off under the cover of night so she could avoid any more incidents like this one. But leaving faster would be good, and she was running out of time to meet Harold.

"Fine."

• • • • • • • • • •

The drive back was under a minute. When they pulled up in front of the house, Ethan hopped out, then heaved the old bike out of the bed of his truck and leaned it up against a tree.

Natalie walked up the front steps and passed the bags over to him while she unlocked the front door with her key.

"You kept the stick?" he asked in a flat tone, nodding to the stick she had fended the snakes off with. It was leaning against the side of the house next to the door.

"Yes. It's a warning. I will swipe at any snakes that come here." She pulled the key out, turned the lock, and opened the door. Then she took the bags from him and stepped inside.

He didn't follow.

"You can come in. Your jacket is just upstairs."

He took a small step in, then another, looking around. "When I was ten, Adam told me this house was haunted."

Natalie snorted a laugh. "Only for me."

He looked like he wanted to comment but stopped himself. He took a few steps, bending to look into the parlour and the dining room. At the staircase, he took in the intricately carved design. "Impressive."

She took a few steps up the stairs, then paused. She was going to leave him in the foyer while she retrieved the jacket. That way, she could just hand it over, say goodbye, and never have to look at his handsome, judgy face again. But she knew that would be rude. He was clearly interested in the old house, and no matter how high and mighty he was about saving the damn snakes, he didn't deserve to be mistreated.

"Do you want a tour?"

His eyebrows inched up, and he tilted his head, as if deep in thought. "A tour?"

Good lord. It was a simple enough question. "Yeah, a tour around the house."

He looked thoughtful for a moment, then a tiny smile tugged at the corner of his mouth. "Sure."

She led him up the stairs, telling him all the little tidbits she had picked up over the months she'd lived there with Elizabeth. Guiding someone along was natural to her. She brought him to Elizabeth's massive room and through the French doors to the third balcony that faced the orchards. Then to the sleeper porch on the east side of the house. And finally, to the third-storey turret.

Ethan stepped into the bright, round room and walked over to the centre window. "Yup," he said, giving the glass a light tap. "This is the window the ghost was in."

She laughed and walked over next to him, peering out. The window was high enough on the house that it could just be seen over the treetops from the street. "Your friend's a real character, eh?"

"You don't even know the half of it," Ethan said with a laugh. "He started his own festival once."

A laugh escaped. "I can only imagine what goes on at that festival. Did he say what the ghost looked like?"

"He just said 'a ghost in a long white dress.'"

Natalie nodded. "Elizabeth used this as a sewing room. He probably saw a dress form with a night-gown on it . She was really short, so she did a lot of hemming."

He turned and looked at her with a smile, and she noticed how his blue eyes were flecked with tiny bits of silver around the irises, and she counted the little wrinkles around his eyes that deepened with his smile.

There were four.

She was standing way too close to his face.

She took a big step to the side, then kept walking toward the stairs. "Come on, my room is this way," she said, walking away and rolling her eyes at how that came out.

He followed her down the stairs, through the long hall, and finally to an open door. She walked in, grabbed his jacket from the chair, and handed it to him. "Thanks again. You were a lifesaver."

"My pleasure," he said, looking down at it without moving.

She was about to tell him to take his jacket and his calm, attractive demeanour and his beautifully crinkly eyes and leave when he looked up at her. He opened his mouth, as if he was going to say something, then paused again, before finally saying, "Would you like to go on an actual tour?"

Natalie stared at him for a beat. Was he asking her out?

"An actual tour?" she asked.

"Yeah," he said, shuffling his feet. "You like waterfalls, right?"

"Yes . . ."

"I thought we could go waterfalling," he said, with an awkward wave.

"Waterfalling."

Ethan nodded. He looked nervous, waiting for an answer.

"Is this like a date—"

"No. Not a date."

He answered so fast she couldn't help but be offended. Not that she wanted to go on a date with him. But would she have said no?

Ugh, probably best not to wonder about that.

Her eyebrows drew together. "Good. Because I don't date."

"Ever?"

She shook her head. "No."

His eyes seemed to look everywhere but at her before he finally said, "Okay, full disclosure. I want to take you around, explain the area, and show you how important your land is to the ecosystem."

"Oh . . . I see. This is part of your crusade to protect the snakes."

"More or less."

She eyed him for a moment, taking in his nervous energy. She couldn't care less about the snakes, but she loved a good tour, and she'd never been "water-falling" before. Not to mention she hated being in that house. Maybe a day away would be nice, even if she had to listen to a sales pitch from the cute doctor about snakes and the ecosystem and blah blah blah.

She walked over to the dresser where her suitcase sat and picked up the yellow pad with the inheritance list on it, scanning for an opening. "Looks like Speeler gave me Thursday off."

Ethan's face lit up. "I can do Thursday morning."

"Fair warning, I won't change my mind about selling this house."

He nodded. "I'll take what I can get."

They walked together down the stairs and through the foyer. Natalie swung open the door to let Ethan out and found Harold Monroe standing alone on the porch, fisted hand suspended in the air about to knock, showing off a sizable sweat stain in the armpit of his beige shirt.

He had dark-red hair, streaked with grey, and big googly eyes that he'd narrowed to slits. He steadied himself to speak, but Ethan beat him to it.

"Eight a.m. good?"

Harold's head whipped between Ethan and Natalie. They both ignored him.

"Fine."

"Perfect. See you then," he said with a charming half smile, then bounded down the stairs to his truck.

She turned her attention to Harold finally.

"You must be Nat—"

She cut him off, raising her voice over his. "You know where the cellar is?"

"Of course I know where the cellar is! This is my—"

"Good. That's where your guns are. Get them and get out."

So much for indifference.

She left him in the house alone and walked down the stairs to where Ethan had left the bike. She couldn't listen to any more words come out of a Monroe. Better to take her chances in the vermin-infested barn.

It was going to be a long two weeks.

EIGHT

E than pulled up through the gates at Monroe Manor, wondering for the twentieth time that morning whether he was making a mistake. He wanted to do whatever he could to save the snakes. He asked Natalie to go waterfalling because he wanted to lecture her about the importance of the land. But a nagging little voice inside his soul accused him of lying.

By omission, at least.

Maybe, in the back of his mind, he'd thought it would be nice to spend the day with her. She was smart and funny, and as much as he tried to ignore it, she was gorgeous. At least she looked that way. Her attitude about the helpless snakes was less than pretty. But he was determined to change her mind.

And that was his mission today. Change Natalie's mind about selling to developers while simultaneously ignoring how brightly her eyes sparkled in the sunlight.

"Piece of cake," he said to himself as he pulled up the driveway. But as he came around the corner to the front of the house and saw Natalie sitting on the porch waiting for him, he wasn't so sure.

She was wearing a plain white T shirt and short black shorts, with acres of tanned legs stretched out in front of her. On her feet were sandals.

He rolled his eyes and stopped the car.

"Morning," she said, hopping into his car with a heart-stopping smile that took over her face.

Ethan blinked away. "You can't wear sandals."

"This is all I have."

"I thought you might say that." He reached to the back seat, pulled up a pair of hiking shoes and socks. "I took these from Amy's this morning. She and Jaclyn left on their honeymoon already, so she won't be needing them. I hope they fit."

"Oh. Thanks," she said, slipping her sandals off her pretty feet and pulling on the socks.

He looked past her at the front porch and saw two metal cages sitting by the door. "What are those?"

Natalie followed his gaze. "Cages."

"Yeah, I can see that. What are they for?"

She looked at him. "The cats," she said, then looked back down and muttered, "if I ever find the damn things."

Horror came to Ethan's face. "Are you really going to lure them into cages and send them off to be euthanized?"

"Adopted," she said, then went about ignoring him.

"You know if they can't find people to adopt them, they euthanize them, right?"

She didn't respond. Instead, she focused all her attention on tying the shoes, then started pressing buttons on the dash. "I'm going to put on the day song."

Ethan shook his head as he put the truck into gear and pulled out of the driveway, wondering why he'd invited this heartless woman on a trip. She hadn't seemed capable of something like that when he was with her at the wedding. She'd said she defended Amy, didn't enjoy seeing good people taken advantage of. But that didn't jibe with her carelessness with her grandmother's defenceless little pets.

Figure her out. Convince her.

He cleared his throat. "What's a day song?" The more information he had, the better strategy he could develop.

"It's a song you play every morning on tour. By the third day, people associate the song with their trip.

After they go home, whenever they hear the song, they remember all the fun they had."

"So this is what you do? You're a tour guide, and you live out of a suitcase?"

She nodded and clicked a few times on her phone, then turned up the volume.

"I chose a song especially for you."

"For me?"

She nodded, then hit Play. The sound of Michael Bublé's "It's a Beautiful Day" filled the truck.

"Why this song?"

"It's about going through a breakup but being happy it's over."

Now she was thoughtfully choosing songs for him? This girl made no sense. Maybe she cared about people, but not animals. She clearly cared for Amy. And Chelsea. And Elizabeth. Maybe he could spin this away from the snakes and tell her about the effects an unhealthy ecosystem had on quality of life.

"You are happy it's over, right? I didn't get to hear the entire story before my dress broke."

He turned to look at her, his memory going back to the feel of her soft skin under his hands. He shook his head to clear it. Thinking about her skin was counterproductive.

"Uh, yeah, I guess."

He needed to get back on track. He glanced over, about to bring the subject to the property, but she was staring at him, her eyebrows drawn together, waiting for an answer to an unasked question.

What the hell were they talking about?

Right, Lindsay.

Focus.

"The relationship was bound to fail from the beginning."

"Then why did you date her?"

It was a good question. He was going to sugar-coat his response, but he was just too sick of the whole thing to bother. "She asked me out, she was really pretty, and I had nothing better to do, so I said yes. It evolved from there."

"I see."

"In my defence, no one told me she was lamentable."

Natalie laughed. "Amy should have. How did it end?"

"She . . . uh, cheated on me."

Natalie nodded. "That makes sense."

He mirrored her nod.

"Did it suck?"

"Well, yeah. You've never been cheated on?"

"No," she said.

"Must be nice."

"I don't date, remember?"

"Right. Yeah," he said, then frowned and focused all his attention on the road.

"What doesn't make sense," she continued, "is why she still went to Amy's wedding."

Ethan winced. "She assumed they still invited her to the wedding, even though we broke up."

"But why would she want to show her face there?"

"Uh . . . she doesn't actually know I know she cheated."

That got her eyebrows up. She stared at him, then did a slow blink and shook her head a little. "What?"

Ethan tapped his phone attached to the dash. They were about ten minutes from the first waterfall on his list, so he filled her in. Told her everything from the beginning, when they started dating, to three months later when he broke up with her. By the end, she was astonished.

"Let me get this straight," she said. "You caught her cheating on you, during one of your baseball games, in the back seat of this truck, with Derek, who is also your teammate, and you just . . . walked away?"

Ethan nodded.

She kept her summary going, this time louder and more indignant. "Then you broke up with her, with-out telling her you knew about the cheating, and didn't tell anyone else, and then she brought the guy she cheated on you with to your sister's wedding?"

Again, he nodded.

"And you kept this truck?!"

"Well, yeah. I just paid it off."

Her face was a mask of shock. If she were a cartoon, this is the part where her head would split in two with a little explosion.

"Do you always make such rational decisions?"

"I strive to, yes."

"You never just do what feels good?"

"I tried that. And we all know how that turned out."

"No. We don't *all* know, do we?" she muttered, looking away out the window.

Ethan tried to block her out, but her reaction was too forceful and brought the debate back up in his mind. He'd thought this thing to death on his research trip, going back and forth. Ultimately, he concluded he made the best decision that he could under the circumstances.

What he needed now was to ignore it, let it blow over, and move on. Then, he needed to find someone who was right for him. He knew he was ready for a serious relationship, and he vowed to himself that he would be more rational in his attempt this time around. No more women who didn't check any of his boxes, regardless of how pretty they were.

They drove in silence for a few minutes before Ethan took a right off the main road into a long gravel driveway. "We're here. Devil's Punchbowl."

He pulled the truck into a parking spot, turned it off, and hopped out. Natalie fell in step beside him. From the parking lot, it was only a fifty metre walk along a paved trail overhung by deciduous trees to the top of the waterfall.

When the waterfall came into view, she sped up and made a beeline straight for the lookout. She leaned over the low wood fence that ran along the edge of the cliff , and stared at the huge semicircle cut-out of land striped with orange, green, and red rock.

"Wow. It's actually a bowl! Look at the colours."

Ethan stepped closer to her, looked over. He'd seen the waterfall dozens of times in his life, but he tried to look at it as if he were seeing it for the first time. It was impressive. The water fell for seven metres, in a long ribbon past multicoloured layers of rock.

"It's beautiful," she said. "I need a picture. Will you?"

Handing him her phone, she propped herself up on the fence, legs crossed, and pulled her long hair forward, making it fall softly over her shoulders down her chest.

He was thankful to be doing a job where she expected him to look at her, because he didn't think he could peel his eyes off her. He felt bad for anyone who only got to see the photo. It didn't do the real thing justice.

He clicked the button a few times, then handed the phone back without a word.

"Thanks," she said, hopping off the fence. She took the phone and slipped it into her purse without looking at it.

They spent a few more minutes walking around the falls, looking at it from different angles. Ethan told her about where the water flowed from and where it went to, and told her what creatures were living around there. He started telling her about the vernal pools nearby, blathering on and on before he realized he was just talking out of nervousness and forced himself to wrap it up.

They went back to the truck, where she put the day song on again, and continued on toward Niagara Falls, stopping at three more waterfalls along the way, collecting pictures. Each time they got back into the truck, she put on the day song. For lunch, they stopped at a farmer's market that Natalie said had good reviews along the lake. They both had the "holiday poutine," made of sweet potato fries, topped with turkey, cranberry sauce, and gravy.

It was delicious.

While they ate at a picnic table overlooking the huge expanse of blue water of Lake Ontario, she asked him about his research trip. He told her about the whale watching tour they went on one day where they saw belugas. He asked her about her travels and was shocked to hear she'd been to ninety-nine countries and six continents. When he found out that she'd been to the Galápagos Islands on tour eight times, he was in awe. He inundated her with questions, but she didn't seem to mind. She spoke passionately about the crystal-clear water and the tortoises, and Ethan made mental notes in the Natalie file he'd started in his head.

Before they left, they bought a box of butter tarts at Natalie's insistence and ate them on the way to the Falls. They were so good, he almost forgot he was listening to the millionth replaying of Michael Bublé. She booked tickets on the way for the Horn-blower cruise, a boat tour that went under the falls.

Once they were on the boat in the churning water, he realized he was actually having a great time. He'd been on the cruise before, with his parents and Amy as a child, but as an adult, it was different. More impressive, somehow. Natalie tried to say something, but the roar of twenty-eight million litres of water rushing over the falls every second drowned out her voice.

"What?" he yelled.

She leaned up close, her soft breath grazing his ear and warming him through the cold, wet air.

"Will you take another picture?"

He nodded, speechless, and she handed him her phone just as the boat became shrouded in mist. Leaning against the railing, she tilted her face up to the sky and held her hands out. He clicked a photo. The water had soaked through the ugly poncho she was wearing, and droplets had collected on her eyelashes.

She should have looked bad; everyone else on the boat did. But her playful expression drew him in. He had to force his gaze from hers again, and although he managed, it was getting harder and harder to do it each time.

• • • • •• • • • ••

Ethan checked the time as they arrived at the last stop on the tour. It was late afternoon, and he still had work to finish up and a baseball game that evening. Normally, he loved his work, would have felt odd not completing it, but he had to admit he wasn't looking forward to it now. Getting away from town for a day of waterfalling had been a fun distraction, even with Michael Bublé.

You're not supposed to be having fun.

He gave his head a little shake as he stopped in the parking lot of the vast conservation area that sat high on the escarpment. He grabbed a backpack with water bottles and put it on. It was a three-kilometre hike uphill.

They left the truck and started their climb. About halfway up, Ethan led them down a heavily wooded, almost nonexistent path.

"You sure you know where you're going?" Natalie asked, crunching along behind him through the knee-high brush.

"Trust me."

They climbed and climbed until they finally reached the top, both out of breath. He expected her to collapse on the ground, struggling for air. Luckily, she seemed to catch a second wind when the lookout came into view. She walked to the edge of the cliff, then plopped down way closer to the drop-off than he thought was safe.

"Oh my god," she breathed out.

Ethan carefully made his way to her and sat down next to her. He opened the backpack and handed her a bottle of water. She drank deeply between laboured breaths, then pushed her sweaty hair from where it had affixed itself to her sticky skin. Her cheeks were flushed pink, and her face was full of awe.

She stared out into the sunny distance, gaze sweeping across the huge landscape surrounding Mapleton. It was a peaceful green mix of forest, farmland, and vineyards.

"Hey, I can see my waterfall!"

Ethan leaned toward her to see through the branches of a sugar maple that blocked his view. "Yup. And there's my pond. You should come see it sometime."

She gave her head an emphatic shake. "Not a chance. I'll look from here, where I'm safe from snakes. I am safe from snakes here, right?"

Ethan rolled his eyes. "Yes." He wanted to defend the snakes, but he knew from experience that would go nowhere, so he changed tactics.

"I came up here two years ago with a land survey-or to assess this entire area and figure out what was going wrong. See how your property lies low, almost in a basin?"

"Yeah."

"The entire property used to be a huge wetland. That's why your relatives built the house up on that hill. But fifty years ago, one of the Monroes drained it to make a field to plant cash crops, and it destroyed the entire ecosystem."

"I didn't know that."

"To be fair, they probably didn't know the effects it would have, either. But the wetlands work as a sponge. They soak up all the rainwater and runoff, slow down the flow, filter the water. Without them, the polluted water rushes into the lake and raises the bacteria levels, which affects everything from fish habitats to the water we drink. The beaches have even shut down because of the poor water quality."

She didn't speak, just sat in introspection for a long time. Maybe he was finally getting somewhere?

"I made a plan for the pond just over three years ago when I moved back to Mapleton. Elizabeth was on board from day one. We've already seen positive effects from it."

"Like the snakes?" she asked, an annoyed look crossing her features.

"You're just biased by your hatred. They are an important part of the ecosystem. Did you know the rodent population exploded after the snake's habitat was destroyed?"

Natalie's face became a mask of horror. Ethan's hope returned.

"By our estimates, the number of mice is a hundred and seventy times what it should be. The mice decimated the food supply. With no food, the birds disappear. When the birds disappear, the bug population increases. Eventually, you end up with what we've got now: a flooded, buggy, rodent-filled mess. If it were to be heavily developed, there would be no recovering."

He watched her as she looked out across the low-lying area, deep in thought.

"I get you want to sell, but, please, consider selling to anyone other than a developer."

She stared at him longer, her eyebrows coming together, then eventually her face fell, but she remained silent. It was the same internal debate he saw play out over her features in Speeler's office when Chelsea quietly begged her to stay.

"Can I ask you something?"

"No," she said, with no resolve.

Ethan smiled. "Why do you hate it here so much?"

"I don't belong here."

"Where do you belong?"

She shrugged. "Nowhere."

Ethan let the words sink in and found himself speechless. He watched her tip her chin up defiantly, as if what she said didn't bother her. But he wasn't so sure.

"Why exactly did you move here when you were younger?"

She glanced at him, stared into his eyes for a moment, then sighed. "My mom died, and I was going to be homeless. Like, really homeless. Not like I am now. There was no way I could afford the rent on our apartment and stay in school. Elizabeth showed up and offered me a place to stay. I'd never met her before, and I hated Robert, but she seemed genuine, and I had no other options, so I moved into the manor with her. But it caused more problems than it solved. For me and for her." She pulled her knees up to her chest and hugged her legs. The position made her look vulnerable, like a devastated angel. He half expected wings to break through her back.

"What happened that made you decide to leave?"

Natalie huffed out a breath and dropped her cheek onto her knees, peering up at him on an angle. "Anne told Elizabeth she didn't want me here."

"Well, that's not your fault."

"I know it's not my fault. But I don't want to be the cause of someone's pain. My mom kept up the affair long after she found out Robert was married. I think Anne has been through enough without me here causing trouble. Every single person in this town had something to say about me. They made up wild stories about why Elizabeth took me in." She paused and seemed to shudder at the memories. "So I decided to leave after graduation and start over on my own. And my life is great now. People out there in the world judge me for what I've done, not who my parents were."

For the first time, Ethan finally got a glimpse of the real Natalie. Not the sharp-tongued girl who acted as if she didn't care, but the outcast who stood up for defenceless people because she knew what it was like to be all alone. He couldn't really relate to feeling alone; he always had a supportive family growing up. But he could relate to feeling judged by everyone in town.

He acted on instinct, reaching his arm around her and pulling her body into his as if he could shield her from whatever was harming her. She stiffened, but after a moment, she relaxed into the embrace and dropped her sweaty forehead onto his chest. They sat for a while like that, in silence, looking out over Mapleton. He thought back and forth about it, analyzing, debating, and came to the conclusion that he was asking way too much of her.

"Sorry, I know the gossip around Mapleton can be vicious. To be honest, I was planning on hiding out at the pond all summer to avoid hearing everyone's take on the mess with Lindsay. I didn't know that people were unkind to you."

She waited a beat, then pulled back and looked up at his eyes. Her face softened with a look he'd never seen on her before. "It's not something I talk about," she said. "Ever."

"Why did you tell me?"

She huffed out a soft laugh. "Because you're so damn persistent?"

He looked down at her, and she was wearing that dazzling smile he first saw at the wedding. He took in her dark eyes, long eyelashes, and full smiling mouth, then forced his gaze off of her and looked out at the distance.

"Or maybe because you're a good person. And you feel safe. And I like your family."

He glanced back at her and was surprised to see that she was looking at him almost as if she wanted him. Was that even possible? She leaned in closer, then reached her hand around his back and dropped her gaze to his lips.

His heart rate kicked up, and he leaned toward her out of instinct. When she didn't back away, it removed all doubt about what she wanted. And he realized how much he wanted her. How much he wanted to pull her to him, lay her down on the cool ground, bring his mouth to hers. His heart was racing as he imagined tasting her lips and feeling her soft curves under his hands.

But then he remembered that she was entirely wrong for him.

And she hated everything he loved.

And, worst of all, she was leaving.

He'd learned his lesson about starting something without thinking. He swore he would never do it again. Getting involved with her would leave him worse off than he was now. He had to be smarter about things this time.

He broke eye contact and pulled his arm away from her. The cool air that replaced her warm body was like a slap to the face.

"We should . . . probably get going."

She nodded, then stood. "Yeah. Probably."

He stood up and backed away from her, putting more distance between them. That's what he needed. Distance would clear his mind. He turned away from the cliff and started back to the path when her voice stopped him.

"Wait, I need a picture here."

She pulled her phone from her pocket, and he stepped back and reached out for it, but she didn't hand it to him.

"Do you want to take one with me?"

"Uh, sure," he said. He wasn't capable of any more denials. The last one took every ounce of willpower from him.

He stood next to her, and she held the phone out to take a selfie.

"Closer," she said. "Now squat." When their faces aligned, she took a picture. He moved, but she held him in place.

"Are you that eager to hear Michael Bublé again?"

Ethan rolled his eyes as she laughed at him, then snapped another picture. Finally, she pulled away and looked at it with a smile.

"That's a good one. Do you mind if I post it to Instagram?"

Ethan laughed and shook his head. "No, I don't mind. You know, when we first met, I thought you were some silly influencer trying to get a picture in the waterfall."

Her smile turned up a notch, and she beamed at him. "Really?"

"Yup."

"And what do you think of me now?"

Ethan's smile slowly retreated as he thought about the question. What did he think of her? He wasn't sure. But he'd be better off not trying to make sense of his warring body and brain.

"I think I need more empirical evidence before I can make a conclusive judgment."

"How very analytical of you, doctor."

Ethan gave a nod. "Come on, let's get this day song over with."

• • • • •• • • • ••

Ethan swung his baseball bag over his shoulder and jogged from the parking lot to the diamond. He was ten minutes late. His team was already on the field warming up. It had taken longer than he thought to drop Natalie off and get his work done. When he got closer, he saw that Adam was sitting alone in the dugout, staring at his phone, waiting for him. They usually warmed up together.

"Hey, sorry I'm late."

He sat down on the bench to change into his cleats.

"Would your lateness have anything to do with the scary hot homeless girl?"

"What?"

Adam lifted his phone and pointed the screen at Ethan.

He was bent over, pulling on his cleats. He glanced up at Adam's phone. It took him a second to register that he was looking at Natalie's Instagram. More specifically, the selfie she'd taken at the top of the lookout.

Her smile was otherworldly.

He turned his attention back to his shoes. "You follow her on Instagram?"

"I do now. Along with about two hundred thousand other people. Did you know she's mildly famous?"

Ethan paused. Two hundred thousand?

Adam turned the phone back to himself and swiped across the screen. "It surprised me, too, but it's easy to see why. You should see some of these pictures. They're amazing."

Ethan let go of his laces and sat up, then snagged the phone out of his friend's hands. He did a quick scroll down through her photos. One after the other was Natalie standing in front of some famous landmark. The Taj Mahal, Machu Picchu, the Great Wall of China. Thrown in the mix were a few photos of her biting into incredible-looking food.

And then there was him. In a boring little town that she hated.

He gave the phone back and finished lacing up his cleats.

"Check out the comments on your picture," Adam said.

"I'd rather not."

"Fine, I'll read them aloud." Adam cleared his throat, then put on the most ridiculous, high-pitched girl voice he could manage. "Damn! Canadian guys are hot!"

Ethan's brows rose. "Someone wrote that?"

He nodded and continued. "Ooo . . . a boy! You never post photos with boys. Who's he?"

"That can't be true."

"Oh, it is, my friend. I looked," Adam said, then went back to scrolling through comments.

She'd never posted a photo with a guy before? That seemed impossible. But she did say she never dated . . .

"Look at this one," Adam said, holding out his phone. "It's just three fire emojis."

"What does that mean?"

"They think you're hot, you knob. What else would it mean? God, you need to get out of your snake pit and start living in the real world. And"—he paused for effect and pointed a finger at Ethan—"you need to get an Instagram account."

"You clearly don't understand the difference between a want and a need."

"I understand the difference, and I stand by what I said."

With a roll of his eyes, Ethan grabbed his glove and water bottle from his bag, then hooked his bag onto the chain-link fence next to Adam's. He tried to walk out of the dugout to the field, but Adam stood in his way.

"So it's getting serious between you two, I take it?"

"There is no it. I took her to see some waterfalls and lectured her about why she shouldn't sell to a developer."

"Wow, you really know how to show 'em a good time, eh? I can't believe you actually had the day off."

"I . . . had to switch something around. It was nothing."

A smug smile pulled at Adam's face. "One thing?"

Ethan nodded. It was actually three appointments and lunch with a colleague, but he wasn't about to volunteer that information.

"It looks like you two had fun," he said, fishing for more information.

"It was fine, other than Michael Bublé."

Adam's brows rose. "Bublé? You guys spent the day looking at waterfalls and listening to Bublé?"

Ethan nodded and made a move to leave. He wanted to put it all behind him. He did everything he could, and now he'd have to wait and hope. As far as Natalie was concerned, the sooner she got her pretty butt on the plane and out of there, the better. He couldn't take much more.

Adam held out a hand to stop him, then waited. Ethan gave in, finally met his friend's eyes, and said, "Something else?"

"Just for the record, she seems great, and I really like her."

"Consider it recorded."

"Seriously. I never told you how much I hated Lindsay, and I regret it."

Adam glanced past Ethan, then his face morphed from sincerity to annoyance. Ethan already knew why. He turned around to see Derek waltzing into the dugout.

"What are you two losers talking about?"

Adam smiled. "Just looking at pictures of Ethan and Natalie."

"Together?" Derek asked.

Adam nodded happily. Ethan knew Adam well enough to tell he was trying to goad Derek. And he knew Derek well enough to know this wouldn't end well.

They were both ticking time bombs.

Derek turned to Ethan. "I should warn you, Natalie Monroe is a huge bitch."

A sick feeling rose in Ethan's gut. He tried to ignore it.

Adam laughed. "Why? Because she refused to dance with you after you groped her?"

"No." Derek's face took on a deep-red hue. "Because she's stuck up. She acts like she's too good for everyone. And she has no reason to. She was just Robert Monroe's whore's kid that Liz took in out of pity. When he found out, he kicked her ass out of the house."

"If that's true," Adam said, "then that would make Robert the bitch. What kind of person abandons their kid?"

Derek was dumb enough to ignore Adam's tone of voice and double down. "She never should have been there. She's nothing but trash."

Ethan could feel his rage bubbling up. He wasn't entirely sure whether it was because he now knew how horrible people were to Natalie or because he hated Derek so much. The why seemed irrelevant, though.

He'd heard enough.

"Are you really in a position to be calling other people trash, Derek?"

"What the fuck is that supposed to mean?"

"It obviously means that I think you are trash."

Derek's hands fisted, and his breathing sped up. "Are you fucking kidding me, talking to me like that?"

Ethan could feel Adam move in closer. The solidarity was nice. But Ethan didn't need any backup. After years of being bullied as a scrawny, nerdy kid, his parents had put him in kick-boxing. The summer he turned seventeen, about a year after everyone else, he shot up a foot and earned his blue belt. He was still pretty lanky, but stood taller than most, and intimidation tactics like Derek's weren't concerning to him.

"The evidence speaks for itself, Derek. I saw the mess you left behind in my truck."

It was almost funny how Derek's entire face changed from rage to shock. Ethan had wondered whether Derek knew he knew and just didn't care. But it was clear now that Derek was arrogant enough to believe he'd got away with it. Derek backed down, turned away without a word. He grabbed his glove and took off onto the field with their teammates.

"Finally!" Adam said, his face cracking back into the natural smile he always wore.

"Let it go."

"I can't. That was brilliant. I mean, it would've been better if you drop kicked that ass-faced motherf—"

Adam stopped short, and a shocked look came over his face. "Gayle!"

Ethan whipped around and came face to face with his mother. Her gentle blue eyes were darting between Ethan's and Adam's, and her fisted hands were on her hips.

"Are you two fighting?" she asked.

Adam plastered an overbright smile on his face. "Of course not!" he said, then pulled her into a hug, lifted her off her feet, and twirled her in a little circle.

She smiled at Adam, but only for a second, before stepping toward Ethan. "What was all that about?"

Ethan looked over her head at Adam and shook his head. Adam nodded.

"Nothing. I didn't know you were coming by."

She pulled back. "It didn't look like nothing. It looked like you were fighting with Derek."

Ethan and Adam stayed stone faced and quiet.

"Nothing to say for yourselves?"

They both shook their heads.

As if unconvinced, his mother pursed her lips. "I came by because I haven't seen you since the wedding."

"Well," Adam said, "he's been travelling."

She frowned and turned back to Ethan. "I wanted to see if you know how to get a hold of Natalie Monroe."

Ethan pulled back, surprised. Why did everyone he saw want to talk about Natalie? "Why?"

"I want to invite her to the house for dinner on Sunday. Your father and I were disappointed that we missed her at the wedding. Aunt Barbara told me you were dancing with her. Is that true?"

"Uh . . . yeah. That is true."

Adam cleared his throat. "Didn't you plan to go to the pond on Saturday?"

Ethan ground his teeth together and glared at him. "Yes."

"And," he continued, "isn't Saturday in two days?"

His mother clapped her hands together. "Excellent. You can just stop by and ask her on Saturday, then let me know what she says." As she walked away, she called over her shoulder, "Tell her I'll make her favourite meal!"

Ethan watched in horror as his mother walked away. Natalie had a favourite meal? What the hell was going on?

"Well, well, well," Adam said with a smug voice. "Meeting the parents, eh? Big step."

"That was not helpful."

"You sure about that?"

"Yes. And she isn't meeting my parents. There is nothing going on between us. She's leaving in a week, and I wanted to avoid her until then."

"If there's nothing going on, then why are you avoiding her?"

Ethan ignored the question and pushed past him to the field.

"You're pretty defensive for someone who claims it's nothing!" Adam called.

Ethan broke into a jog, ordering himself to calm down. It was just dinner. He'd invite her but not offer her a ride. Her filling up the space of his truck was too much. They would eat; she would leave, and he would never see her again.

This was going to be fine.

Just fine.

NINE

Natalie was sitting on the floor in front of the buffet in the parlour. She was going through the list of items, and prepacking them for pickup. It was Saturday, which meant she had five pickups that day, two of which had already come, but it also meant she was finally getting some help. Chelsea was on her way, thank God. After encountering ten Monroes, she was ready for a break.

She finished wrapping up the eighth—yes, eighth!—tea set in newspaper, carefully placed it in a cardboard box, marked the name on the top, and pushed it aside. At least it gave her something to focus on instead of Ethan.

The eight tea sets would be collected over the next two days, along with several pieces of jewellery, a recipe book, three quilts, a violin, a box of tomato seeds, many weapons, and a weird mustard-yellow figurine of an old woman holding a fish.

Natalie pulled the hideous figurine off the top of the buffet and held it up in the light. Why did people want crap like this? The knick-knack would be bad enough on its own, but then you'd need a shelf to put it on, and cleaning supplies to keep the dust off, and a shelf to keep the cleaning supplies on, and then you'd have to clean the cleaning supplies shelf.

Ugh.

It seemed like a horrible waste of time. She'd lived the last ten years with nothing, and she was just fine.

She shook her head and shoved the offensive thing into a box. Then her mind drifted back to Ethan for the tenth time that morning, and she wondered whether he had stuff like that in his house. She imagined his house would be full of comfortable furniture, books, pets, and plants, with enormous windows that looked out into gardens he carefully tended. And she was willing to bet that if someone gave him a figurine as a gift, he'd keep it forever and take care of it.

She wanted to see his home. Wanted to be invited into his life. He was just so calm and genuine and solid. When he'd put his arm around her at that cliff and held her tight, she nearly begged him not to let go. She wanted him to lay her down on the soft ground and press his body into hers under the canopy of trees. Replace some of the bad memories of Mapleton with some good.

But he definitely wasn't the type to invite someone into his life temporarily, as was clear from his relationship with Lindsay. He should have treated Lindsay as a one-night thing, then moved on.

But he hadn't. And that was very telling.

When he first told her he walked away without confronting her, she thought he was weak for not sticking up for himself. But the more she thought about it—and she thought about it a lot—the more she realized that wasn't true at all. It was easy to tell an asshole they were an asshole. But it took serious resolve to show kindness to someone who deserved none.

Still, there had to be a better way of going about it.

Natalie admonished herself again for thinking about Ethan, taped up the box with the old woman inside, and wrote the name across the top in Sharpie. She picked it up and brought it to the foyer next to the other boxes waiting to be picked up. Then did the same with the eight tea set boxes.

She put a check mark next to the names to show she'd packed them up. She only had a few more things to locate and pack. Chelsea wanted to go through the house and see whether there was anything she wanted that hadn't been claimed before the house and its remaining contents went to an auction.

The only big hurdle left to jump was the cats.

She'd ordered cages that trapped animals inside as soon as they passed through, as well as three bags of cat treats. She set them up in the kitchen before going to bed, but when she woke up that morning and checked, they weren't there. The treats remained completely untouched.

She suspected there were too many mice in the house keeping the cats well fed. They didn't care at all about treats. So she got on her phone and ordered fifteen mousetraps to set around the house, as well as six cans of tuna. If she could kill and dispose of the mice fast enough, the cats might take the bait. If that didn't work, she'd have to rethink the entire plan.

She'd just finished up when her attention was snagged by a flash of red through the front window. The next Monroe wasn't due for another half hour, so Natalie figured it must be Chelsea's little rust-bucket pulling up.

She dropped her phone on the counter and walked to the door. When she grabbed hold of the handle to swing it open, a little rap on the outside of the door stopped her. She could see Chelsea through the window, still at the trunk of the car, pulling out a duffle bag.

What the hell made that knocking noise?

She pulled the door, looked down, and came face to face with a boy.

He was little, like only a few feet tall. She had no idea how old he was. He was wearing a tiny blue baseball cap, a little T shirt with a skateboarding dog on it, grey shorts, and blue running shoes over striped socks that were pulled up almost to his knees.

"Ben!" Chelsea called, slamming the trunk. "I told you to wait for me." She came up the stairs carrying a backpack and a pillow, both covered in Spiderman.

Natalie stood frozen in shock. Did Chelsea have a son? Impossible. She was way too young. Maybe she worked as a nanny in between classes to pay the bills?

"Do you live here?" Ben asked.

Natalie stared down at him. He had blond hair poking out of his hat and blue eyes. The same blue as Chelsea's. In fact, his entire face looked like hers, right down to the deep dimples in both cheeks.

"Do you?" he asked again.

"I . . . no."

"Well, I'm here for a sleepover. We're going to have a pyjama party! Mama brought popcorn, candy, a movie, my pillow, my sleeping bag, my toothbrush, my toothpaste, my dino, my pajamas, my . . ."

He carried on like that, listing the entire contents of his backpack for nearly a minute before Chelsea found her voice and interrupted him.

"Ben, can you take these things inside, please?"

"Okay, Mama." He grabbed his pillow and backpack and skipped past Natalie and inside.

Natalie turned to Chelsea. "Mama?"

"Yes," Chelsea said, tipping her chin up.

"You have a son?"

"Obviously."

"How old is he?"

"Four."

"So you had him when you were . . ." Natalie tried to make her brain work but couldn't even manage basic subtraction.

"Eighteen."

"What about his dad?"

"Not really in the picture."

"Why didn't you tell me?"

"I'm telling you now."

"I mean before."

The worry on Chelsea's face broke. Her brows dropped into a frown; her mouth went flat. "I didn't really think you'd care."

Natalie's face crumpled, then her gaze dropped from her sister's eyes. When she'd left, Chelsea was young and had a loving mother in her life. Natalie had never worried about her at all.

"I didn't want to bring him here, but my mom is sick and couldn't take him for the night, and my friend who usually helps out is working."

Natalie let that bit of information sink in, then closed her eyes and dropped her head.

"You never even called me," Chelsea said, her voice cracking. "Never added me on social media. You changed your name so I couldn't even find you."

"Chelsea, I . . . I didn't realize . . ."

"That I'd be upset that my sister disappeared? I figured that would be obvious."

Natalie's shoulders slumped as she let out a long exhale. "Fuck."

Chelsea's gaze snapped inside, then back to Natalie. "Language! He repeats everything."

"He's not even here."

Chelsea leaned in close, let her face move a fraction into a little smile. "He's everywhere." She turned on her heel and walked down the stairs toward her car.

Panic flooded Natalie's brain. "Where are you going?"

Chelsea laughed. "I'm not leaving. I'm just grabbing stuff from the car. I got us coffee and Timbits."

Ben popped his little face from behind the door. "Timbits!" he yelled.

Natalie jumped back, startled, and had to bite back the curse that nearly slipped out.

"You can have one now," Chelsea called to him. "But the rest are for our pyjama party."

He sagged against the door, but his smile stayed in place. He looked up at her. "You're coming to the pyjama party, right?"

"Uh . . ."

His eyes widened to saucers, and his smile dropped.

"Yes. I'll come. Count me in," she said, patting his little head and hoping that would make the smile return.

It worked.

His face melted back to its happy state, and Natalie breathed a sigh of relief.

"Come on, you two," Chelsea said, walking past them on the porch and into the house. "Bedtime is seven, so the party starts at four. We're ordering pizza."

Ben threw his hands in the air. "Pizza!" he shouted as he ran after the box of Timbits. She was certain this was the cutest kid that ever existed, wondered what he'd looked like when he was a baby. And wondered how Chelsea was managing raising a kid while being in film school.

She glanced over at the clock. Two in the afternoon. There were still a couple more hours of Monroe pickups to deal with. She closed the door behind her with a smile on her face. Who knew she'd actually look forward to a pyjama party with a four-year-old?

Only one problem. She didn't own pyjamas.

· · • ● · ● ● · · ·

At three thirty in the afternoon, Natalie slipped into an old nightgown she found in Elizabeth's dresser drawer. She had ten to choose from, each more horrifying than the last. She wasn't sure what was more out of character for her—wearing an old lady nightgown, putting on pyjamas at three thirty in the afternoon, or just having pyjamas on at all.

She usually wore nothing to bed when she was on tour and staying in private hotel rooms. In between tours, at hostels, she slept in her bra and panties. Pyjamas were the first thing to go from her suitcase.

She'd selected the least horrifying option, a stiff white cotton nightgown that covered every inch of her skin, besides her face, hands, feet and ankles. It would have come down to Elizabeth's toes, but Natalie was a few inches taller, so it stiffly stuck out in a ring six inches off the floor. She looked in the mirror and stared at her dreadful reflection until the frilly lace and pink rosettes strangling her neck started tickling her jaw.

How did Elizabeth sleep in this?

She'd considered taking scissors to it, probably would before eating, but she figured it would get a laugh out of Ben and Chelsea. And after the afternoon they'd had, they could all use a laugh.

Having Chelsea and Ben there had made dealing with the three Monroes that afternoon more bearable. Chelsea seemed unaffected by their horrible comments and disgusted attitudes, and Ben was downright delightful. He was bright and curious and had the most addictive laugh. He'd even brought a brief, albeit strained, smile to Hattie Monroe's face, and Natalie suspected that face hadn't turned joyful in at least two decades.

She was smiling as she left her room and walked down the stairs. She couldn't wait to get his little pyjama party of three started. It was so opposite of her normal, she almost felt as if she was on vacation.

Eating pizza, drinking a juice box, watching a kids' movie, and tucking little Ben into his bed was the perfect way to unwind after a day.

She found Ben in the living room in his little superhero pyjamas, complete with cape, and Chelsea in her flannels. They were cuddled up on the old couch, with the movie ready and waiting on the screen.

"Nat, can you grab the—" Chelsea stopped mid-sentence when she turned enough to take in Natalie's nightgown. A second passed before she burst into laughter. "Ben, look at Aunt Natalie!"

Ben's eyes bugged out, and he let out a little giggle. "You look so cool!"

Chelsea let out a snort through her laughter.

Natalie tried to look annoyed but failed miserably. "I like your definition of cool, my man."

He jumped up and inspected the lace sticking out around her wrist. "You look like the big bad wolf in grandma's bed."

Chelsea bent over laughing and wiped at the tears coming down her cheeks. "She looks like one of the Golden Girls." The remark came in fragments through her laughter.

"I did this for you."

Ben's squeaky laughter ceased just long enough for him to say thank you.

A knock on the door split into their laughter. Chelsea wiped her eyes again. "That must be the pizza," she said, then frowned in the clock's direction.

"I'll get it," Natalie said. "Give the delivery person something to gossip about in town."

She walked to the front door just as another knock sounded. She grabbed the handle and pulled the door open with a dramatic flourish, but to her surprise, it wasn't the pizza.

It was Ethan.

Natalie's jaw dropped as Ethan's dirt-smeared face morphed from an irritated look to one of shock. He raked his gaze from her eyes, down her body, then back up again. Finally, a grin overcame him.

"Hey there, Sandra Dee."

Natalie swung the door closed, but Ethan's hand shot out and held it open.

"Oh, no, you don't," he said, then a laugh came out. Then another. Before long, he threw his head back and clutched his abs with his other arm.

She used his distraction to her advantage, put two hands on the door, and pushed it harder. "Go away," she said.

"I'm not going anywhere," he said, holding the door firmly open with little effort. He was a lot stronger than he looked. "What the hell are you wearing? Is this another one of your weird suitcase things I don't understand?"

Natalie huffed out an annoyed breath. She refused to stand there losing more ground, uselessly pushing the door closed, so she stepped back, crossed her arms, and gave him a slow, annoyed blink.

"We're having a pyjama party. I borrowed this because I don't own pyjamas."

Ethan lifted a finger under his glasses to wipe a tear away as his laughter slowly stopped. "You don't own pyjamas?"

She shook her head. "Suitcase."

Ethan audibly swallowed. His gaze dropped down her body as he reached his hand back to rub his neck. "Uh . . ."

Ben's feet came slapping down the hall behind her, pulling her attention from Ethan's searing gaze. She turned to look at him as he stopped in his tracks. "You didn't bring any pizza?" he asked Ethan.

Ethan stared at him for a moment, then looked up at Chelsea, who followed behind Ben. "Hi, Ethan," Chelsea said. "We thought you were the pizza delivery. This is my son, Ben."

Ethan barely missed a beat. He held his hand down in a fist. Ben bumped it with his own little fisted hand. "Hi, Ben, I'm Ethan."

"Hi. Are you here for our pyjama party?"

"No. I'm just here to talk to Natalie."

"Aunt Natalie," Ben corrected.

Ethan looked up at her. "Right."

She stared at him for a moment, wondering what he wanted to speak to her about. He'd already given her his entire explanation about saving the town's watershed. She'd figured she wouldn't be seeing him again. A thought that was both a relief and a discomfort. Seeing him stand in front of her now, it was impossible to deny that she was happy to see him again.

"Come on, Ben," Chelsea said, a little too loud. "Let's have those Timbits."

"Timbits!" he said, then ran off to the living room.

"Good to see you again, Ethan," Chelsea said, before leaving Natalie and Ethan alone once more.

"Uh," Ethan started, looking around as if he were lost. He was awkward, but, somehow, it lent to his attractiveness. She wanted to feel his body against hers again, then wondered what he would do if she leaped at him, and shook the thought away.

"Why are you here?" she asked. She meant for it to come out rude, but it came out breathy.

He cleared his throat. "To ask if you'd like to come to my parents' house. For dinner. Tomorrow night."

"Oh," she said, taken slightly aback. A smile came over her face. Was he asking her out on an actual date? "Is this a date? Or part of your continued effort to save the snakes?"

"No, neither," he said, with a shake of his head. His gaze dropped from her eyes down to his mud-caked boots.

He looked nervous. Maybe because she'd told him she didn't date and he was trying to frame it another way. She quietly hoped that was the case and knew without a doubt that she would say yes. She looked at his eyes as they rose back up to hers.

"My mom wanted me to ask you."

Natalie stared at him for a long moment. "Your . . . mom."

"Yes."

"Gayle is asking me out?"

Ethan huffed out a small laugh. "Yeah. She said she missed you at the wedding and wanted to catch up. She's making your favourite meal."

Disappointment washed over her. She couldn't blame him for not wanting to get involved with her. He was a long-haul type. And she wasn't. They were just incompatible. She selfishly wanted more than what she could give.

She swallowed, trying to look at the bright side of things. Natalie loved Gayle. She would hang out at her house with Amy all the time. She was a very sweet lady and an absolute master of chicken pot pie.

"All right, I'll come. What time?"

"Dinner's at six."

"Okay."

He stood in place. He probably wanted to ask her whether they'd talked about selling. But he didn't. After a few awkward moments, he gave a half wave and returned to his truck. He reefed open the door, hopped in, and drove off.

"Okay, then . . ."

She closed the door and looked down at what she was wearing. "Ugh."

She turned and leaned against the door. Chelsea stood in the foyer across from her with her hands on her hips. "What was that?"

"Nothing. We need to talk about selling the house."

"I'd rather talk about what just happened. Did Ethan ask you out?"

Natalie's shoulders slumped. "No. His mom did."

Chelsea cringed. "His mom?"

"Yeah. He's actually Amy's brother. I was close to his family when I lived here. I'm going over for dinner tomorrow night."

Confusion marred her pretty face. "Have you guys been spending time together?"

"Yes. He's been trying to convince us not to sell to developers."

"Us? He hasn't tried to convince me of anything."

Natalie rolled her eyes. "I'm sure if you were here, he would have taken you waterfalling to convince you."

"Waterfalling? You two went waterfalling?"

"It wasn't a big deal."

She said it, but knew it was a lie. It had been a big deal. For her, at least. She never opened up to people the way she did with Ethan on that cliff. And never accepted comfort like that, either. All of her interactions were surface level, with people who were very temporary. No one ever knew how alone she was in life.

"He wants the Monroe property to stay a wetland. Maybe we can hold off selling to developers? See if there's a family that would buy it instead?"

Chelsea nodded. "Honestly, I'd feel better about selling, knowing the house won't get torn down. But I've been wanting to move apartments, and my savings won't last that long. Maybe we could give it a couple of months, and if no one offers to buy it, then sell to a developer?"

Natalie nodded. "That seems fair. At least we can say we tried." She'd tell him tomorrow at dinner. He'd just have to be happy with that.

"You look disappointed, Nat."

"I'm not."

"I know disappointed when I see it. I watch actors trying to pull it off all the time."

"Fine. I am. A little. Maybe."

Chelsea smiled. "You like him."

"You'd have to be a complete psychopath not to like him. He's a genuinely good person."

Chelsea nodded. "True. He's a real 'my rock' type, you know."

Natalie snorted. "Rock? He's like the goddamn Canadian Shield."

Chelsea laughed. "I knew it! You don't like him the way Grandma liked him. Or Speeler, or Ben, or me, or the snakes, or the people in town. You *like* him, like him."

"Doesn't matter. He's not interested in me."

"He is. Actors try to pull off that look, too. Most fail. I should record him talking to you and play it back so that they can see exactly what smitten looks like."

Natalie rolled her eyes. "Fine. I think he is interested. And I do like him. But he won't ever act on it, and I can't expect him to. I'm leaving, and he doesn't seem like he wants a one-night stand."

Chelsea cocked a brow. "Have you asked?"

A smile broke out on Natalie's face. "Not verbally."

"Maybe you should."

Natalie laughed. "Maybe when I'm dressed better."

"I doubt he'd turn you down, even in that atrocity."

A knock came from the other side of the door, and Natalie pushed away from it.

"That must be the pizza. You get it," she said to Chelsea as she walked past. "I don't want to be seen like this anymore."

She went to the living room and sat down on the couch next to Ben. He was happily staring at the TV with colourful sprinkles crusted onto his sweet little face. She put an arm around him and hugged him, dropping a kiss on top of his little head. Then she reached into the box on the coffee table, grabbed a chocolate-glazed Timbit, and shoved it into her face.

As the crumbs tumbled down the front of her hideous nightgown, she silently vowed to give herself extra time to get ready before dinner the next night. At least she'd look her best if she was going to throw herself at him and get shot down.

TEN

"Ethan, can you light the candles and take the appetizers out?"

His mother was in the kitchen, pulling on oven mitts. She opened the door to the oven, and a waft of savoury chicken pot pie billowed out, filling the whole room. The smell was almost as incredible as the "bake-sale brownies" she'd made earlier for dessert.

Turned out, Natalie had pretty good taste in favourite meals.

"Are candles really necessary?"

They never had candles when it was just Amy, Jaclyn, and him. Candles felt too formal. Too romantic. He already knew this was going to be a disaster, but as long as he didn't look at Natalie or talk to Natalie, he could conceivably get through it. Candles would set a mood that added to his difficulty.

He'd just have to wolf down the meal, say good-bye, and never see her again. The thought made his stomach drop, but he wasn't sure whether it was relief or dread.

His mother stuck the tip of her knife into the golden crust of one of the pies. "This dinner is important to your father and me. We miss Natalie."

"How much time did she spend here?" he asked, pulling the matches from the junk drawer and lighting the candles on the table.

"Oh, she was here a lot. Always for dinner on Sundays. Amy told us that was when Robert would visit Elizabeth. We loved having her. It was very sad when she left."

Loved having her?

God.

Ethan rolled his eyes and dropped the matches back into the drawer, then slammed it shut.

"Did you know she was the reason Amy came out to us?" She asked as she slid the pie back in and closed the oven door. "She was more scared than Amy that day. Thought we would disown her. I guess she'd seen a lot of homeless teens on the streets growing up. She even offered to take Amy in."

Ethan looked away from his mom, hoping she'd stop talking about how great Natalie was. "Uh, well . . . I guess that was nice of her."

"It's hard to find friends like that," his mother said. "Ones who are there for you when you need them most. I know you two are at odds with the property, but she's a good person with a tender soul, Ethan. She grew up hard and had to deal with a lot at a very young age. When she left back then, it was no surprise. There was nothing here for her besides an awkward relationship with her grandmother and gossip around every corner. You could just see it scraping away at her heart."

Ethan took a deep breath, then exhaled. "Right."

"She'll leave again, and you'll just have to figure out what to do with the property after it's bought by the new owners. It's not fair of you to pressure her to stay, though I would love to see her more."

He took another deep breath and was just about to confess to his mother that it wasn't only the property that made him feel sick about her leaving when the doorbell rang through the house.

"Oh, she's here! Will you get the door? I have to toss the salad, and I don't know where your father is."

Ethan shook out his tense shoulders and walked to the door, giving himself a silent pep talk on the way. He could get through this if he could just think of her as a snake-beating cat killer, instead of a beautiful, misunderstood girl with a big heart whom his parents loved. Bracing himself, he opened the door and looked up.

And found Anne Monroe standing on the porch. She was wearing white and navy blue, as always, and had a fake smile pulling at her surgically enhanced face.

"Dr. Pierce. It's a pleasure to see you."

She stuck her hand out at him, and he took it, confused. "Hi."

"I'm going door to door to speak with voters ahead of tomorrow's election."

He looked up and down the street but didn't see anyone else. Just a big white Cadillac parked in front of the house with its four-ways on. "You do that alone?"

"Not usually."

"Okay . . ." He looked back over his shoulder, hoping to catch one of his parents for her so he could escape. No luck.

"I think everyone is busy right now. I'll let them know you dropped by."

"I came to speak with you, actually."

"I don't live here."

"Well, you weren't home, and I heard your family is big on Sunday dinners. I thought I'd find you here."

She smiled as wide as her face would allow, as if following him was a totally normal thing for a mayoral candidate to do. It was a creepy thing to do, but she made it worse by lying about it, then changing direction immediately.

He took a step back. "Okay. What is it?"

"I wanted to ask you about the Monroe property." She glanced around before stepping closer to him and lowering her voice. "There's a great deal of talk around town about . . . the heirs."

"Uh huh . . ."

"And I've been slipping, ever so slightly, in the polls. I believe it's because of the gossip circulating."

"Okay. What does that have to do with me?"

"Well, I can't get any solid information about their plans for the property. I know you've inherited the pond, and you've been spending some time with one of them. The older one. Do you know if she plans to stay?"

Ethan swallowed down a lump that formed in his throat. "They plan to sell."

Anne's smile returned. "Excellent. That's excellent news. Will they do it soon?"

"I don't know."

Anne's facial features unnaturally jerked around, from concentration to concern to glee. "Doesn't matter, I guess. I forgot to mention, when I retake office, I plan to allow a portion of the budget for environmental restoration. You can apply for some grants, and I will see to them. Personally," she said with a wink.

Ethan's grip on the door tightened. "I don't need a grant. I need the property to remain undeveloped. Speeler told me he petitioned your office to change the land zoning, but you blocked it."

"It isn't fair to take private property owners' rights away. Besides, it would be better if those two were on their way."

"Better for who?"

Her smile dropped, and a hardness took over. "Everyone. Have a wonderful dinner, Dr. Pierce. I hope I can count on your vote."

Anne turned away just as a movement on the street caught the corner of Ethan's eye. He looked over, and coming around the corner down the sidewalk was Natalie, in a yellow dress holding a bottle of wine. When she saw the back of Anne, she quickly ducked between the houses into the backyard.

Anne seemed to sense something, like a shark smelling blood but not sure where it was coming from. She slowly turned toward Ethan's gaze, but Natalie had already concealed herself.

"Uh, we'll see," he said. "Thanks for stopping by. Good luck."

Anne's face whipped back to her forced smile. "Okay. Good evening."

She strutted to her car, got in, and took off.

Ethan waited.

Then waited some more.

Finally, he got sick of waiting, pulled on his sneakers, and went off the porch to find Natalie. When he came around the corner between the houses, he found her hiding in between the ten-foot-tall hydrangea bushes that were covered in huge white and pink blooms. She was clutching the bottle to her chest with both hands and deep breathing.

"Uh, the coast is clear."

She opened her eyes and forced a sheepish smile. "Hi."

"Hi. You okay?"

She nodded but didn't answer.

He narrowed his eyes at her, assessing. "How can you have so much guilt about your mother's affair? You won't even look Anne in the eye."

She shrugged and looked down at her sandalled feet, then softly kicked at the wood chips.

"I really don't think she deserves your sympathy, Natalie."

"She looks like she bounced back well, after I left."

With one hand, Ethan gently pried the wine bottle from her grip; with the other, he cautiously clapped her upper arm in a friendly gesture. He knew the dangers of getting too close, but he couldn't leave her hiding in the bushes looking ashamed.

"You did nothing wrong, and you're not responsible for ensuring Anne's happiness. She could have left him."

Natalie looked up and stared into his eyes without a word for a long moment. He watched the back and forth play out in her eyes and could almost feel the torture she was putting herself through.

"Ethan . . ." she said.

The sound of his name on her lips rendered him completely lost. She was so beautiful. Her hair was down around her shoulders, and he knew how soft it was from experience now. And the mix of her sweet-smelling perfume and the flowers that surrounded them messed with his brain. He stared into her eyes, waiting. "Yeah?"

She took a step closer to him, smiled, then reached her hands out and rested them on his forearms. They drifted up to his elbows, then down to his wrists and gently squeezed. "Thank you for being so nice to me."

His skin warmed under her hands, and he moved closer, closing the distance between them. She rose on her toes, hesitated slightly, then leaned forward and grazed her soft, dewy lips across his cheek.

A bolt of white-hot light shot through his blood. He reached his free hand up the back of her neck, through her silky hair and pulled her in close until his lips were millimetres from hers. The warmth radiating from her skin was soaking into his brain, and he couldn't recall why he'd ever thought this was a bad idea. He inched toward her as she tipped her face up to meet his, and slowly closed the distance until his lips softly grazed hers in an almost kiss that made his heart spiral.

All he could think was *more.*

He leaned in, deepening the kiss as she opened for him. A soft moan escaped her lips, and he spiralled more, down down down out of control until the smack of a slamming screen door broke through his daze.

"Ethan?"

He jumped back from Natalie, looking over to find his mother standing on the porch. She couldn't see them, so he stayed put, hoping she'd give up and go back inside and he wouldn't have to explain why he was in the landscaping, groping their dinner guest.

He laid a finger over Natalie's snickering, swollen red lips and stayed still. A few seconds passed with his mother muttering to herself on the porch about everyone disappearing. Finally, she gave up and went back inside, letting the door slam behind her.

When he moved his finger away, Natalie smiled her blinding smile at him and laughed. She was impossibly pretty. His heart pulled him toward her, but his brain fought back. Now that he'd been slapped to reality, he remembered why this was a terrible idea. He took three big steps away from her and a deep breath. Distance was what he needed, he reminded himself. When he got too close, things got out of hand.

"Yeah, it's all funny now," he said. "Just wait until Adam finds out. We'll never hear the end."

"How would Adam know?"

"He has spies."

Natalie looked at him like he was a weirdo. "Did you ever get caught bringing girls back here when you were younger?"

Ethan huffed out a laugh. The question was absurd. "Of course not. Girls weren't interested in me when I was younger. Even now, everyone in town still looks at me like I'm a nerdy little kid always covered in dirt."

She tilted her head and looked up at him. "Do you mean a nerdy hot doctor always covered in dirt?"

He laughed. "Hot? That's definitely not the descriptor they'd use. But I'll take it over scary, homeless snake charmer."

"I don't think I ever called you scary."

"It was implied. You yelped when you first saw me."

She let out a breathy laugh that grazed along his heart. "I was startled. But I'm lucky you were there. You saved me."

She smiled at him, held his eyes for a long moment. He wanted to take her back into his arms, push her up against the wall, press his body into hers, and finish what they'd started.

But he now knew without a doubt that he couldn't shield his heart from her. She'd leave, and it would devastate him. Better to ignore it, avoid it, and move on. He broke eye contact, cleared his throat and took a step back.

"We should go in," he said with all the conviction he could muster up.

Natalie's smile fell away, replaced with a confused furrow to her brow, but she said nothing. She nodded once, then sidestepped him and walked toward the front porch, leaving him wondering whether he'd just made the best possible decision, or the worst.

• • • ● • ● • • ••

Natalie stepped into the house and took an exaggerated inhale of the chicken pie- scented air, a smile returning to her face. Ethan closed the door behind him and watched as she took off her sandals and walked in.

"I hear you spent a lot of time here in high school."

Natalie's smile faltered at his voice but mostly stayed in place. "Yes. I loved it here. It's like family houses you see in movies."

She sounded stiff, missing her usual sarcastic, playful tone. Unease filled his chest, and he nearly choked on it.

"Natalie," he began, not really sure where he was going with it. She turned, waiting for him to continue, but he had no idea what to say. "About the bushes . . . in the bushes, I mean. I know you're leaving in a while, and I—"

"Natalie?"

His mother poked her head around the wall from the kitchen down the hall and interrupted them.

Again.

Natalie took off running—literally running—down the hall. "Gayle!"

His mother threw her arms open wide, and the two of them hugged each other tight, swaying back and forth, saying how much they missed each other. When they finally released each other, Ethan's father, Mark, came in from the basement, and Natalie ran into his arms for a hug, and the entire exchange began again.

Ethan watched in . . . awe? Horror? He wasn't sure. All he knew was that the unease in his chest was growing, taking on a life of its own, clouding his brain and causing him to doubt every decision he'd made regarding her until that point.

"Come in, come in, dear," his mother said, looping Natalie's arm with hers. "Dinner is ready. I made chicken pot pie."

Natalie smiled. "You remembered my favourite meal?"

"How could I forget? I think of you every time I make it. It was so nice to have two kids to feed after Ethan left for school."

Natalie smiled at his mom, then released her and walked to the back door on the other side of the dining table. Ethan wrenched his gaze and focused on the wine bottle still gripped in his hand. He went to the counter, pulled out the bottle opener and four glasses, then set about pouring. It was good to have a task to concentrate on, to stop his mind from spiralling into visions of her being there as his date, not his mother's, and what it would be like to kiss her without worrying about protecting his heart.

His hand shook as he reached for a glass, knocking it over.

"Careful, Eth," his father said. He took the wine bottle from Ethan's hand and finished the job. He handed him two of the glasses and tilted his head toward Natalie.

Ethan walked to Natalie and handed her a glass. She gave him a polite smile and went back to staring out into the backyard. "The gardens look beautiful in summer," she said. "I only saw them in the winter."

"Oh yes," his father chimed in. "Ethan did a great job with them. He still tends them now."

"Really?" she said, giving him a quick glance. "I didn't know you did this."

Ethan nodded silently, then took a swig of his wine.

"Remember how crazy he used to make me with the gardens, Gayle?" his father said. "It's all he would ever talk about. Every damn weekend I was out there with him digging."

His mom laughed. "Remember when he made you reroute all the eavestroughs so they'd empty into the rain gardens?"

His dad shuddered and took a drink.

"Rain gardens?" Natalie asked.

No one responded, so Ethan piped up. "Yeah," he said, pointing through the window. "Those two gardens collect and filter the runoff, kind of like the wetlands."

Natalie continued staring out the window. "I can just imagine what the gardens look like at your place," she said.

"Uh . . ."

Images of Natalie in his home flashed through his mind— laughing in the kitchen, cuddled on the couch, falling back onto his bed with her hair fanned out over his pillow. . .

He shook his head and worked to clear them.

"Actually, I don't have any gardens."

She turned to finally look at him. Two tiny lines formed between her eyebrows. "Why?"

"The real estate agent said most people shy away from overly landscaped yards. Too much work."

"Oh. Are you planning on selling?"

"I don't have any immediate plans to sell, no."

Natalie gave a humourless laugh and shook her head. "Always so practical."

Ethan was about to protest when his dad clapped his back with a laugh. "You hit the nail right on the head, Natalie. Ethan won't blow his nose without knowing the consequences and having a Plan B. He's always been that way, even as a toddler."

Ethan slowly turned his head toward his father, then narrowed his eyes at him. He'd never told his dad to shut up before, but he was seriously considering it now.

"See?" his dad said with a laugh. "Even now, he's working through how to get me to shut up in the most efficient and painless way possible."

"Mark, stop," his mom said. "Everyone sit."

Ethan turned and reached for the chair he'd sat in since he was a small child. Then he saw Natalie's hand do the same.

Natalie smiled up at him. "This was always my spot."

With a small laugh, he shook his head and walked around the table to sit in Amy's chair. "I didn't know I'd been replaced after I left."

His mother gave his back a pat. "We missed you very much. It was wonderful having Natalie here."

Natalie sat down and squirmed a little in her seat. She looked mildly uncomfortable. He remembered her saying she'd never had a home, but it seemed as if she'd found one with his family. He suddenly had an overwhelming sense of relief that his parents had been there for her when she was going through the loss of her mother.

"So, Natalie," his father said, pulling Ethan's attention. "What have you been up to? I've always wondered where you went after you ran away from us."

Natalie gave a small smile. "I went to Florida."

"Florida?"

"Yeah, I got a job on a cruise ship. I worked on the ship and travelled the Caribbean for two years."

"Really. That sounds exciting. Then what?" his father asked.

"After I saw every country there, I quit, moved to Peru, and got a job on an alpaca farm near Cusco."

Ethan nearly spit out his wine. Everyone turned to him. He started to make an excuse but gave up. "You worked on a farm?" It seemed impossible. She couldn't even stand the sight of little snakes.

Natalie laughed. "Yes. I got a job on a farm. They gave me free room and board, and I travelled around on my days off."

"Then what?" he asked.

"Well," she said, smirking at him. "I hated it. So I quit and got my first job as a tour guide in South America. It was much better. I could travel more and make more money. After I'd visited every country in South America, I quit. I figured I'd move to Europe after that, but I was in Chile at the time, so I took a boat tour to Antarctica first."

"You did?" his father asked.

"Yeah. It was really cool."

"Did you move to Europe after that?" his mother asked, picking up a big knife and slicing into the pie.

"Sort of. A guy I worked with on the cruise ship contacted me. He sailed yachts back and forth from the Caribbean in the winter to the Mediterranean in the summer, and he was looking for a crew, so I joined him."

Ethan had to overcome his shock before he could speak. "You sailed a yacht across the Atlantic?"

Natalie nodded.

"Incredible. What was that like?" his father asked with an astonished smile.

Natalie laughed. "It was incredibly boring. And we were constantly worried about running out of food. But it was in the middle of the Atlantic that I set a goal to see one hundred countries and all seven continents before I'm thirty."

"Wow," said his dad. "How far have you come?"

"I'm at ninety-nine countries and six continents. But I'm starting a new job in Australia soon."

"Is that the continent you're missing?" his father asked.

Natalie nodded. "Landing in Sydney is going to feel amazing."

Ethan's chest tightened.

"Well, that is wonderful, Natalie!" said his mom. "You've created a very exciting life for yourself. You should be proud. When do you leave Mapleton?"

Ethan held his breath, not sure he wanted to hear her answer. She glanced his way, but he avoided her eyes and took a drink.

"I'm leaving on Tuesday."

It was like taking a roundhouse kick to the temple. His chest pain increased as he swallowed.

"I'm glad you made time for us before you take off on another adventure," his dad said.

Tuesday.

She was leaving Tuesday.

Forever.

He'd never see her again. Never feel her again. Never hear her again.

"Ethan?"

A moment passed before he finally registered his mother's raised voice calling his name. He looked up and found all three sets of eyes staring at him from around the table. "What?"

"The lifter?"

He looked down at his hand and found the silver lifter clutched in his fist. He loosened his grip and passed it over to his mother, who looked at him with her eyes wide. She probably thought he'd lost it.

As the word Tuesday ricocheted around his brain, he was pretty sure he had.

ELEVEN

Natalie hopped into the passenger side of Ethan's truck and closed the door. After dinner and dessert, which were both delicious, Gayle insisted she take enough leftovers home to last until Tuesday. Then she insisted Ethan drive her home.

He didn't look happy about it.

In fact, he'd seemed upset the whole evening. Ever since their near kiss while hidden in the garden, he'd been switching between lustful gazes in her direction and annoyed shakes of his head. She'd never seen anyone fight something they clearly wanted so hard. And she'd never understand why he wouldn't just give in so they could both find a release for all the built-up tension.

It was just a kiss, just one night. No pressure. No big deal.

Ethan waved to his parents standing arm in arm on the porch before getting into the truck and slamming the door. Natalie had assured them all that she didn't mind walking, that she regularly walked tens of kilometres a day on tour, but they wouldn't take no for an answer. She comforted herself with the fact that Monroe Manor was only a three-minute drive away.

"You're not going to play Bublé again, are you?" he said when he put the truck into reverse.

Natalie rolled her eyes. "This isn't a tour. And that wouldn't be the right song for this situation, anyway."

"What would the right song be?"

Natalie felt a smirk take over her face. She just couldn't help herself. She could think of a hundred songs about unreleased tension and frustration in the anticipation of sex.

Her thoughts must have shown on her face, because Ethan squirmed in his seat and adjusted his glasses, refusing to look over at her. She rolled her eyes.

She would have accepted his rejection if she'd known he wasn't interested, but knowing he wanted this as much as she did but was too stubborn to give in felt like a challenge.

And she was ready to lay it all on the line.

He came to a stop in the driveway but didn't put the truck in park. Natalie unbuckled her seatbelt and opened the door, then picked up her leftovers. She knew she should just say thank you for the ride and walk away forever, but she couldn't. She didn't want to leave without making it abundantly clear what she wanted.

"Would you like to come in?" she asked.

His deep-blue eyes widened slightly behind his glasses, and he opened his delicious mouth to say something, but hesitated. His awkward rejection would have been funny had it not been so humiliating.

She waited for his response, but it never came.

"It's just sex, Ethan. One night," she said with a shrug.

"It's . . . probably not a good idea," he said, looking pained.

Natalie's heart plummeted, but she nodded. "You're right. It is a bad idea. I just hoped you might like to do it anyway."

She gave him a smile and stepped out of the car. "Thanks for the ride," she said over her shoulder without looking at him. She went inside and closed the door behind her.

She shut her eyes and took a deep breath, her body threatening to sag. But she straightened herself up, ordering herself to get it together. In two days, she'd be on a plane, headed back to England; two weeks after that, she'd be in Australia, starting her life over again.

She told herself to look forward, but she couldn't fight the frustration that seeped through. It had been a while since she'd found someone she was attracted to, and actually spoke English. Leaving without feeling more of Ethan's hands and lips made her want to throw her chicken pie across the room, and if it hadn't been so delicious, she would have. She took a step toward the kitchen to put the pie in the fridge when a loud knock came from behind her.

She stared at the door for a moment, wondering whether she could believe her ears, when the knocking began again. Harder this time. So hard, in fact, that it sounded like a fist was about to break through the hundred-and-fifty-year-old solid oak door.

She grabbed for the handle and wrenched it open to find Ethan standing on the porch. His owl-like eyes were long gone. In their place was determination.

He stepped in without a word, took her face in his hands, and kissed her.

Need exploded through her body. Mixed with relief and excitement. She gave in, let him take her mouth with his, slide his tongue against hers. He raked his fingers through her hair, making her moan with relief.

Finally.

He broke the kiss and pulled back to look at her. His eyes darted between hers, waiting for her response. She lunged toward him, taking his mouth once more, almost afraid he might change his mind again. Being in his arms felt comforting and natural. Like putting a blanket on when you're cold.

She wasn't sure she could get enough.

He leaned forward and kicked the door closed behind him, then he backed her against the wall, his hands reaching for her leftovers and placing them on the few boxes left stacked against the wall. Thankful to have her hands free, she reached for his waist, felt around his hard stomach, ran her hands under his shirt and up his long, warm back. He groaned deep in his throat, reached a hand behind his neck, and pulled off the shirt, discarding it on the floor.

She felt his chest, shoulders, back. He was solid, corded with long hard muscles under his warm skin. His dark chest hair perfectly covered his chest and ran down the centre of his abs in a narrow line that disappeared under his boxers. She couldn't stop touching him. She leaned forward and kissed him under the hollow of his throat.

"You changed your mind?"

He smiled and kissed her once, softly on the lips. "I came to my senses."

He reached for her and lifted her off her feet. A gasp came from her throat as she wrapped her legs around his waist and kissed across his cheek to his ear and down his neck as he walked them to the stairs and started climbing them.

When he got to her bedroom door, he loosened his grip, letting her slide down to standing. He pulled her purse over her head and dropped it on the floor, and then he pulled her with him into her bedroom until the backs of his legs hit her bed and he sat with her standing in front of him. He reached for the buttons that went down the front of her dress.

"I want to see you. Feel you," he said.

She placed her hands on his, stilling his fingers. "Ethan?"

He looked up at her with a burning need, mixed with something deeper she couldn't quite put her finger on. "Hmm?"

The intensity of his gaze made her burn up, but she wanted to be certain he knew what he was getting with her. "Are you sure you want to do this?"

He smiled, moving his fingers to undo the top button that sat right over her cleavage. "Are you having second thoughts?"

She shook her head. "No. I just don't want you to regret doing this. With me. After I leave."

He undid the rest of her buttons silently before looking up into her eyes. "I've been trying to convince myself that I don't want this, that you aren't right for me. But I can't believe my own lies anymore. I want you. One night is better than no nights."

He stood and grasped the straps of her dress, one in each hand, and slid them down her arms, letting the dress flutter to the floor around her feet.

She looked down at what he was seeing, a plain nude cotton bra and matching panties, the kind most women probably wore when they were sick or on their period. Not the kind of underwear one wore when one was finally going to have sex for the first time with a man they were wild about.

But it was the only underwear she owned. Seven bras, fourteen panties, all identical and thin enough to roll up into the corners of her suitcase.

"I sometimes wish I had prettier things to wear," she said. "Lace, or colours, or prints . . ."

She trailed off when his finger came under her chin and tipped her head up.

"It doesn't matter what you wear," he grazed his fingers along the thin fabric covering her breasts with careful caresses. "A broken dress, an old lady's nightgown, plain underwear," he said with a laugh. "You're always sexy because it's the things you say and who you are that make you that way."

She closed her eyes, leaned into his touch, dazzled by his deep, rumbling voice. He took his time, letting his hands softly explore her skin, touching every millimetre of her body. Her face started burning up. Her brain felt as if it had been lit on fire.

Ethan turned her around and unclasped her bra, slipping it forward off her outstretched arms. Then he gathered her hair in both hands and let it fall, cascading down her back like a waterfall, sending tingles rushing to every corner of her body, cooling the places that had flamed beneath his touch.

She could barely breathe, couldn't think.

"So soft," he said, almost too quiet to hear. She fell back against his chest, giving in to the full-body sensations he was inciting. He leaned forward and placed soft kisses along her shoulder as both of his hands slid around her, cupping her breasts, grazing across her nipples. Then he trailed his fingers down her stomach, slipping under the fabric of her panties and making slow, soft circles with the pads of his fingers.

She sank deeper into the pleasure, revelling in the warm, solid wall his chest made against her back. He moved his lips, his tongue to her ear, kissing, sucking until she shook with pleasure, crested, and fell apart in his arms.

She was so dazed that she nearly dropped to the floor when he turned her back to face him. Gently laying her down on the bed, he reached into his pocket, pulled out his wallet, and took out a condom. Unhurried, with his eyes pinned on hers, he unbuttoned his jeans and pushed them down, along with his boxers. He leaned up over her, slid a finger under the elastic band on her panties, and gently coaxed them down her legs and over her feet.

She was in a trance as she opened for him. He knelt between her thighs and put the condom on. He leaned forward and kissed her mouth, trailing kisses down her neck, over her nipples, along her stomach. She squeezed her eyes shut, unable to fully process her feelings. He was moving slowly, taking his time with her, savouring every kiss. She was pretty sure her brain was melting.

"Open your eyes, Natalie," he said, the low rumble of his voice dancing along her skin. "I want to see you."

She did as he said, her eyes meeting his right above her, his warm, heavy body pressing her into the mattress. He kissed her lips, as he slipped inside her, a moan releasing from him. His eyes fluttered shut in pleasure for a split second, then were back on her. She couldn't breathe.

He moved in long sensual strokes, taking pleasure from her as he gave it. His face intensified. His meditative strokes built her up again, and she wrapped her legs around his hips, pulling him deeper with every thrust, unable to get close enough to him.

His movements quickened. His tight control slipped. "Natalie," he said. "I'm—"

She reached her hands up to his hair, down his neck, and over his shoulders. His body fell deeper and deeper into his need, spurring on her own. She stared into his dark-blue eyes, heavily lidded and saturated with pleasure. As she rose once more into an endless orgasm that ripped through her body, she called out his name.

The tight clench she had on him finally eased as he found his own release and collapsed on top of her, breathless.

She couldn't think, couldn't move, wouldn't dare speak, fearing what might come out. She lay still under him, calming her breath, coming down off the high he'd brought her to.

When her breaths evened out, and she regained consciousness, she tried to muddle through all the feelings she was having. It had been incredibly intense, and part of her felt a little terrified. But mostly she was relieved that this thing between them had finally happened and felt almost vindicated at how good it was.

This was usually the awkward part where she'd get up, get dressed, and say goodbye. But she didn't want that this time, and she didn't feel awkward at all. She felt content.

Happy, even.

Ethan lifted himself up and fell onto the bed next to her, leaving a cold, hollow sensation on her body. She told herself to get up, ask him to leave, but couldn't face the hypocrisy. She'd told him to go for what he wanted without worrying about the consequences, so, perhaps, she should do the same.

She looked over at Ethan, eyes closed, face in a deep state of relaxation, and she allowed the grin she'd been fighting to break through. Then she rolled toward him, pressed her body along the side of his, and laid her cheek against his chest. The last thing she heard before sleep took her was the gunfire heartbeats pounding inside Ethan's chest.

• • • • • • • • • •

Sweltering heat roused Natalie out of her dead sleep. When she opened her eyes, she found herself tucked against Ethan's body. She peeled her sweaty face off of his chest and carefully sat up, trying her best not to wake him up. She slid across the bed, adjusting the blanket, then slowly stood and turned to look at him.

He slept with a peaceful look on his handsome face. He was wearing his boxers, which meant he must have got up after they had sex, cleaned up, put his underwear on, then got back into bed with her. He could have slipped out unnoticed, but he didn't. A smile pulled at the corners of her mouth as she stared down at him. He sucked in a breath, rolled, and spread his fingers out to the space she'd vacated. His eyes cracked open.

"Mmm . . . morning," he said, then yawned.

She wanted to crawl back in, feel him again, but she told herself to stay put. They had an understanding. One night only. "Morning."

He sat up, letting their blanket fall down his chest and pool around his waist, then reached a hand up and slid it through his rumpled brown hair. He twisted, reached for his glasses on the nightstand, and slid them on.

When he looked at her and smiled, she realized she was standing in front of him, completely naked.

She turned to her suitcase for a bra and panties and put them on.

He had a smirk covering his face as he stood from the bed and stretched his arms over his head, making his muscles contract, his abs stretch.

Her mouth dropped open. She looked away.

"So . . ." she said, unsure where she was going with it. Part of her wanted to tell him to leave. Part of her wanted to pull him back into bed for more sex and snuggles. She'd never been so conflicted after a one-night stand, and it made her realize she was completely out of her element.

There had been something almost decadent about the sex she'd had with Ethan. As if all the sex she'd had before was waxy dollar store chocolate. Then she finally tasted a creamy, ganache-filled, melt-in-your-mouth gourmet delicacy. Her mouth watered just looking at his long body and calm eyes, and a fresh wave of need flooded her veins. She shook her head and reached for a T shirt in her suitcase but changed her mind and took a tank instead.

Get it together, dammit.

"Wouldn't it be easier to use the dresser?" Ethan asked.

Natalie cleared her throat and shrugged one shoulder. "I like my suitcase."

"I see. Uh, would you like to—" Ethan stopped midsentence, tipped his ear toward her door. "Did you hear that?"

Natalie pulled the shirt down over her head, stuck her arms through. "Hear what?"

"I think it was . . . meowing," he said.

She gasped. "I finally got 'em?!" She dashed out of the room, leaving Ethan standing alone in his boxers.

She'd set the cat traps in the kitchen again before leaving for dinner the night before and filled them with piles of treats and open cans of tuna. She'd even put a blanket over them, convinced they were smart enough to recognize a trap by sight alone. She hadn't even thought to check them, with all the sex.

Happy to have a distraction from all the dishevelled sexiness, she made her way down the stairs, around the corner, and into the kitchen, then pulled up short.

An orange marmalade cat sat in the middle of the floor in front of one cage, screech-meowing at its door.

Ethan came into the room behind her. "He's not in the cage."

Natalie stepped around the cat, grabbed the blanket that stretched over the cages, and pulled it off. One of them was empty, but inside the other was a cat that looked almost identical to the one on the outside, but something was slightly off. She squatted to inspect it. Where the cat's eyes were supposed to be were two empty slits.

Her mouth fell open.

Ethan crouched down next to her. "Oh. He's blind."

The cat outside the cage started hissing at her, then carried on its incessant meowing. She stood and backed away while continuing to stare at the blind cat.

When she'd contacted the humane society and told them about donating the cats, they'd told her it would be difficult to find them families, but they'd try. Now, seeing they were nearly feral and one was blind, she knew they wouldn't be able to find people to adopt them.

They would almost certainly be euthanized.

There was something about trapping and murdering a blind cat that seemed too horrific for her to do.

Ethan cleared his throat. "I think he's worried about his brother."

Natalie looked up at Ethan, who was staring at her with his brows raised.

"Brother?" she asked, guilt flooding her heart.

She had no clue what to do, but she knew she couldn't kill the damn things. She took a deep breath, trying to summon some bravado to act like she didn't care, then gave up. Her shoulders slumped forward. "Fuck."

She unlatched the cage door and watched as the blind cat followed the meowing of his brother and left the cage. They reunited, then scurried off down the hall and disappeared.

She walked to a chair and fell into it, rubbing her pounding temples with her fingers. "What am I going to do now? Abandon them? Sell them with the house as a package deal? Find a barn somewhere to sneak them into and leave them to fend for themselves?"

Ethan's soft chuckle came through. He moved behind her, slipped his big warm hands under her hair onto her shoulders, and began massaging her. "For what it's worth, I think you did the right thing, letting him go."

Natalie moaned. She wanted to say something snarky to him, but his hands just felt so good. Comforting.

"Do you want to go get some breakfast?"

She tensed. "What?"

"I'm sure you heard me," he said, then leaned down to her ear. "Let's get breakfast," he said, kissing her neck and ear.

"Mmm . . . that's not how one-night stands work."

Ethan laughed his low, rumbling laugh she was starting to crave. "No?"

He started massaging again, and she gave in to it, leaning back with another moan. "No. You're supposed to put on your pants awkwardly, say something douchey, and bolt out the door."

"Not really my style," he said.

She rolled her neck, revelling in his touch, feeling every last bit of tension melt away. "You don't think breakfast is a bad idea?"

"I do," he said. She could almost hear his smile coming through his words. "But I'd like to do it anyway."

"Sex changed you."

Ethan laughed. "It's just breakfast, Natalie."

"I've been trying to avoid town. And crowds."

"Don't you live in London, with like, seven million people?"

"It's closer to nine, I think."

"Well, there are only four thousand here. So."

"But those four thousand know everything about me. So."

"What's the worst that can happen?"

"I get tarred and feathered and run out of town."

Ethan laughed. "I'll protect you. My parents forced me to take Muay Thai lessons for eight years after a kid at school beat me up." He placed a kiss on the top of her head, and she let out a deep breath along with a laugh.

"What's Muay Thai?"

"It's basically kick-boxing. I got to a blue belt around the same time I hit a growth spurt, so the bullies left me alone, and I quit. But I assure you, I can fall right back into it. It's just like riding a bike."

"Hmm . . . no wonder you're a lot stronger than you look."

Ethan smiled. "I'm going to choose to take that as a compliment."

She stood and, against her better judgment, but unable to stop herself, walked into his arms, taking him into a deep, exploring kiss. When she pulled back, she dropped a kiss on his chest, then rested her cheek in the same spot.

"Okay."

"Okay, as in, yes, to breakfast?" he asked.

"Yes."

Ethan reached for her hand, tugged her out of the kitchen. "Perfect, let's get dressed. The café in town has breakfast poutine."

What?

"Breakfast poutine?"

He laughed. "Guess I should have led with that."

She nodded and let him lead her up the stairs.

TWELVE

E than walked down Main Street toward Brin's Café, holding Natalie's hand and grinning from ear to ear. It wasn't until Lindsay's Aunt Carol passed by with a scowl that he realized he was making a bold move. He'd all but forgotten about Lindsay, a nice perk of spending so much time with Natalie, but the drama with his ex-girlfriend hadn't slipped the minds of the people in town. That was obvious.

They walked along, passing several pedestrians, almost all of whom regarded them with varying levels of interest. He couldn't tell whether they were shocked at seeing him with someone else so soon or wondering who the beautiful, mysterious girl was. Or maybe they knew who she was and were shocked to see her around town.

He looked over at Natalie and smiled. She gave him a matching smile, then looked away. He stared at her profile for a moment more, feeling incredibly lucky to be with her. He was pretty sure that taking her up on her offer to go inside, even with all the uncertainty, was the best thing he'd ever done.

Was it a terrible choice?

Probably.

Did he care?

Nope.

He watched her as they walked, taking in her square jaw and dainty nose, memorizing her, until her smile fell, then disappeared, and a blank, dead-eyed stare took over.

Ethan turned to see what she was looking at and spotted Anne. She was standing on the sidewalk, surrounded by a small crowd and signs that read Polling Station. A reporter from the local paper was standing with her, interviewing her. She spoke animatedly with a huge smile. But when she looked over the reporter's shoulder and caught sight of Ethan, hand in hand with Natalie, her smile immediately broke. The reporter twisted to look at them, then whipped back to Anne, firing off a question and sticking a recording device in her face.

Ethan winced. "Come on. Almost there."

He dragged her past one more storefront, a surf shop, then ducked into the café.

And came face to face with Adam.

"Eth!" Adam said, booming through the cafe and drawing everyone's attention. "And . . . Natalie! Wow." His eyes darted between Ethan's and Natalie's as his grin expanded.

Ethan narrowed his eyes at his best friend. He would get the hint, but he would probably ignore it anyway.

"Good morning," Natalie said.

"Yeah, I bet it is."

"Wow," Ethan said. "Really?"

He was about ready to grab Adam by the jacket and push him out the door when Natalie's laughter broke through his annoyance.

"You bet right. Want to join us for breakfast?" she asked. Her delicate face was glowing and full of mischief.

"Oh," Adam said. He looked shocked. He spared a glance at Ethan, then back at Natalie. "No, no thanks. I gotta get going."

Natalie's smile melted into a cool stare. "Good. See ya."

Ethan snorted a laugh. It was impressive the way she so easily managed people like that. She knew Adam wanted to give them a hard time, but she also seemed to know that, when push came to shove, he'd never actually interfere.

Only one problem; she didn't know Adam well enough. He loved a good mind game.

He planted his feet and tilted his head. "There's a baseball tournament on Thursday, Natalie. Our team is playing. You should come cheer us on. It's going to be fun. Food trucks, open bar, a band, fireworks . . ."

Natalie's smile dropped. "Oh, I can't. I'm actually leaving tomorrow night."

Adam's face fell. He turned to Ethan and likely read his face in an instant.

Yes, she's leaving, and yes, it sucks.

"I see," Adam said, turning back to Natalie. "Well, then. It was very nice meeting you. Safe travels."

Natalie's blank face nodded a little as Adam clapped Ethan on the shoulder and walked out the door.

The reminder that Natalie was leaving stung. Part of Ethan wanted to leave with Adam. Go home to lick his wounds and try to move on. The other part screamed to soak up as much time with her as he could. He'd thought the same the night before when she'd walked away from his truck and closed the door. But he just couldn't walk away, even though the end was inevitable.

"Natalie?"

She tilted her eyes up to meet his. "Yeah?"

"What are you doing for the rest of the day?"

"Uh, the last four Monroes are coming to collect their junk between ten and eleven. That's it, really."

"You want to hang out after?"

A smile came over her face. "Hang out?"

"Yeah. One last day before you leave. We can go to the beach, have a picnic, get ice cream. It'll be fun."

She narrowed her dark eyes at him and smirked. "Is this a bad idea?"

Ethan laughed. "I honestly can't tell anymore."

She looked out the window at the polling station before turning back to him. For a long beat, she just stared at him—long enough for him to question his choice at least ten times.

"Okay. I'm in."

He smiled and leaned down, kissing her breathless until a loud throat being cleared reminded him he was in public. He pulled away from Natalie and looked up. Behind the counter stood one of Lindsay's best friends, Dani, wearing an apron and a scowl.

Dammit. He forgot she worked there.

"Ethan," she said, nose scrunched as if she'd just smelled a dead body.

Ethan sighed. This would for sure come back to bite him. But he decided to deal with it the way he'd been dealing with everything else for the past twelve hours; he pretended it wasn't a problem and decided to worry about it later.

"Dani," he said with a polite nod. "We'll have two coffees and two breakfast poutines, please."

· · ◆ · ◆ ◆ ◆ · · ·

After casting his vote and rescheduling his appointments to the following week, Ethan hastily threw together a picnic lunch for two, grabbed some towels and a Frisbee, and packed it all up into a bag. Then he changed into his navy-blue swim shorts and threw on a grey University of Toronto faculty T shirt, sunglasses, and his favourite Blue Jays hat. He jogged out the door and drove to Monroe Manor, arriving just before lunch. Natalie was sitting on the porch waiting for him, as she had been the day they went waterfalling, back when he hadn't yet allowed himself to see how perfect she was.

Then his eyes had opened, two days before she was getting on a plane and leaving forever.

She wore a blue dress he hadn't yet seen, her black sunglasses and her gold sandals, with a towel folded over her forearm.

"Hi," she said, hopping up into the truck with a smile. She leaned over for a sweet kiss that made his skin blaze and his heart ache.

"Hey." He shook off the dread and reminded himself to focus on the now.

He drove the winding road down to the beach. The parking lot was full, and the long stretch of soft sand was heavily dotted with colourful umbrellas and chairs. White sailboats drifted in the distance on the calm, sparkling blue lake. He found a spot and parked his truck, slung the bag over his shoulder, and took Natalie's hand.

They walked along the paved path that led from the parking lot to the beach until Natalie stopped abruptly and stared down at a lush garden that filled the spaces where two paths converged.

"Hey, this has your name on it," she said, pointing down at a metal plaque staked into the soil.

"Yeah, this is a pollinator project I worked on three years ago. Before I turned my focus to the watershed. There are fifteen gardens in total along the paths."

He pointed up and down the path in both directions. Each of the gardens had a small flowering tree that hosted butterflies and caterpillars and was underplanted with carefully chosen purple, pink, and orange wildflowers. He hadn't been to the beach yet that summer; he'd been avoiding it, knowing that Lindsay came often. But he knew the gardens would look good. They were well established by now and thriving without his attention.

He took a few steps and pointed past the parking lot. "We also did a dune restoration project over there."

Natalie looked at the sand dunes rising from the ground where the beach gave way to the luxury homes that the most affluent of Mapletonians had built along North Shore Drive. There was an enormous area that he'd fenced off and planted with grasses. He was happy that it was coming along successfully.

"Wow," she said, giving a contemplative look. "You really care about Mapleton, don't you?"

Ethan shrugged. "It's home, and I know how to make it better, so I want to. Come on."

He took her hand and led her past the jungle gyms covered in children, the basketball courts, and the famous Mapleton Beach Bar Patio that was packed with people eating and drinking and soaking up the warm sun. They found an empty spot close to the water in between an older lady on a beach chair under an umbrella reading a novel and a young family with two toddlers digging in the sand. They laid out their towels and took off their sandals.

"Are you hungry?" Ethan asked. "I packed some sandwiches. Hope you like turkey."

"I love turkey," she said with a smile and fanned herself with her hand. "But it's too hot. I want to swim."

She reached for the bottom of her blue dress and pulled it up over her head, revealing a black bikini with ties at her hips and behind her neck. Then she pulled a hair tie off her wrist and tied her long brown hair up on top of her head. She turned around and took a few steps toward the water, her bikini bottoms doing little to cover her pretty, swaying ass.

"You coming?" she asked.

He looked up at her face, saw she was smiling over her shoulder at him. He should have been sorry for staring at her butt, but he couldn't untie his tongue enough to offer an apology. Instead, he pulled off his T shirt, jogged to her side, and wrapped his arm around her, tucking her perfectly into his side. They walked into the lake together through the tumbling waves, the smoothness of her warm skin against his in the cool water sent a shot of adrenaline through his heart. He'd had to take deep breaths just to get through it.

They swam for a while together. Ethan led her out to the big sandbar about ten metres from the shore. After swimming, they ate their lunch on the beach, then played catch with the Frisbee before walking hand in hand to the Peach Creamery; an ice cream parlour right on the beach that was known for making delicious, fresh peach ice cream with all-local ingredients.

When the beach had mostly cleared out, and it was well past dinnertime, Ethan reluctantly suggested it was time to go. It was so easy to pretend this moment wouldn't come, but he knew he was on borrowed time with Natalie. Now that his time was nearly up, the shitty feeling he'd been suppressing started bubbling up from his heart again and seeping into his brain.

He packed up their stuff and, holding hands, walked back to the parking lot, wishing for the millionth time that day that this was just the beginning and not the end. At least he could comfort himself with the fact that Natalie looked as if she was struggling with it, too. When they arrived at Monroe Manor and she got out of the truck, she hesitated.

"Do you want to come in? Have supper with me?" she asked.

Ethan smiled as the knot that had been forming in his stomach untangled slightly. He hated the idea of saying goodbye to her now. It was obviously coming, but he would happily kick this can down the road as long as he could. "Yes."

He followed Natalie inside to the kitchen where she pulled out a bottle of red wine and a box of Kraft

Dinner. "I don't have much food left, and there's no point in buying more, since . . ."

Ethan nodded. He didn't want to hear the end of that sentence. To distract himself while Natalie started the Kraft Dinner, he reached for the remote on the counter and turned on the TV to the local news channel.

"I wonder what happened with the election."

Natalie grabbed a pot from the bottom cupboard, filled it with water, and put it on the stove just as the commercials ended and the same reporter who had interviewed Anne on the sidewalk that morning came onto the screen.

"In case you've missed it, the results are in," she said. "There's a new mayor in town."

Ethan's jaw dropped as his head snapped toward Natalie. Her skin had already taken on an algae-greenish tinge.

"She lost?"

Ethan nodded. "Looks like it."

Natalie walked to the dining table and sank down into the chair as the camera cut away from the reporter and landed on Anne standing behind a podium. She cleared her throat and started her concession speech. It was short, to the point. She thanked those who'd volunteered and voted for her, then walked off the stage.

Ethan turned off the TV. He opened the bottle of wine and poured two glasses.

"Here," he said.

Natalie took the glass but didn't drink. "Do you think she lost because of me?"

"No. I think she lost because she wants to keep Mapleton exactly the way it's always been, while her opponent realizes we need to move forward, grow, build."

"Did you vote for her?"

Ethan shook his head. "There's something . . . I don't trust her."

Natalie's brows rose, and she opened her mouth, likely to disagree, when her phone started ringing on the table. She picked it up, looking at the number, and reluctantly answered with a drawn-out "hello" that sounded more like a question than a greeting.

Ethan couldn't make out who the caller was from Natalie's side of the conversation, only that she wasn't happy about what she was hearing.

Her eyes went wide, and her mouth opened and closed as if she didn't know what to say. "What . . . what does this mean?"

She shook her head, squeezed her eyes shut. "I'd rather you just tell me now."

He didn't know what was happening. Who would call her with terrible news? Maybe her boss to tell her she'd been fired and should stay in Mapleton forever?

Nah.

He'd never get that lucky.

"Fine. Bye." She stabbed the red button on the screen, then tossed her phone on the table.

"Who was that?"

She didn't move. Only stared at the wall across from her as if she wanted to punch it. "Speeler."

"What did he say?"

She twisted her head toward him slowly, as if it weighed fifty pounds, then stared into his eyes as if she didn't believe what she was about to say.

"Anne and Emily are contesting the will."

THIRTEEN

N atalie woke up Tuesday morning, after a night of spotty sleep, and got dressed. Speeler had been annoyingly brief the night before, insisting on discussing the ramifications of Anne and Emily's legal action in person. At least he'd scheduled their appointment for eight a.m., so she could get it over with quickly and figure out how to deal with it.

Hopefully, before her flight that night.

She went to the barn, pulled out Elizabeth's old bike, and started for Speeler's office. When she arrived, she saw Ethan right away waiting patiently in front of Speeler's door and wearing navy pants and a button-down shirt.

He was so calm, so patient.

She leaned the bike against the red-brick wall and walked to him. She wanted to walk right into his arms, press her face against his chest, but she knew it would be an overstep of the boundary they'd laid. They'd had one day and one day only to do whatever felt good before she left.

And she *was* leaving.

"Good morning," she said to him.

He took a step toward her, then paused, and finally retreated. "Morning."

Just then, Chelsea's little car pulled up and stopped. She got out and walked up the sidewalk, wearing baggy jean overall shorts covered in floral graffiti over a white crop top, with Timberland boots on her feet. She looked like a nineties flower child rapper .

Somehow, she pulled it off perfectly.

"So," she said, stopping in front of them. "Anne's pissed off she lost the election and decided she'd like to take it out on us?"

Speeler's crusty throat cleared behind her, making Natalie jump. She turned to find him standing in the doorway. "It would appear so, Ms. Davenport."

He turned and stepped inside, then barked over his shoulder, "Don't just stand there."

Natalie, Ethan, and Chelsea trotted behind him, through the lobby, down the hall, and into the godforsaken conference room where this whole mess had begun two weeks earlier.

He sat at the top of the table, took a drink of coffee, shuffled some papers, and then cleared his throat again.

She wanted to scream at him to get on with it. The rising dread was filling her ears with a rushing noise she could no longer ignore.

"So, as you all know, Anne's hare-brained lawyer called last night to tell me she is proceeding with legal action to contest the will."

"Can she do that?" Chelsea asked.

"Anyone can contest a will. The question is, will she succeed?"

The clock ticked for two eternal seconds. Finally, Natalie lost her cool. "Well, will she?!"

Speeler sat back in his seat, taken aback at her outburst. "It's certainly possible, Ms. Alvarez. But even if she doesn't succeed, we may still lose."

Natalie tried to understand what the hell he was saying but came up short. The blank looks on Ethan's and Chelsea's faces made her feel a little better about her total confusion.

"I'm sorry. What does that mean?" Ethan asked.

"Anne is claiming that the original will Elizabeth had, which named Robert the sole beneficiary of the entire property as well as the shares Elizabeth held in Monroe Corp., is still valid, because . . ." He paused for a moment, adjusted his glasses. "Because she claims that you two are not Robert's children."

Natalie's head started spinning. She wanted to run away again. She couldn't believe she'd found herself in this room again, listening to this bullshit.

"Why would that matter?" Ethan asked. "Elizabeth could have left her entire property to a complete stranger. She left part of it to me, and I'm not family. That's her right."

"That's true," Speeler said. "But she's claiming that Ms. Alvarez and Ms. Davenport unlawfully convinced Elizabeth to rewrite the will."

"That's not true at all!" Chelsea said.

"I know, Ms. Davenport. But she has the financial means to drag this out for a long time."

"So I was right?" Chelsea asked. Her eyes blazed, and she pounded a fist against the table. "She's only doing this because she lost the election? Inventing all manner of crap to convince people she's a victim?"

"I believe so. These plans have been in the works for the past week. She told her lawyer to call as soon as the results were in. If she won, she would drop it. But if she lost, she would proceed."

"Why wait, though?"

"Well, I suspect it's because there would have been a lot of terrible publicity had she proceeded during an election. She has nothing left to lose now."

"What about Emily?"

"Anne likely added Emily on without her even knowing, possibly for sympathy. Based on what Elizabeth told me, Emily has been deeply under her mother's thumb her whole life."

Natalie wanted time to process it all, but there were just too many questions firing off in her head.

"What about the Monroes?" Natalie asked. "You said she claims to be the rightful owner of the shares they inherited?"

"Exactly right. I'm sure that's part of the reason she put it off as well. Because of the way the original will had been written, a distinction cannot be made between the property and the shares. She has to contest it all."

Natalie winced. "I can't imagine they'll take this lightly."

For the first time, Speeler looked more tired than grumpy. He took another drink from his mug, then stretched his neck. "No. They won't. It certainly complicates matters. I'm waiting to see how their lawyer responds. Victor Monroe is shrewd. He may choose to make a deal with Anne and fight alongside her—that's what I would advise him to do if I were his counsel."

"What are you saying?" Ethan asked.

"I'm saying, if the Monroes align with Anne and decide to fight us, we won't win. You won't get the pond. Ms. Alvarez and Ms. Davenport won't get the property. There's no way we can fight them both."

They all sat in silence with varying looks of horror on their faces. They all had something major to lose. Ethan, the pond; Natalie, her peace and freedom; and Chelsea . . . well, Chelsea would probably lose out the most.

Natalie watched her sister as she swallowed several times, blinking back tears that welled up in her eyes.

"So we can't sell," Chelsea said, dazed.

"No," Speeler said. "Not until the matter is completely settled."

Natalie chanced a glance at Ethan and found him staring at her with a guarded expression. Then looked at Chelsea and found the same thing. Lastly, she looked at Speeler, who was staring a hole in her head.

"What?" she asked the room.

"We should ask you that, Ms. Alvarez. What are you going to do?"

"Well, I'll do what I can to help you fight it, of course. But I'm needed in London tomorrow and Sydney at the beginning of next month. I'm sure whatever you will need of me can be accomplished remotely?"

Speeler nodded. "That will be fine."

"Can you estimate how long it will take?"

"Could be as little as six months, but I've seen these things drag on for years. It all depends."

Silence fell again before Chelsea broke it once more.

"Can I move in?"

Natalie's eyes popped, and she twisted her head.

"Yes," Speeler said, just as Natalie yelled, "What?!"

Chelsea turned to Natalie. The tears that had fallen had dried, and a determined look settled on her face. "I want to move in with Ben. And I want you to stay with us, too."

Natalie feared this meeting would permanently freeze her face in an expression of shock. She noticed Ethan's head abruptly twist in her periphery and felt his dark-blue eyes boring into her temple. She opened her mouth to say something when Speeler cut her off.

"I'm certain there is a more private place you can discuss your personal matters. I have another appointment at eight thirty."

He stood from his chair, gathered his papers and mug, and exited the room.

They were officially dismissed.

· · • • · • • · • ·

Natalie stepped out of Speeler's office and onto the sidewalk, then sucked in a deep breath of fresh air.

"I will never set foot in that place again," she said, stabbing a finger in the office's direction. Only bad things happened in that office. Things that did irreparable damage to one's life.

She felt Ethan walk out behind her, his quiet presence dominating the circle the three of them formed on the sidewalk. He had his hands in his pockets and regarded her with a curious expression.

"I'm going to go," he said. "Let you two discuss things." Before he walked away, he turned to Natalie. "If you leave tonight, will you call me and let me know?"

"I *am* leaving tonight," she said.

"Please, Nat. Just hear me out," Chelsea said.

Ethan's face softened into a tender smile. Leaning in, he kissed her on the cheek. When he pulled back, he stared into her eyes for a long moment. "Bye," he said. Then he turned and walked to his truck.

"Bye," she said in a daze, watching him walking away from her and wondering why he didn't believe that she was leaving. Maybe he thought—

"Did you and Ethan . . ." Chelsea interrupted her thoughts. "Did you end up asking him?"

Natalie sighed, then nodded and tried to act as if it meant nothing to her. "Yes," she said, allowing herself to feel the loss she experienced, just for a second. She'd had one-night stands plenty of times, with exciting sexy men from all over the world. But she had to admit, she'd never felt anything like she felt with Ethan before. He clearly didn't understand how to have meaningless sex.

"Wow. Good for you," Chelsea said, giving her a pat on the back. "He's hot. And smart. And kind. Hard to find a triple-threat like that."

"It was only once—well, twice—and it's over now. I'm going back to London, then Sydney. Sticking to my plan."

Chelsea looked down the street, walked over to a black metal bench that was flanked with enormous planters filled with purple flowers, and sat down. Natalie followed and sat next to her. After a few moments of quiet contemplation, she broke the silence.

"Why do you want to move into the house? I know you wanted to move apartments, but can't you just put it off a little while?"

Chelsea sighed. "I already signed a lease for a new place and used most of my savings for first and last month's rent."

"What's the hurry?"

"It's in a much safer school zone for Ben."

"Ben's starting school?"

Chelsea nodded. "In September. I'm supposed to move at the end of next week, but I can't afford it without selling the house." She sat for a moment, staring down. Her eyes welled up again. "I can't stay where I am. My apartment is falling apart. It's in the worst neighbourhood in Toronto. I'm afraid to walk around at night. I hate that Ben is growing up there."

Natalie put her arm around her sister and held her. She didn't enjoy seeing anyone struggle like that, but especially not her sister. The inheritance had built up so much hope in Chelsea, only to have it all ripped away. But what could they really do? They were at Anne's and the Monroes' mercy.

Chelsea sat up, wiped her wet cheeks. "Natalie, I don't want to sell the Manor. I can't stand the thought of it being destroyed. Mapleton is perfect for me and Ben. Have you seen the elementary school here? It's adorable. And safe. And the beach is right there. And the property has so much space for Ben to run and play."

"I hear there are snakes."

Chelsea waved a dismissive hand, set her stubborn jaw. "I want to live here."

"Maintaining a property that size is a lot of work and a lot of money. It's not exactly in pristine condition. You really want to do all that?"

"To give Ben a nice place to live? I'd do almost anything."

"But the people here, Chels . . . They don't like us."

She shrugged. "If I worried about what people thought of me, I would never have got as far as I have. I'm fine with being hated by people I don't know."

Natalie looked away. It was easy for Chelsea to say that. Her mother had left Robert immediately when she found out what a slimy bastard he was. Unlike Natalie's mom, who'd stuck around for decades, destroying lives. A mental image of Anne's disappointed face during her concession speech popped into Natalie's head, and she had to make an effort to clear it. She couldn't flippantly dismiss them like that when she was the one in the wrong.

But she could understand Chelsea's perspective.

Mapleton would be a good place for Ben to grow up. Ethan had grown up here, and he turned out to be one of the best people she'd ever met. He loved it so much he moved back and started improving it.

She reached for her temples and dug her fingertips in. "Okay. Move in. If it means that much to you, we won't sell it. I didn't even want the damn place, and I'm leaving. I don't really care what you do with it."

Chelsea smiled, then it faltered. "I want you to stay with us."

"Chels—"

"Mapleton isn't like it was before. You're an adult now, not a grief-stricken teen. I want you to be a part of Ben's life. I want him to know his aunt. I want . . . to spend time with my sister."

Natalie blinked several times. "I want to be a part of your lives, too. It won't be like it was before. We can video chat whenever you want, and I'll come back and visit. Every year."

"If you stay, we can be a little family. We can celebrate Thanksgiving and Christmas together. I want you to be at Ben's birthday parties."

She thought of how she currently celebrated holidays, alone in a hostel with nowhere to go, no traditions to take part in, not even a single ornament to hang on a stupid tree. She usually requested to work those days, but more often than not, she was just alone. But she was hardly the only one alone. Plenty of people were alone on the holidays.

"Families live apart all the time," she said.

Chelsea sighed. "But it sucks, though. And what about Ethan?"

Natalie opened her mouth to say something, but nothing came out. If she was being completely honest, she felt a little queasy about getting on that plane and never seeing him again. Or worse, seeing him around Mapleton when she would come to visit. Planting gardens, waving to people on the sidewalk, holding hands with the love of his life and making her laugh.

Bile rose in her throat, and she nearly gagged on it.

He deserved to find someone like that. Someone who would treat him better than she did. She wanted that for him. After a couple weeks of training and touring in Australia, she'd get over the sadness and look back at this summer spent with Ethan and be flooded with happy memories. And so would he. Maybe one day, when she was done with travelling and ready to settle down, she could find someone just like him.

Hopefully.

Chelsea cleared her throat and put on a smug expression. "That look says it all. It's easy to leave sisters and nephews behind, but love is a whole other thing."

"Love is a very strong word."

"Yet completely appropriate."

Natalie was about to protest when Chelsea sprang up from her seat. "I gotta go. I have a class at ten thirty, and I have to pick up Ben from my friend's place and drop him off at daycare."

When Natalie stood, Chelsea threw her arms around her in a tight hug. "Please think about staying. Even just until you have to leave for Australia? Do you really need to go back to London?"

"I don't know . . ."

"We'll have fun together. I promise. Just call me later, and let me know what you decide. I'm going to call the new landlord and get my money back and tell the movers my new address."

She walked back down the sidewalk, got in her car, and drove away.

Natalie stood on the sidewalk, alone and lost. Eventually, she got on Elizabeth's old bike and headed for the Manor, but at the intersection where she should have turned left, she took a right instead, and headed for the sparkling lake. She slowly biked along the paths that stretched for several kilometres along the beach, passing by each of the fifteen gardens Ethan had planted, each one bursting with bright flowers and buzzing with activity from bees and butterflies. When the paths ran out, she biked up to the street, then came back along Main Street past the quaint cafes and specialty boutiques.

Mapleton had a certain charm to it, and if she forced herself to look at it objectively, she could see it for what it was: a hidden gem. She'd visited many small towns all over the world, and this one was right up there with the others. It had a quirky beach town vibe, somewhat historic architecture, and it sat on a stunning natural landscape. If tourists around the would knew it existed, they'd come from far and wide and eat it up.

She turned at the intersection and biked the five minutes back to Monroe Manor. She walked into the house, marched up to her bedroom, and plopped down on the edge of the bed, staring at her suitcase on the floor next to the dresser.

Then she looked over at the empty drawers right next to it.

With a sigh, she picked up her phone and dialed Jess's number. It rang only once before she answered.

"Nat! Are you back in London already?"

"No. I'm still in Canada. Where are you?"

"Dublin. When is your flight coming in?"

"Actually, there's something that came up." She shook her head. That sounded like a total lie. She ordered herself to get it together. "I can't come back to London."

"Oh. Is everything okay?"

"Yeah, I just . . . I can't leave yet."

"I see. Will you be in Sydney on the first?"

"Yes. Absolutely."

"Okay, good. Man, how great will it feel when you land in Sydney for the first time?"

Natalie smiled. "It's going to feel so satisfying. I can't wait!"

They spoke for a few more minutes before hanging up. When she put her phone down, she stared at her suitcase again. If she was staying for two more weeks, maybe it made logical sense to unpack. She hadn't done that since she lived on the cruise ship and knew she'd live in the cabin for four months.

She reached into her suitcase and picked up one pair of her unremarkable panties, folded them in half, then opened the top drawer and carefully set them down inside. After staring at them for a few minutes and noting that the sky hadn't fallen, she picked up the rest of her measly belongings and finally unpacked her suitcase for the first time in nearly ten years.

Fourteen

E than tapped his fingers on his full beer bottle and scanned the sizable crowd at the baseball complex while Adam sat on the other side of the picnic table, looking at him in horror. They'd just finished their last game of the tournament and won, coming in first place. He'd played well, hitting three home runs and making a handful of catches that, if he were a less humble man, he'd brag about all night.

He should have been on top of the world and celebrating with his teammates, but he was too nervous to celebrate.

"Hey, know what's even better than tapping your beer?" Adam asked.

Ethan rolled his eyes and took a long drink before continuing his tapping and scanning.

"Man . . . you're a mess. It's just a fucking pond, Ethan. It's going to be fine."

"Pond?"

"Yeah, isn't that why you're all"—he gestured with his hand toward the bottle—"tappy?"

Ethan cringed. He hadn't given the pond much thought after hearing Natalie was leaving, then being given a glimmer of hope when Chelsea asked her to stay. He'd convinced himself she'd stay when he left her on the sidewalk. Then he went home and doubted he'd ever see her again. He'd been in turmoil for hours before pulling out his computer and distracting himself by reorganizing his desktop.

But he never once thought about the pond.

"This isn't about the pond at all, is it? It's about the hot homeless girl."

"Don't call her that."

Adam rolled his eyes. "Apologies. Didn't you know she was leaving all along?"

"Yes. But I guess she delayed leaving."

"Oh, well, that's good, right? Is she coming tonight?"

Ethan nodded, took another drink, then looked around at the crowd. Adam did the same, but they didn't see her. They did, however, spot Lindsay and Derek standing at the bar, taking shot after shot.

Adam looked back as his eyebrows shot up. "Those two are a train wreck waiting to happen. Hopefully, Barry cuts them off soon."

Ethan shrugged. "Not my problem."

"Thank fuck." He took the throat of his beer bottle and clinked it on Ethan's. "So how long is Natalie staying?"

"I don't know. I asked her to call me, but she sent me the shortest text possible, instead."

He pulled out his phone, opened the conversation, and passed it to Adam.

"'Hey, didn't leave,'" Adam recited in his fake girl voice. "'See you Thursday.'" He looked up, and his smile had turned back to a look of horror.

"What?" Ethan asked. Maybe she'd said something else? Texted back since and said, "Nevermind!"?

Adam scrubbed his face with his free hand. "You replied, 'Great!'?"

"Yeah. So?"

"Great? That's the worst . . . Why didn't you call her? Tell her you love her? Ask her to grow your babies in her womb?"

Ethan ripped the phone from Adam's hands and looked down at the screen. "I added an exclamation mark."

"That means nothing. You clearly want her to stay. You're a mess over this."

"I do, but I don't know how long she's going to be here. Telling her any of those ridiculous things you just said will make it worse if she's just going to leave anyway."

Adam narrowed his eyes, evaluating. "I think you're getting this all wrong."

"Yeah? And what qualifies you to make that judgment?"

Adam scratched the back of his neck, shrugged. "Fair point," he said with a laugh. "But something about this just doesn't sound right to me. You know who we need? Amy."

Ethan rolled his eyes and drained his beer. If he was going to deal with Adam, he was going to need more alcohol. "Amy's in Barbados. Another?"

"Yeah," Adam replied.

He'd taken a single step toward the bar when he caught sight of Chelsea walking between the picnic tables, scanning the crowd. She was impossible to miss.

"Chelsea's here."

Adam twisted on the bench, looking over his shoulder. "Who's Chelsea?"

"Natalie's sister. Over there. Baggy pink dress, gold hair thing, weird boots."

He looked for a split second, then stood abruptly. "Is she single?"

"I don't know."

"But she's only in town temporarily, right?"

Ethan slid an annoyed look Adam's way. "Right."

"Good. Introduce me."

Ethan wasn't sure he wanted Adam hitting on Chelsea, at least not without warning her first, but he wasn't about to waste precious time talking about it. Besides, something told him Chelsea would handle Adam just fine. He marched toward her with Adam by his side.

"Chelsea!" he said with a wave.

She had an ice cream cone in each hand and had just licked around it when she noticed him. She swallowed, then her face broke into a grin. "Ethan! Hey. Wow. Nice shirt. Very you," she said, dripping sarcasm.

Adam barked a laugh and clapped Ethan on the back.

Ethan had forgotten about his horrendous baseball shirt. As captain of the team, Adam got to choose the team name, so of course, he went with the most ridiculous name he could think of and printed it on lime-green shirts. When Ethan had first seen it three years ago, he'd refused to wear it.

Eventually, his teammates forced him.

"Yeah, it wasn't my choice."

"The Masturbatters," she read. "Classy."

Ethan laughed. "I don't know what's worse, the name or the colour."

"It's a toss-up."

Adam cleared his throat. "I think they look good."

Chelsea's gaze drifted away and slid over Adam. She looked at him the way most women did, with a sense of shock, followed by appreciation, then apprehension, and finally, curiosity.

Uh oh.

"This is my friend, Adam. He's responsible for the shirts."

Chelsea nodded. "Hey. I'd shake your hand, but . . ." She gestured with her full hands and a shrug.

"Two cones, I like your style," he said with an easy smile. "Do you want to come sit down with me? Have a drink?"

Chelsea stared at him for a moment, then looked around. "Oh, I don't think . . . Sorry. Not tonight."

"Hmm . . . maybe another time. How about tomorrow?"

Chelsea shook her head. A drop of melted ice cream dripped off one cone and onto her hand, and she licked it off.

A low noise came from deep in Adam's throat. He opened his mouth to speak just as Mrs.— Ms. P. sauntered past.

"Hey, Adam!" she said, then her smile dropped. "Fuck you."

He turned to her with his brows raised, then snapped his head back to Chelsea. "Wow. Ms. P. has terrible timing."

Chelsea burst into laughter, a full head-back laugh that made Ethan laugh, too.

"That depends on who you ask," she said. "Was she an ex? It sounds like a name you'd call your teacher."

Ethan burst into laughter so hard, a snort came out. His muscles started aching, and he had to bend in half and wrap his arms around his abs.

"She was . . . It's complicated," he said it in a tone that seemed annoyed, but he was wearing an enormous smile. Ethan knew he'd think the whole thing was hilarious, too, but he was too busy pursuing a pretty girl to let anything distract him.

"So what about Saturday night? You're new in town, right? I can show you all the best spots before you leave."

Chelsea stared at him as if he'd just told her the number purple piloted a lightbulb.

Adam stared back, narrowing his eyes in deep concentration. Ethan was pretty sure he had no idea he was being shot down.

He'd probably never experienced it before.

Ethan wiped a tear from his eye that had escaped during his laughter. "Is Natalie here?"

"Uh, yes," she said. "Somewhere."

Just then, Natalie appeared from behind the crowd, wearing short black shorts, a white tank top, and gold sandals, holding Ben's little hand. Her face split into the largest grin he'd seen yet. It was like glue, hastily holding the pieces of his broken heart together .

For how long? He hadn't a clue. He was just happy to see her when he worried he might never again.

"Mama!" Ben said. "Aunt Natalie showed me the diamond and let me run around all the bases."

"Cool, buddy. Here, I got you an ice cream cone," Chelsea said, handing the cone to Ben. She looked up at Adam, then raised an eyebrow.

Adam stared down at Ben with the same wide eyed, horrified look he'd given Ethan about the ex-clamation mark.

Ethan winced. The funny exchange had turned into an awkwardness that was too much to bear. He should have told Adam about Ben before they walked over there. Adam wouldn't even date a woman, let alone get involved with kids.

"Uh, so . . ." Ethan started. He didn't know what to say or do, just that he wanted it to end.

Adam cleared his throat, peeled his eyes off of Ben and looked up. "Hey, Natalie. Good to see you again. I gotta go. Nice to meet you . . . Chelsea."

He turned and walked back to the picnic table with their teammates.

"What the hell was that all about?" Natalie asked.

"Language."

"Well?"

Chelsea gave a little shrug as she licked her cone. "I'll tell you later. Ben and I are going home. It's almost bedtime. Nice to see you, Ethan. Have fun."

She took Ben by his free hand, and they walked away together toward the parking lot. When she was completely out of sight, Natalie turned to him.

"Did you let Adam hit on her?"

"Let?" he asked with a smile. In fact, his smile totally took over his face. He was so damn happy to see her, even if she was pissed off.

"What?"

"Nothing."

"I like your shirt," she said with a smirk.

Ethan laughed. "Are you trolling me?"

She laughed and nodded.

She was so pretty, he couldn't stop looking at her. "Wanna meet the other Masturbatters?"

"Yes, I really do."

He threaded his fingers through hers and walked, only to feel her arm pull taut. She hadn't moved. He looked down at their joined hands as she pulled him gently back to her, rose onto her toes, and kissed him.

Relief washed over him. Being with her, hearing her voice, touching her lips, was the best feeling in the world. Way better than winning a stupid tournament. He put his hands on her hips, then slid them to her back. When he heard a loud whistle—probably Adam—and realized they'd drawn attention to themselves, he pulled back.

"Come on," he said with a laugh.

He'd taken two steps toward his team when he felt a cold, damp hand grip his arm. He looked down at the long, red fingernails digging into his skin and shuddered.

"Ethan, can we talk?"

He turned to meet Lindsay's mascara-smudged, tear-filled eyes.

"I don't think that's a good idea." He made a move to step around her, but she stepped in his path, wobbling and nearly falling over in her high-heeled shoes.

Derek stepped into view beside Lindsay, his face its normal rage-red.

"I think you're drunk, Lindsay. We have nothing to talk about. Do you want me to call you a cab?" he asked.

"I . . ." She did a long blink as a sob escaped. "I don't want to break up with you, Ethan."

Yikes.

Ethan looked around at the crowd that had formed, then at Natalie, who was standing off to the side, looking uncomfortable. He didn't want to deal with drunk Lindsay. He wanted to hang out with his friends and the girl of his dreams for however long she was going to stay.

He gently took her by the arm, trying to lead her away from the curious crowd and save her from herself, when Derek appeared in his path and blocked his way.

"Where are you two going, Ethan?"

Why had he never punched Derek before? The guy's face brought out Ethan's most violent side. "She needs to go home. I'm going to find her a ride."

Lindsay wrenched her arm free from Ethan's hand. "No! I want to talk. About us!"

Ethan looked around. The crowd had doubled. They couldn't look away from the train wreck, and honestly, Ethan couldn't blame them.

Derek came toward Lindsay, gripped her arm tight in his fist, then started dragging her toward him, but she resisted, leaning away from him and nearly falling.

"Whoa," Ethan said. "What are you doing?"

Lindsay wrenched free from Derek and fell into Ethan, latching onto his body and sobbing into his chest. He held up his hands, not wanting to touch her, and completely clueless about what to do next.

He looked around, hoping an answer would fall into his lap, when Derek lunged at him. Derek fisted his hand, pulled back his arm, then exploded forward, aiming for Ethan's face. But Ethan threw up his forearm at the last minute and blocked the blow. Lindsay was screaming into his chest. As annoyed as he was, he didn't want her getting punched in the face, so he turned with her and started walking away. He needed some distance and a plan.

"I won't fight you, Derek," he said over his shoulder, and he took Lindsay by the elbow and started leading her toward the parking lot. Maybe he could find one of her friends to take her from there.

He'd got a few steps when Derek grabbed his shoulder and spun him around. Rearing back his fist, same as before, he aimed for Ethan's face. Ethan could see it coming a mile away. He even had time to roll his eyes before ducking. He had to admit it was satisfying to watch Derek trip and fall to the ground with the forward momentum that never connected, but he'd rather the whole thing just be done.

Derek let out a war cry from the ground, jumped up, and charged again with the same fist and the same move that hadn't worked twice before .

Ethan could have easily shot out his foot to Derek's kneecap and taken him down, but he didn't want to lower himself to Derek's level and start fighting over a girl he wasn't even interested in. So he waited until the last second and was about to dodge his fist again when Derek froze midair, then flew backwards.

Adam's face appeared over Derek's head. His usual happy-go-lucky expression was long gone. He looked ready to kill. He held on to the neck of Derek's shirt in his fist, gagging him.

"It's time you go, asshole," Adam said, dragging him away from Ethan, but Derek resisted.

"I'm not going anywhere!" Derek yelled, flailing around and swinging his fists, trying to hit Adam.

Ethan was watching Adam struggling to pull Derek back, and he didn't notice Lindsay until she reached her hands up to touch his face. He took hold of her hands and removed her from him. He took a step away.

"Please, Ethan," she said through tears. "Please."

Ethan shook his head. "No. You need to go home."

"What the fuck, Lindsay?" Derek yelled, still struggling in Adam's grip. "Don't you get it? He doesn't want you."

"Shut up, Derek!" she said.

"He knows, you ditz," Derek said, his whole disgusting face morphing into sinister enjoyment.

Lindsay froze, then swayed on her heels. "W-what?"

"Ethan knows you cheated on him with me," he said in the loudest possible voice. Then, because he was the worst human on earth, he added, "In the back seat of his truck."

There were literal gasps from the crowd behind him. Lindsay looked up at Ethan, then around at the crowd, before letting out a wail and running off.

Before she was even out of sight, Derek started laughing.

"You're such a little fuckwad," Adam said. He kicked out Derek's ankle, making him fall to the ground, then started dragging him across the pavement toward the parking lot. "You know you're off the team, right?"

"Good! I don't want to be on your fucking team, anyway! You think you're so much better than everyone because you own half the town . . ."

Derek continued screaming insults as Adam dragged him around the side of the bar, and his voice quieted in the distance. Ethan was about to go with them to make sure Adam would be okay when Max, Jake, and Connor—three of his teammates in matching horrible shirts—pushed through the crowd and followed them around the bar.

Ethan took a deep breath and looked around. The crowd had dispersed, giving him glances with varying degrees of pity that made him want to puke. This was exactly what he'd been trying to avoid.

"You okay?" Natalie asked, appearing behind him with concern pulling at her eyes.

"Uh, yeah."

"I know that was . . . awkward, but at least the truth is out. Right? No more elephant following you around town."

"I guess. I just . . . don't know what to do now."

She nodded, looked around at people still staring at him, then back. "Well, if I were you, I'd run."

He thought for a moment. "You know, I think running is a great idea. Wanna come home with me?"

Natalie's grin stretched over her face, lit from within. "Yes."

And just like that, his night did a one-eighty.

• • • • • • • • • •

Ethan pushed open his front door, then stepped aside so Natalie could go in. She toed off her sandals and took a few steps into his house, taking it all in.

"This isn't at all how I pictured your home."

He dropped his baseball bag on the floor in the corner, then hung his keys up on a single silver hook he'd drilled into the wall next to the closet. "You've pictured my home?"

"Mmm-hmm."

He looked around the house the way she did, trying to see it objectively. It was a nice enough place. Older, but he'd done a lot of work to it already. He'd replaced the horrible pink carpet with oak floors, painted all the walls, redone the bathroom, and replaced the kitchen cupboards, countertops, and appliances.

But he'd painted all the walls the same boring beige colour, had barely any furniture, and had never bothered with curtains, art, or any of the things that might have given off the impression that an actual person lived there.

"How often did you picture it?" he asked, taking off his shoes.

"Mmm . . . I've definitely given it more thought than I should have." She said it like a confession, and it made the glue holding Ethan's heart together harden a bit more.

"So you don't like my house?"

"It's not that I don't like it. It's . . . kinda like your shirt." She ran her hand over the black letters, pausing over his heart and resting there. "It's just not you. It's . . . boring."

"The shirt is boring?" he laughed, reaching up and resting his hand over hers.

"No. Your house."

"I am boring, though."

She shook her head. "You're not boring. You just like things that most people find boring."

"That's essentially the same thing."

"No, it's not. You like nature, right?"

"Yeah."

"Well, to people who don't like nature, you would be boring. But to other nature lovers, you would be super interesting. Truly boring people are the ones who never do anything."

"Hmm," he said. "I guess I never thought about it that way."

He closed the distance between them, reached up, and raked his fingers through her hair. The feel of her soft strands in his hands had become the best feeling on earth. Natalie's eyelids fluttered closed, and she leaned into him. She always seemed to relish his touch, which was perfect, because he loved touching her.

"So what would you suggest for my house, then?"

"Well, for starters, I pictured you living in the woods, not suburbia."

Ethan laughed. "Like a homeless person?"

She let out a soft chuckle that ended with a sigh when he traced her ear with his fingertip. "In a house in the woods, I mean. With lots of windows and an enormous deck."

"That actually sounds amazing."

She hummed an agreement. "I imagined you'd have an outdoor fireplace in a little clearing, too. With some comfy furniture where you could cuddle up under a big blanket and look at the stars."

He leaned down, kissed her softly on the lips. The picture she described came across so clearly in his mind, but he could see her on the couch next to him. He was smart enough to know it was pure fantasy, but it raised about a million questions.

He pulled back. Watched her eyes slowly open. "What would your ideal house be like?" he asked.

A little crease formed between her eyes. "I've never really given it much thought."

"I'm guessing it's not a twelve-bedroom Victorian manor?"

She laughed. "Definitely not, but . . ." She looked down, tilted her head a little. "I think it would be nice to have a bathroom."

Ethan smiled. "Bathrooms are pretty standard in homes."

"I mean, I would like to have a really nice bathroom. With a long counter that I could leave all my stuff on without having to pack it all away every day. And a great big bathtub with jets and one of those pillows that sticks onto the side of the tub."

"That's it? A bathroom."

"Yes. And slippers and a bathrobe and very fluffy towels. I'm talkin' like—" She gestured with her fingers, showing her desired thickness. "Oh! And I'd like tacky souvenirs all over the place. Bobble-heads and magnets and snow globes. Even if it means I have to dust. It would be nice, I suppose, to collect things when I'm travelling."

He smiled as he skimmed his hands down her body, leaned down, and kissed her again. She ran her hands up his back, just as she had before, and took off his hideous green shirt.

"Much better," she said, throwing the shirt on the floor. "Now you look like you."

He couldn't hold back any longer. He pulled her to him, covered her mouth with his. The only piece of furniture in the room was a large sectional that ran along the wall, but he wanted her in his bed more than he wanted his next breath, so he broke the kiss, took her by the hand, and led her down the hall.

He kicked open the door and drew her to the bed where he took her in his arms once more and gently laid her down. She pulled him down with her, wrapping her legs around his waist and kissing him as he reached for the hem of her shirt, lifting it up. He hadn't known whether he'd ever feel her skin under his hands again. Now that she was here, in bed with him, he couldn't keep his hands off her.

He reached for the button on her shorts. "This okay?"

She nodded, then lifted her hips off the bed so he could slip them and her plain nude panties out from under her. He slowly pulled them down her long tan legs and discarded them on the floor as they both let out a collective moan.

His baseball pants were uncomfortable and confining, and he strained against them, but he forced himself to ignore the urge to tear them off. He knelt down between her legs, pushed her tank top up, and kissed around her belly button, across her skin to her hipbones, down her smooth inner thigh, then back up the other one as she squirmed.

She was propped up on her elbows, watching, until he took her with his mouth, and her eyes rolled to the back of her head, and she fell back onto his pillow.

He was as lost in her as she was in him. Her moans and little gasps, her thighs twitching, it was all too much for him. He licked and sucked, stroking her thighs as her hips lifted from the bed. Every muscle in her body tensed, holding tight, until she found her release with a half scream, half gasp, and let go.

The sight of her on his bed, half-naked and blissful from the orgasm he'd just given her, made his body flame. He'd never seen a more beautiful sight in his life. He had to have her. Now.

He climbed onto the bed, slid open the drawer on his nightstand, and pulled out a condom. Stretching out next to her, he kissed her. She opened her eyes and smiled.

"Whoa," she said with a little shake of her head. "That was intense."

She slowly rose up onto her knees and reached for the zipper on his pants. She leaned over him, kissing down his stomach, then further down as she lowered his pants.

Tingles raced across his skin, and his eyes rolled to the back of his head as she put her hands on his chest and straddled him, the soft weight of her pinning him to the bed.

When he opened his eyes, she was staring down at him. Her dark eyes intense, staring into his. She reached down for the bottom of her shirt and pulled it over her head, then unclasped her bra and slipped the straps down her arms.

He reached for her, gliding his hands up the sides of her torso, then cupping her breasts in his hands and brushing his thumbs across her nipples.

"Beautiful," he said. "You're so incredibly beautiful, Natalie. I—"

She cut him off by kissing his mouth. He only had a moment to wonder whether she knew what he was going to say, before she reached for the condom, ripped it open, and slid it on him. When she lowered herself down onto him and he disappeared into the smooth heat of her, every word in his throat died, every thought in his head evaporated.

She rode him slowly, torturously, setting an excruciating pace. She stared into his eyes for a long time, her face going slack even as her eyes burned. Part of him wanted to flip her over, hold her tight, and bury himself into her. But he didn't dare give up the sight of her above him. He bit his lip and watched her move, her faced steeped in pleasure.

She fell forward, her mouth going to his neck, sucking, kissing, adding shivers to the rush of sensations coursing over his skin, before moving up to his ear. She nibbled his earlobe, licked the shell of his ear, moaned, and clenched, continuing her slow assault.

And he couldn't take it anymore.

"Natalie," he said, just once. A warning? He wasn't sure.

He linked his arms around her waist, bent his knees, planted his feet, and thrust into her, slightly faster than her pace, trying to find some relief without scaring her.

She gasped and held on, whispering into his ear. "Yes, Ethan. More."

Thank God.

He went faster, then freed one hand, slipped it into her hair at the base of her neck, and tilted her head gently back so he could see into her eyes. She rose with the pleasure, her face tightening.

"Yes, Ethan."

He stared into her eyes, taking in her pleasure as her breath came faster, matching his. She leaned forward, her breasts in his face. He took her nipple into his mouth and sucked as her mouth opened, and she crested. A strangled, breathy noise escaped from her throat. She gripped, convulsed, tightened around him, spurring on his own orgasm. It ripped through every corner of his body lightning fast and held him there in strangled pleasure that rolled on and on.

He held her tight to him. Even long after their bodies had eased into a warm, languid state and their breath had returned to normal. When she finally moved, he held her tighter in place, not ready to face being without her.

He looked into her eyes, searching, trying to tell her without speaking the words. He'd always suspected that he'd have a hard time getting over her when she left, but in that moment, he knew. All doubt was gone. He'd never manage it.

"Stay . . ." he said with a thick voice.

She smiled and kissed him, then cuddled into his side and sighed as his arm came around her shoulders and he kissed her forehead. Her face relaxed, her breathing evened out, and, when he was certain she'd drifted off to sleep, he whispered the thought he'd had from the moment he got her text the night before.

"Stay forever."

FIFTEEN

Anne's head was pounding as she walked through the front double doors of her North Shore Drive mansion and stepped onto the polished marble foyer floor.

The morning had been a nightmarish ordeal. She couldn't get out of attending the Mayor's brunch, a Mapleton tradition where the incumbent Mayor shakes hands and makes nice with the newly elected Mayor after weeks of campaigning against each other. At the start of the campaign, she'd looked forward to it, convinced she'd walk into the room with her head held high, accepting congratulations from local bigwigs on another successful run. None of her contenders had been any actual competition for her.

But then Elizabeth went and fucking died.

She'd been looking forward to the day the old battle-axe finally took leave. But the timing couldn't have been worse. It was incredibly frustrating that even in death, Elizabeth seemed to have the upper hand.

She clicked along the floor, not bothering to take off her heels, and headed straight for the mirrored sideboard along the dining room wall, where she kept the liquor. She'd already taken four painkillers that morning, but nothing cleared a headache like a couple glasses of wine, followed by a few gin and tonics.

Her campaign manager, and long-time best friend, Tina, came through the door just as she emptied the rest of last night's half-consumed bottle of pinot noir into her glass and took a long drink.

"Anne, isn't it a little too early in the day for that?"

She swallowed and shook her head. "What did you hear?"

Tina looked away as Anne took another long drink. She'd known Tina since they were children in school, over forty years, and could tell when she was so uncomfortable that it closed up her throat. She also knew from experience that yelling and threatening her wouldn't work to force the words out.

Tina had a very long fuse, but even she had a limit to what she'd take.

Anne reached for another bottle and the opener and helped herself to another glass while she waited. Finally, Tina found her voice.

"The poll results came in. It's just as you thought. Ninety-six percent of people who didn't vote for you cited 'scandal' as the reason."

Anne threw the corkscrew across the room. It sailed through the air, hit the floor with a clank, then skidded along before crashing into the bottom stair.

Tina's brows shot up, and she took several big steps back.

"What else?"

"Everyone's talking about the baseball tournament last night. Apparently, Susan Carlisle's daughter, Lindsay, with the red hair you say looks trashy, made a big scene. She and Derek were drunk and fighting again. It came out that Lindsay actually cheated on Ethan Pierce with Derek, and . . . they did it in the back seat of Ethan's truck."

Anne rolled her eyes closed and squeezed the bridge of her nose. "Why am I supposed to care about this? Get to the point, dammit!"

"Mom?"

Anne snapped her head up and came face to face with Emily. She stared in shock for a moment, wondering whether she was seeing things. Then remembered bits and pieces of two nights ago when

Emily came home from Toronto and said she was staying for a while. She should have known better than to come home so late in the evening when Anne's memory was more likely to be fuzzy.

"Emily. What is it?"

"Are you drinking again?"

Anne looked down at the glass and bottle in front of her and then back up at Emily. "It seems pretty obvious that I am. It's not a big deal."

"That's what you said the last time."

"It's under control. When are you going back to the dorms, Emily?"

"Back to the dorms? Mom . . ."

Emily stared at her for a long moment, then glanced at Tina before looking back. "I graduated. In the spring. You came to the graduation. I'm here for the summer now. We talked about this two nights ago."

Anne had a flicker of memory cross her mind. She remembered it was a long conversation, but for the life of her, couldn't remember most of it. She had probably explained why she came back to Mapleton and what her plans were, but Anne couldn't be sure they'd had that conversation.

"Of course, dear. I meant, have they moved your stuff out of your dorm already?"

Emily's face took on an exhausted look. She looked too old and dumpy for a twenty-five-year-old. And she was gaining weight again, too.

"I moved out in April. I'd tell you more, but you won't remember it, anyway."

"It's fine, Emily. You look tired, and I can tell you haven't been eating right. You're gaining again. I'll book us into the spa next week. You need a facial."

Without another word, Emily turned on her heel and left the room. Her daughter was angry with her, but one day, she'd thank her.

As soon as Emily left, Tina turned on her. "Anne, you've really upset her. She doesn't like seeing you like this."

Anne rolled her eyes. "She's fine. She loves the spa."

Tina walked out of the room. The sound of the garage door opening and then slamming shut a moment later jarred her aching head. When Tina returned, she was holding several empty wine and gin bottles.

"You're getting out of control again, Anne. Did you drink this morning before you came to the brunch?"

Anne ignored her. "Tell me the rest of what happened with Susan's daughter."

"Maybe you should take some time off. Get some help. Or just get out of town. You could go the cottage in Muskoka for a couple weeks."

"That's the last thing I need."

Tina's face fell. "What do you need, then?"

"What I really need right now is my best friend to help me with some information so I can make a plan."

Tina stared at her for a long moment. Anne knew Tina didn't like drinking, but she never told her no. Never.

"Afterward ," she started with a quiet voice, "Ethan and Natalie left together. Apparently, they kissed and looked very cozy. People are saying it's serious."

Anne reined in her temper, took another drink. "I think she was at Gayle and Mark's house on Sunday night for dinner. I didn't see her, but I just know."

Tina nodded. "Uh, there's one other thing I found out."

"What?"

"Chelsea Davenport has an appointment this week with Mrs. Landet to enrol her son, Ben, in kinder-garten at Mapleton Elementary."

"Enrol . . . she's staying?"

Tina nodded.

"At the house?"

Another nod.

"With Robert's grands—" She couldn't even get the rest of the word out. The anger took over.

Then the disgust.

Then the panic.

She clutched her chest as it tightened under her hot, creeping skin. "I have no choice now . . ."

Her brain started turning a mile a minute. She had to get rid of them. Now. And she knew how to do it. It just wasn't ideal. It could easily backfire. But she couldn't let them stay and coexist with her in Mapleton. They were a constant reminder to the whole town that her marriage was a sham. Her husband had penetrated every vagina he could find, and she was a complete and utter failure.

"Maybe it's time to just walk away," Tina said. "You've fought this for so long. I think you should focus on taking better care—"

"I can't walk away. I have to carry through with my plan."

Tina threw up her hands, stood from the table. "We talked about this, or do you not remember that, either?"

"I can make it work." She worked to steady her breathing. She needed to get out of her head and let the anxiety recede so she could think again.

She strode out of the dining room, through the foyer to the untouched kitchen. She leaned against the spotless island counter, then remembered she'd forgotten to eat again that morning and pulled an apple from the bowl.

Tina followed her, leaned on the opposite side of the island. "You can't make this work, Anne. You're not thinking clearly. This will backfire. Unless . . ." She looked up, hopeful. "Did Victor's lawyer call you back?"

"He did, but they aren't interested in making a deal. I'm going to have to do this alone."

Tina rolled her eyes. "How?"

She bit into the apple. "I can . . . do what we talked about before."

"That's not a plan. That's a scheme. And I'm sorry, but I won't be a part of it."

"Tina . . ."

"No."

"No?"

"That's right. No." She pulled the keys from her pocket and walked out of the kitchen. Pausing in the doorway, she said, "I love you, Anne. You're my best friend. But going through with this is crossing a line. Call me when you need a ride to rehab. Other than that, you're on your own."

With that, she walked out and slammed the front door behind her.

For a split second, Anne wondered whether Tina was right. But the doubt passed quickly, and she could clearly see exactly what needed to be done.

She took another bite of the apple, chased it with a swig of wine, then gathered up the empty bottles and brought them back to the garage. Being alone in this was fine. Better, actually. She had a lot of practice taking care of everything on her own, being Robert's wife.

She drained the last of the wine. At the front door, she threw her purse over her shoulder and pulled her keys out. She checked her face in the entryway mirror for any signs of inebriation—she didn't need another DUI that her lawyer would have to get her out of—put on her sober, happy, politician face, and walked out the door to her Cadillac.

It was finally time to pay Natalie a visit.

Sixteen

"**A**re you sure you won't come to the pond?"

Natalie shook her head and tried to put on a disgusted face. She was smiling too widely to pull it off. She'd blissfully spent the morning in Ethan's bed, talking and laughing and relieved that she'd bought herself another two weeks with him. Eventually, they'd had to get up to eat. Then, Ethan said he needed to water his trees, so they drove back to Monroe Manor together.

"I told you, I will never go out there."

"Do you know how many snakes there are in Australia?" Ethan asked, pushing his glasses up his nose with a finger. He was so cute. She reached up and kissed him, unable to resist his soft lips and scratchy cheeks.

She didn't want to think about Australia. Or snakes. She just wanted Ethan to take care of the pond and come back and watch a movie with her on the couch under a big blanket, as they'd planned.

"Probably a lot less than there are out there."

"Completely incorrect. There are tons."

Natalie rolled her eyes. "Literal tons? Someone has estimated their cumulative weight?"

He laughed his happy, crinkly eyed laugh. "I wouldn't doubt it. There are gigantic snakes there. The scrub python can grow over seven metres long and weigh as much as sixty pounds."

Natalie narrowed her eyes at him. "Did you look that up?"

He smiled and nodded. "It's the largest in Australia but far from the scariest. The eastern brown snake is smaller but has much more potent venom. Same with the taipan, and the common death adder, and—"

"Okay, that's enough talk about venom and death. My tour is on the East Coast. Cities and beaches and reefs and shrimps on the barbie. Not snakes."

Ethan's mouth quirked into a sad half smile. It was the first time his smiling face had broken all morning, and it made her stomach roil. "It shouldn't take me too long."

Her brain screamed at her to say something, get them back on their happy track. She was thrilled to have more time with him, like extending a vacation at the last minute. But he seemed to view it as putting off something terrible.

He walked to the door, put on his boots, and left.

She stood for a few minutes, wondering whether she should go after him, make sure they were on the same page. But by the time she decided she should, he'd already be at the pond. And she meant what she'd said; she was never going back into those snakes again.

She turned to get some snacks from her stash in the kitchen when there was a knock on the door.

Maybe Ethan was back? Why would he knock?

She walked to the door and opened it and found Anne on the porch. She was dressed in a short-sleeve cream cashmere sweater, with wide, white, perfectly pressed pants and nude heels. Gold and sapphire earrings dangled elegantly from her earlobes, just visible through the tendrils of her blond hair.

Natalie's jaw dropped.

"Natalie, is it?"

Natalie swallowed the lump in her throat and managed a nod.

"I don't think we have ever formally been introduced. I'm Anne. Robert's widow."

Natalie stood frozen in place. Only her eyeballs moved to look out over the grass toward the pond, but Ethan was long out of sight. Chelsea and Ben weren't there, either. They'd gone out shopping for orange paint that Ben had requested for his new room. She was completely alone.

"May I come in?"

Natalie still couldn't speak, but she couldn't very well slam the door in this poor woman's face. She should have looked before she opened the door. She stepped aside, opening the door wider. Anne walked into the house, taking a few steps into the foyer, and looking into the parlour, then the dining room. When she silently turned back to Natalie, she had a calm smile on her face.

Natalie waited a few moments, hoping she'd say what she came to say, but she calmly stood waiting without a word. Natalie assumed Anne was there to yell at her to leave, or worse, to cry and to beg her to leave, but she did neither. She just stared until Natalie became increasingly and visibly uncomfortable.

Then she smiled.

Natalie couldn't help but feel there was some play for power happening between them, on Anne's end at least. Natalie had no power in this situation, and she was growing impatient and desperate for the exchange to end.

She cleared her throat, swallowed. "What brings you here?" she finally squeaked out.

Anne's smile widened. "I'm here to make you an offer."

Natalie returned a blank stare. "An offer?"

Anne nodded. "Yes. I'd like to buy this property."

"But you're contesting the will. It isn't mine yet to sell."

She tipped her delicate square chin up. "I'd prefer to settle this out of court and without Victor Monroe getting involved. Less attention that way."

Natalie blinked. She wanted to ask why she was bothering to contest the will in the first place, then, but moved on. The fewer words spoken between the two of them, the better. She just wanted to get out of there. "Okay . . ."

"I'll purchase this property for five million."

The fog clouding Natalie's brain cleared when she heard the number. "It's worth twelve."

"Yes, but I'm willing to sign an agreement with Ethan Pierce that the land won't be developed. That's a very generous offer for him. If the will goes to court, he may get nothing."

Natalie's heart squeezed. "I don't understand why you want this house."

"I want my daughter to have it."

Guilt closed up her throat once more. It had never sat right with Natalie that Elizabeth had cut Emily completely out of the will.

"There is, however, one condition I need from you," Anne continued.

Natalie's eyes widened. "What?"

"I need you to leave Mapleton. Immediately. Your sister and nephew, too. And I need your assurance that none of you will ever come back again. My daughter and I can't live in peace when you're all here. We'd finally started to heal after Robert's death, and now with you both here, the humiliation is ever present. "

Natalie stared at her for a long moment. Her mind was spinning. Two weeks ago, she'd have jumped for joy. Promising to never come back would have been a piece of cake for her back then. But the longer she stayed, the harder it was becoming to leave. And then there was Ethan . . .

"I'm not sure . . ."

Anne took a step forward, placed a hand on Natalie's shoulder. Concern pulled her impeccably shaped brows together. "Mapleton isn't the right place for you. I think you know that already. It's a tight-knit community, and believe me, no matter how hard you try, in a town like this, you'll never escape who you are. People will never let you forget that you're Robert's daughter. Do you want your nephew to face this, too? Children can be so cruel. Emily certainly learned that."

Natalie's stomach lurched at the mention of Ben. She knew what the kids would say about him at school, knew the kind of shadow he would grow up under in town. She'd dealt with the same thing.

Anne took a step back and let out a sympathetic sigh. "I heard you made a rather pleasant life for yourself, travelling the world. That's something most people only dream of. You're smart enough to know you're better off out there where no one knows your past and people won't judge you for what your mother did."

Bile rose in Natalie's throat. She never had to think about what people thought of her out there. But in Mapleton, everyone talked about her. She'd overheard everyone from the librarians to the grocery store clerks gossiping about who she was. That was the problem with small towns.

She already knew that the only way to silence the judgment was to put distance between her and it. Running was incredibly effective.

Besides, going to Australia had always been the plan. She was happiest when she was travelling. And she had an incredible opportunity waiting for her. An opportunity that, at one point, she could only dream of. If she took Anne's offer now, it would mean everyone would win. And no one would be forced to deal with the pain of this situation any longer.

Five million was a lowball offer, but it was still plenty of money for Chelsea and Ben to have a very comfortable life away from the cruelty of Mapleton. And Ethan would get his pond, and his snakes would keep their home. He'd be better off with someone else, anyways. Someone who could love him for longer than two weeks.

She looked up at Anne. The woman who her mother had treated so terribly. Maybe accepting this offer would help ease some of the guilt she'd been living with since she found out Robert had been married.

Natalie took a deep breath, about to agree, when she saw Mi's fur pass by in her periphery, the other Mi following. "What about Elizabeth's cats? Mi and Mi. I inherited them, but I obviously can't take them with me, and they can't be adopted."

Anne looked over her shoulder, then back. She plastered a huge smile on her face. "Emily will take good care of them. She loves cats."

Natalie nodded. "Good. Chelsea and Ethan will have to agree, but I'm happy to sell you the property."

Anne smiled, then swayed a little with what looked like relief. "Excellent. I'll have my lawyer draw up the paperwork and send it over to Mr. Speeler."

Natalie nodded. The lump in her throat returned, but she couldn't swallow it away. She knew she was doing the right thing, but for some reason, it made her feel as if she were drowning. An overwhelming urgency to move, to go, to run, started flaring up in her brain.

Anne walked to the door, then paused. "You'll be leaving shortly, then?"

Natalie's eyes darted between Anne and the opening between the trees past the grass where Ethan had disappeared. Maybe if she hurried, she could get out of there before he got back. Saying goodbye to him was going to be torture. He knew she was leaving eventually, anyway. She could just scribble a note for him and make it easier for them both. And she'd leave one for Chelsea, explaining that she had Ben's best interests at heart. Chelsea looked at

Mapleton and saw a wholesome life. Natalie knew better.

"Yes," she said. "I'm going to go right now."

She closed the door behind Anne, her mind spinning. She threw up a silent prayer that she'd never have to look her in the eye again, and pulled her phone from her pocket as she ran up the stairs to start packing. A quick call to Speeler, a couple notes for Ethan and Chelsea, and a new flight, and this whole mess would be behind them all for good.

Seventeen

B y the time Ethan made it to the pond, he'd covered enough ground to make the trip three times. He'd stopped more times than he cared to admit and retraced his steps back to the house to speak with Natalie about how he felt, only to think better of it and continue to the pond. Eventually, he made it there with two buckets, forced himself to fill them from the pond, and give his new trees a much-needed drink.

He looked up at the dark sky, but the forecast only called for a few millimetres of rainfall, which would never be enough to soak the trees to the roots. So he began the mindless task of filling buckets and hauling them around to the fifty trees he'd planted.

His mind wandered to that day he'd started planting the trees, when he'd come back from Hudson Bay looking like a mess, and first heard Natalie screaming in the woods. He laughed to himself, remembering how he thought she was just some silly Instagrammer, then he met her and realized she was actually the person who held his fate in her hands, then later realized she actually was an Instagrammer, but not silly at all, and in fact, smart and funny and exciting, and possibly the best person he'd ever met.

He couldn't believe how wrong he'd got her.

He emptied a bucket onto a scrawny little pine tree, watched the water quickly seep into the ground and disappear, and he made up his mind.

He was going to tell her he loved her and ask her to stay in Mapleton. With him. Forever.

He just needed to think about what to say, exactly.

He filled more buckets, brainstormed, watered each tree, and by the time he'd finished, he had a fully fleshed out script written in his mind, ready to be delivered.

He smiled to himself as he walked back to the house, but as he rounded the corner and emerged out of the tree line, his step faltered at the sight of a taxi idling in the driveway.

Why would a cab be there? Maybe Chelsea's crappy little car finally gave out, and she had to call a cab to get home?

Jogging to the front door, throwing the buckets into the bed of his truck as he passed it, he took the stairs two at a time and walked straight into the house without knocking.

"Natalie?"

No answer.

He walked back to the kitchen, called her name again, but she was nowhere to be seen, so he jogged up the stairs and pushed open the door to Natalie's bedroom.

And that's when he saw her, hunched over the dresser, taking fistfuls of clothing and hastily shoving them into her suitcase around her mother's jewellery box and photo albums.

His heart ceased. "Are you . . . packing?"

He hadn't even realized she'd unpacked.

Natalie glanced at him for a fraction of a second. She looked back down and squeezed her eyes shut. "Yeah."

"Why?"

"I'm leaving."

A sick feeling slithered up his spine. He had a million questions, but it was hard to wade through them all while being tortured, watching her fill her suitcase.

"Why now, suddenly?"

She stopped with her bras midair between the drawer and the suitcase, just for a second, then smashed them down haphazardly on top of her swimsuit. "Suddenly?" she asked, still not meeting his eyes. "I've been trying to leave ever since I got here."

She pushed past him into the hall, and he stood there, dumbfounded, watching her leave the room. He had the idea of going to her suitcase and emptying it back into the drawers, but he stopped himself. He didn't want to fight with her. He wanted to go to the couch and hold her, as they'd planned. He was at a complete loss.

Think.

He needed to tell her how he felt, convince her to stay before she finished packing up and disappeared from his life.

She stormed back into the room, arms full of a toiletry bag and little shampoo and soap bottles. She opened her arms overtop of the suitcase, let it all fall in, then zipped it up. His heart stopped beating.

"Natalie, I don't want you to leave. I should have told you before, but I—"

"Stop, Ethan. Don't," she said, her breathing coming short and fast. She clutched the neck of her T shirt and pulled it from her throat, sucking in panicked breaths.

"It's going to be okay. We can talk about this and figure it out," he said.

He stepped toward her with his arms open, but she shot a hand out to stop him, then shook her head. She bent down, picked up her suitcase, and pulled up the handle.

"I can't talk. I have to go. This is why I wanted to leave before you got back."

Ethan stood stock-still, staring at her, letting her words percolate through the pain. "Wait a minute. Were you going to leave without even telling me?"

"No." She reached over to the dresser, grabbed a torn scrap of paper that had once been an envelope, and handed it to him. "I wrote you a note."

Ethan stared down at the paper in her hand that she'd haphazardly scribbled a few words on as an afterthought. His blood started boiling. "You wrote me a note?"

She casually nodded, as if it were no big deal. "For you and Chelsea. To explain—"

"You wrote a fucking note?!" he screamed. Rage exploded inside him. He was angry with her, no doubt. He never would have said goodbye to her with just a note. But he was far more angry with himself.

For the first time since he'd met her, he didn't want to be close to her. He wanted to be as far away as possible.

Natalie flinched. "Ethan—"

"No," he said, shaking his head. "Not another word."

He knew she would leave, and he was stupid enough to let himself fall completely in love with her anyway. Here he was, trying to tell her he loved her, to beg her to stay with him, and she didn't even care enough about him to tell him she was leaving in person. She was going to disappear from his life while he was at the pond. Maybe that's why she didn't want to go out there. She was looking for an opportunity to ghost him.

A calm feeling washed over him as he completely shut down and disengaged. It was the same thing he felt when he saw Lindsay and Derek in the back of his truck. A refusal to care about someone who cared so little about him.

"I'm done." He turned on his heel, started for the door.

"I made sure that your pond—"

He didn't hear the rest of her words. Tuned her out as he walked out of the room, down the stairs, and outside.

When he got into his truck and turned it on, he started for home, but then he thought better of it. There was no way he could face his house now. It was filled with memories of her. And his bed . . .

He shook the memory off. As he glanced down at his key chain, the spare key Adam had given him caught the light and glinted at him. He made an abrupt U turn that caused several angry honks and headed toward North Shore Drive.

Eighteen

"And that wraps up East Coast training!" Alira announced.

A cheer roared through the coach bus as it pulled up to a stop in front of the Sydney tour office. Natalie couldn't bring herself to add to it, though. Landing in Sydney hadn't felt nearly as triumphant as she imagined it would have, and the last two weeks of training had been a battle. But she knew that if she just kept moving, focusing on what was next, she'd be fine.

Being with a dozen other guides and drivers during the day was easier. They'd shared their adventures and gone to all the tourist hot spots and the off-the-beaten-path places Alira had curated into the trip to show their travellers. They'd tried amazing food and toured incredible landmarks. She'd even forced a smile in some pictures for her followers.

But it was in the quiet moments at night, alone in her hotel room, that her mind would haunt her. It always landed on the burned-in image of Ethan shutting down and walking away from her. It replayed the disappointment that had soaked through his voice when he asked whether she was going to leave without telling him.

She didn't even want to think about how Chelsea would have felt, coming home to an empty house with cans of paint, ready to make it a home for Ben, and finding a note saying her sister had bailed on her and taken a huge loss on the house. She made every effort to block it out.

She knew what she did was right. Get out fast before anyone got hurt, let the lawyers work out the details so they could all move on. It was best for everyone. They were all getting what they'd wanted from the start. But it was brutal to feel this emptiness. It reminded her of the feeling after she lost her mother and knew she was alone.

Keep moving.

She stood from her seat, collected her things, and started filing off the bus with the others.

"Don't forget to meet back here at six tonight," Alira said. "We have reservations for dinner, and then we're going out for some drinks to celebrate."

Natalie nodded and forced a smile as she passed Alira and stepped down off the coach. She wasn't in a celebratory mood, but it was part of her job to always be upbeat. She pulled out her phone and checked the time. Two o'clock. She had plenty of time to check into her hotel and find a party dress to wear out that night.

She thought back to the night her one-and-only party dress had broken and how the warmth of Ethan's jacket had engulfed her.

"Natalie!"

She looked up and found Jess running toward her. She threw open her arms and grabbed Natalie in a big hug.

"I thought you weren't coming in until tomorrow."

Jess looked her up and down. A frown formed. "I took an earlier flight. I wanted to spend an extra day in Sydney before we leave on tour."

Natalie nodded.

"Everything okay? You look . . . sad? I've never seen you sad before."

She tried to pull the sides of her mouth into a smile, but it was way too much effort. "I'm fine. Alira made plans for dinner and drinks tonight. You in?"

"Absolutely."

"Cool. I need to check into my hotel and buy a dress. I was going to go to the QVB. Do you want to come?"

Jess smiled. "Yeah, I want to see the Queen Victoria Building. I hear the shopping is amazing. Lead the way."

They walked a block to the hotel, and Natalie filled Jess in on the training and told her about some things they'd see on tour. She checked in quickly, and then they hopped on a bus to the historic shopping mall. Natalie could feel Jess's eyes on her the whole time, analyzing, questioning.

"So . . ." Jess started as they walked into the first store with dresses in the window. "How was Canada?"

Natalie shrugged, picked up a black dress. When she turned it in her hands and saw it had thin, criss-cross straps and no back, she quickly returned it to the rack and moved on.

"It was . . ." How did you explain that you had both the best time and the worst time? That you were thankful that it had happened and also full of regret? "Uh . . . busy."

Jess's face showed her trying to work through what that meant. "I saw your Instagram post. At Niagara Falls."

Natalie's hand froze midair, reaching for a gorgeous satin eggplant fit and flare. She shook off the memory of Ethan's arm around her at the cliff and picked up the dress by the hanger. "Yeah, the falls are really something, eh?"

Jess laughed. "A few weeks back in Canada and you're sounding like a Mountie. Eh?"

Natalie narrowed her eyes. "Do you know what a Mountie is?"

She laughed harder and shook her head. "Nope."

Natalie rolled her eyes, looked at the dress, then draped it over her forearm to bring it to the change room.

"Something isn't right, Nat."

"Why?" she asked, holding the dress up again. "Purple isn't my colour?"

"I don't mean the dress. It's beautiful. And, side note, any colour is your colour. What I mean is that you seem off. Are you missing Marco?"

Natalie reared back. "Marco?"

"No? Then it must be the cute Canadian guy from your post? The one with the glasses and the blue eyes and that smile."

Natalie looked away. Ethan did have exceptional eyes. Kind eyes. And an unbelievable smile. Not to mention his hands . . .

She mustered the energy to shake her head and reach for a light orange, knee-length fitted dress that had a long slit up one thigh. It was equally beautiful as the purple. She draped it on her arm and kept walking.

"What was his name?"

Natalie swallowed. "Ethan," she choked out. "He was just . . . temporary."

Jess stepped closer. "Natalie, you can't lie to me. You seem . . . really down. Maybe you're homesick."

"It's impossible to be homesick when you don't have a home."

"Maybe he was your home."

Natalie's heart ceased as she forced her head to shake convincingly. "I'll be fine. I just need to keep moving."

"Haven't you been on the road for two weeks? More than that. Where did you go after you left Canada?"

"I extended my layover in Dubai."

Jess's eyes closed for a moment. "What did you do there?"

"Slept."

Natalie spotted a bright-red halter dress, which she picked up, only to be struck by more Lindsay vibes than she cared for. She immediately put it back and picked up the same style in a saturated magenta.

"Did you go out while you were in Dubai? Go down to the beach? Sightsee?"

"Nothing has really changed since I was there last."

She located the change rooms and headed for them with her three dresses, hoping two of them would look terrible on her so she wouldn't have to choose. Now that she was back to suitcase living, she only had room for one.

"Maybe moving all around the world isn't the right solution for this problem, Nat."

"Why wouldn't it be? It worked last time."

"But that was a different problem, right? You had no one. Ethan seems like someone."

She paused and turned to Jess. "He was wonderful, and I'll admit, I miss him. But it's a lot more complicated than that. In Mapleton, I'm trash. Nothing more than Robert Monroe's whore's kid."

"Natalie!"

Natalie shrugged as if it didn't bother her. But she knew Jess would see through it. "That's what they call me." She turned and walked into the change room, then closed the curtain.

"Well, fuck 'em!" Jess yelled from the other side. "You're allowed to exist."

Natalie smiled for the first time in almost three weeks. She hadn't realized how similar Jess and Chelsea were. But the smile was fleeting. She pulled her yellow dress over her head, kicked off her gold sandals, and slipped the purple dress on. "I'm better off alone than surrounded by people who make me feel like shit."

"True. But being alone is hard. And you've been doing it for longer than I thought possible."

Natalie pulled back the curtain and did a turn.

"It's stunning," Jess said.

Natalie went back into the room and changed into the orange to show Jess.

"Gorgeous."

Another couple minutes, and she came out in the magenta.

"Perfect. They all look good."

She looked at herself in the mirror, then at the dresses hanging in the room. "I don't want to choose one."

Jess nodded. "Maybe you should think about renting an apartment in Sydney so you have a home on your days off. Then you can buy all the dresses."

Natalie shook her head. "It would only make things worse. I don't want to sit in an empty room all alone. Better off in hostels."

"I'm worried about you, Nat. I had a friend once who was really down, and I never asked or did anything to help him, and he . . ."

Natalie took her by the shoulders. "Jess. I appreciate your concern. But you don't have to worry. I'm not going to off myself. I've been through worse. I just need some time."

She turned back into the change room. Stared at the dresses. A sadness washed over her, thinking of her dresser in Mapleton filled with all of her clothes.

She shook her head. "I'm taking the orange," she said. She pulled off the magenta and hung it on the hanger just when a notification sounded on her phone. She pulled her phone from her purse and saw a new email from Speeler.

The breath left her chest in a fast whoosh. She plopped down on the small stool in the corner of the change room and clicked on the email. It was the final agreement of sale. She gave it a quick read-through.

When she got to the final sale amount and saw that it wasn't five million dollars—it was five hundred thousand— her jaw dropped.

"What the fuck . . . ?"

"What's wrong?" Jess asked.

She threw her yellow dress back on and pulled back the curtain. "There's a problem with the sale of the house. Speeler emailed me last week and said the purchase agreement had been sent off. It was exactly what we agreed on. I thought it had all been taken care of. "

Jess's face split into a grin. "Oh, my God. Is it fate?"

"No. It's fucking Anne Monroe."

Jess narrowed her eyes at the name in solidarity. "I hate her. Who is she?"

"My dead biological father's widow."

Jess looked up, squinting and confused, before she finally cringed. "Yikes."

Natalie nodded. "She offered a decent amount to buy the property my sister and I inherited, but it seems like she dropped the price."

"Wait, wait. You have a sister?!"

Natalie looked up. "Uh, yeah. Half sister. A different 'whore's' kid. The town hates her and her mom, too."

"Oh my God, stop saying whore right now. And the town should focus their judgment on your father, not all of you. He's the one who couldn't keep his tallywacker in his trousers. Was he at least a good dad to you?"

Natalie scoffed. "He never even spoke to me. Not one word. I was completely unacknowledged."

Jess's face fell. "Seems to me the town should have shown you sympathy. This shame is not yours to carry, babe. No one should treat a child that way."

Natalie let that sink in. She scrolled back up the document, searching for the mention of the property not being sold to be developed, but couldn't find it anywhere. She frantically scrolled down, past the amount to the very bottom of the document, and what she saw made her sinking heart drown.

Both Chelsea and Ethan had scrawled their signatures on the lines next to their names.

"What the hell?"

"What is it?"

Natalie looked up at Jess. All the energy she'd been lacking came rushing back. But it wasn't her normal excited energy.

She was fucking pissed.

"I have to make a phone call."

Nineteen

"Ethan!"

Ethan opened one eye, saw Adam standing over him, hands on his hips in his hideous lime-green shirt and grass-stained baseball pants. He closed his eye again and twisted his body away, burying his face in the back of Adam's sofa.

"This is the third game you missed. We lost. Our sub missed three catches you would have made easily."

"Sorry," he mumbled into the cushion, but he didn't mean it. There was no way he was going to those baseball diamonds. In fact, he had no plans to leave Adam's house at all. He'd been working from Adam's home office, sleeping in his basement, working out in his home gym. He'd occasionally stepped onto the back deck, but the view of the sand dunes and blue lake made his chest hollow out.

Adam sank into the chair next to the couch, rested his elbows on his knees. "It's been three weeks. I'm getting worried about you."

"I'm fine."

"You're clearly not. Have you been to the pond?"

"What's the point? I signed Anne's settlement offer yesterday. So did Chelsea. Speeler is sending it off to Natalie, but it's taking a bit with the time change. After she signs, it's over. I'll have to wait and see what Anne does with the property. She'll probably sell it immediately to a developer and turn a nice profit at Chelsea's expense."

Adam huffed a breath and stood, then walked to the kitchen. He pulled two beers from the fridge and came back but stalled with his hand around the cap.

"Let's go out for a beer. I want to pop into Eighteen-Twenty and see how things are running," he said.

Ethan sat up, gave Adam's hand a pointed look. "You are holding the best beer in Canada. Why would we go there and drink crappy beer?"

"Are you calling my beer crappy?"

"Uh . . ." Ethan tried to think of a way to backtrack. He'd forgotten Adam and Max had just purchased the most centrally located pub in Mapleton a week ago. The location was perfect. The beer and food were not. "It could probably use . . . some . . . tweaking."

Adam broke into a grin. "My thoughts exactly. It's going to be amazing once we get it renovated and Max fixes the menu. The beer is a whole other thing, though. I'm glad you introduced me to Tipped Canoe. I looked into their head brewer. She's a genius. I'm hoping that if we throw enough money at her, she'll join us."

"I'll keep my fingers crossed for you."

"I'm also interviewing for a replacement for Derek," Adam said.

Ethan squinted at Adam. "Interviewing? You can't interview people for rec league baseball."

Adam shrugged, then walked back to the kitchen. "If they want in, I need to know they aren't douchey assholes," he called over his shoulder as he put the beers back in the fridge.

Ethan was just reaching for the remote when Adam came back and ripped it from his hands.

"No more Netflix. You're making my bat cave into a lair for the depressed," Adam said, looking around. "Maybe we should throw a party to clear out the bad vibes."

"We?"

"Well, yeah. You practically live here now."

Ethan rolled his eyes, stretched his long legs back out across Adam's enormous sectional.

Adam seethed. "We're going out."

"Tomorrow."

"Amy's back tomorrow. You have your family dinner thing. Or are you going to miss that another week, too?"

Ethan shook his head, then dropped his shoulders. "I can't go back to my parents' house alone. I don't want to go anywhere."

"You weren't half this depressed after you broke up with Lindsay, and she was your actual girlfriend. You didn't even sell your truck. And she fucked Derek in there."

Puke surged up in Ethan's throat.

"And what about that hot French girl . . . Celine? Ciel? Soleil?"

"Camille."

"Right. You dated her for like two years in university, then she went back to Montreal, and you never saw her again. Did you mope around my house for three weeks after that?"

"No."

"Exactly. And do you know why?" Adam leaned toward him with a deranged, wide-eyed look.

Ethan rolled his eyes. "Because you still lived with your dad then, and he used to scare me?"

"No. Because you love Natalie! You should have fucking told her, man."

"We've been through this. She was already packed."

"Then you should have screamed it at her!"

Ethan stood up from the couch with a huff and lumbered toward the fridge. "You don't get it. It's complicated. And it's over now. Do you really think I'd magically be over it if I had told her?"

"At least it would be off your chest. Right now, it's just sitting there, festering. Like some kind of flesh-eating disease." He shuddered as he walked to Ethan, grabbed his arm, and started pulling him toward the door.

"We're going out. Life is meant to be lived! You need to see some people, maybe meet a new girl. I'm not taking no for an answer."

Ethan reluctantly let Adam drag him along. "Fine. One crappy beer. No girls."

Adam smiled. "Deal."

· · · · ● · ● · · · ·

The second they walked into the bar, Ethan regretted letting Adam drag him there. The place was packed. People were seated all around the enormous bar in the centre of the room and filled almost every table. Luckily, there was a Blue Jays game on that had gone into extra innings, and all eyes were glued to the big screens around the bar.

Adam walked through the crowd, saying hi and waving to almost everyone, while Ethan followed behind, avoiding everyone's eye contact. When they got to the only empty table in the place and sat down, the music changed, and a familiar, upbeat tune started playing.

Ethan's brain turned, trying to place the familiar song as he took off his jacket and sat.

"Hey, isn't this Bublé?"

His eyes widened as Michael Bublé's perfect crooning voice struck up with the music, and he started singing about a woman he was happy to be rid of.

He shot up out of his chair, nearly knocking it over, and grabbed his jacket. "I'm out."

Adam lunged forward and grabbed onto his jacket, pulling it from his hands, and pointed at the chair. "You made a deal. You haven't had a beer yet. It's just a song. Tune it out."

Ethan exhaled and slumped back into the chair. He tried to tune out the song, but it was impossible. Natalie had said the purpose of the day song was to remind you of all the fun you had on your trip. He was transported back to that cliff with her by his side, her knees up to her chest, his arm around her shoulders as she cracked open her soul for him. He could feel the warmth of her skin against his. One thing was certain—the day song did its job.

"It's psychological warfare," he muttered.

"What's that?" Adam asked.

Ethan shook his head.

The song mercifully ended just as a pretty waitress came bouncing over in a tiny black skirt and low-cut black shirt that stretched across her chest.

"Hey, Adam," she said, leaning toward him and completely ignoring Ethan.

"Hey . . ." Adam hesitated.

"Lacey."

"Hey, Lacey, how's it going?"

Lacey giggled a little, leaned in closer. "Better now. I hear you're my new boss."

Ethan rolled his eyes, but it was more of a whole-body roll. He could just imagine what Natalie's reaction would be if she were there with him. Her dark eyes would crinkle the way they did when she was amused, and the corners of her mouth would pull up into a pretty smirk.

"Uh, yeah. I guess," Adam said. "We'll take two pints of the session IPA and some nachos."

"'Kay!" she said, then twirled away and walked to the bar with swaying hips.

Ethan stared at Adam, who was looking at him instead of at Lacey. "You know, when I said 'no girls,' I meant for me."

Adam waved a dismissive hand and looked out over the crowd. "She's too young. And technically, she works for me. You know how I feel about employees—"

He stopped midsentence, his eyes going wide.

"What?" Ethan twisted in his chair, followed Adam's gaze, and his eyes immediately landed on bright-red hair. Before he could look away, Lindsay made eye contact and waved.

He raised an awkward hand, then turned back to Adam.

"Did you just . . . wave?" Adam asked with a murderous look.

"She waved first."

"The only appropriate response is to flip her off."

"You know, this wouldn't even be an issue if I was still on your couch. I shouldn't have come here."

"Here are your beers," Lacey said, putting coasters down on the wood tabletop, then placing two frosty glasses down. "The nachos will be out in a few minutes."

"Thanks," Adam said, then looked away.

But Lacey refused to take the hint. She flipped her tray under her arm and shifted her weight onto one foot to angle herself toward Adam.

Ethan picked up the beer, took a drink. "Blegch . . ." He shuddered as he forced the vile beer down. "It's undrinkable."

Lacey went on ignoring him. "You know, Adam, I'm off in about twenty minutes, and I don't have any plans for the rest of the night."

Ethan had heard enough. He picked up the disgusting beer, tipped his head back, and drained it.

"What are you doing?" Adam said, looking around Lacey's hip toward him.

After swallowing the last drop, once he was certain he wasn't going to throw it up, he put the empty glass back down on the coaster. "You said one beer. I'm leaving. I won't wait up for you."

"I didn't mean the physical beer."

Ethan shrugged. "You should have been more specific." He stood, grabbed his jacket, and turned.

"It was implied! It's the spirit of the beer!" he called out over the sound of the pub, but Ethan kept walking.

He loved his friend, but he wasn't ready for this yet. He had made it out the front door and three steps across the parking lot, when a voice stopped him.

"Ethan!"

He turned to find Lindsay coming out the door after him. "Uh, yeah. Hi." He kept walking, but she followed.

"Wait. I was hoping we could talk. About what happened."

"I can't stay here. It's all good. Let's just forget about it."

"No, Ethan. We can't just forget it."

He turned with a sigh. "Fine, what is it?"

She glanced around. There were packed tables on the patio area, and of course, they had drawn a few eyes. "Can we go somewhere private? Can we meet at the beach?"

"I don't have my tru— I came with Adam."

"Do you want a ride home?"

"Have you been drinking?"

Her mouth formed a sad smile. "No."

"Okay. I'll take a ride, then."

He walked with her to her car and got into the passenger side, and she pulled through the parking lot. Just as she passed the front door, Adam stepped out of the bar and looked around.

Their eyes met through the glass as Lindsay pulled out of the parking lot. Adam stood frozen in place, then his jaw dropped. His head began shaking, and he said something. He was probably thinking the unthinkable, but Ethan couldn't explain. Instead, he shrugged and gave a little wave as Lindsay hit the accelerator and carried on down the street, leaving Adam standing in the parking lot, dumbfounded.

TWENTY

N atalie left a voice mail for Speeler, but then Jess pointed out that it was two a.m. in Mapleton and that he wouldn't be able to return her call for at least another six hours. So they met the group for drinks and dancing.

It was a fun night with an awesome group of people, but Natalie couldn't peel her mind off of Ethan and Chelsea and Ben for long enough to enjoy it. She just kept wondering why they'd sign that.

She was still wondering at midnight, lying in her hotel bed staring at the ceiling. It was eight a.m. in Mapleton, and she was growing impatient. She set a five-minute timer on her phone and set it on the nightstand. Five minutes was plenty of time for Speeler to get settled in his office, get his messages from the receptionist, and call her back.

Two minutes later, her phone rang.

She dove for it, saw Speeler's name on the screen, and answered.

"Finally!"

"Excuse me, Ms. Alvarez. You're the first call I made."

"Good. What the hell is this crap you sent me?"

"That is Anne's offer."

"This isn't what we talked about. She offered five million and said she would sign off on not having the land developed."

"Well, it appears as though she lied. Her lawyer countered with this offer. I sent back a counter-offer, with an addendum to protect the land from being developed, but she refused it."

"But why would Ethan and Chelsea sign this? It's bullshit."

Speeler's face flashed in her mind, twisted in annoyance. "Because, Ms. Alvarez, you left them no choice. They can't fight this without you. Even with you, there was a ninety percent chance they'd get nothing. This way, Ethan is guaranteed his pond, and Chelsea gets something. Anne had them bent over a barrel."

Natalie squeezed her eyes shut. "Is she going to give the house to Emily at least?"

Speeler snorted. "Emily knows nothing about this. Anne is already in contact with a developer that she knows from her time in office. They're going to offer a quick closing, and Anne is going to walk away with millions."

Natalie's head shook. "I don't understand why she'd do this."

"She isn't who you think she is. Look, I may over-step my role here, but Elizabeth told me all about your history when she changed the original will ten years ago. You were ashamed of your mother . . ."

Natalie was ready to hang up the phone. "I can't listen to this—"

"But Anne isn't a victim. She's manipulative. Eliza-beth once described her as 'emotionally violent.'"

Emotionally violent.

Natalie let out a breath. "What about the Mon-roes?"

"Victor's lawyers have been quiet. So far . . ."

She didn't like the idea that Anne had manipulated her. But it was hard to deny that was the case. She'd stayed in Mapleton because the thought of leaving made her want to cry. When she unpacked her suit-case into her dresser, she'd had an overwhelming sense of relief. But speaking with Anne had pro-pelled her into a full-blown panic attack, and she'd fled Mapleton faster than a jet-fuelled cheetah .

She wanted to leave Mapleton because of Anne. But then she met Ethan. The memories of him left a weight resting on her lungs. She hated leaving him, hated feeling alone. Especially now that she'd had a taste of the alternative. She'd justified it when Ethan and Chelsea were both going to get what they wanted. But now . . .

Her throat closed, and she swallowed. "I can't sign that. I won't do that to them."

"Good."

"But I can't go back there. At least, not like before."

"I'm afraid I'm not following you. Are you coming back or not?"

Natalie looked around her empty hotel room, at her suitcase on the rack, at the empty bathroom counter. She closed her eyes and remembered the laughter around Ethan's parents' dinner table, and the weight lifted off her chest a little. Maybe she *was* homesick. Maybe Jess was right, and Ethan was her home. She wanted Ethan permanently, and she also wanted all the things they talked about: a bathroom, a warm pair of slippers, a couch, a fuzzy blanket.

Once she allowed herself to picture a home with Ethan, she craved it. More than she wanted to travel Australia. More than she wanted to avoid Anne. More than anything.

"Yes," she said and couldn't believe the conviction in her voice. But she smiled anyway. "I'm moving back to Mapleton. But I need to deal with Anne. And I think I might know how."

"I'm all ears, Ms. Alvarez."

"Here's what I'm thinking . . ."

TWENTY-ONE

Lindsay parked in front of Adam's house, then turned in her seat to face Ethan. He'd planned to let her speak and get this over with. But as soon as she began, a million thoughts came to mind.

"Ethan—"

"It was really shitty, what you did to me. I never would have cheated on you."

"I know," she said, her dainty face a mask of remorse. "I'm so sorry, Ethan. Derek and I . . . we dated in high school, and I was heartbroken when he left. I always thought he was the one, you know? When he moved back, I was already dating you, but he told me he wanted to get back together. I was stupid enough to think he cared about me. But he's actually a huge asshole. I guess I just didn't see it."

Ethan thought about Natalie's opinion of him. "I'm told he was deplorable back then as well."

"I know that now." She wrung her hands in her lap. "I really wish you'd said something when you caught me."

"I thought about it, but I didn't think it would make a difference. It would've just given people more to gossip about. I wanted us both to save face. It was a solid plan until you brought him to Amy's wedding."

"That was mostly his idea, but I was angry with you and went along with it. I thought things were good with us."

Ethan stared at her, eyes wide. "You thought things were good? You cheated on me."

"But I loved you, Ethan. I just made a mistake with Derek. I thought we had something special."

Ethan cringed, then shook his head. He hated conversations like this. But he took a deep breath and finally faced it.

"I'm sorry, Lindsay. We didn't have something special," he said. "We have nothing in common, and I always got the sense that you wished I was different."

He hadn't known how bad things were with Lindsay until he'd been with Natalie. Maybe one day, she'd find genuine love, and then she'd understand.

"You won't find anyone who likes snakes, Ethan."

He laughed. "I know that. But it's not about snakes or hobbies. It's . . . fundamental. Like acceptance and understanding. It's hard to explain."

Lindsay nodded. "Do you think we could try again?"

He was depressed enough about his prospects to say yes. The loneliness was tough, and it didn't help that the girl of his dreams had fled the country like a wanted criminal. But he wasn't about to repeat his mistakes. He needed to learn from them, move forward. No one's perfect, but some people are so glaringly wrong for you, it's impossible to ignore.

He slowly shook his head. "I don't see a point, Lindsay. I'm sorry. It would just never be right."

Lindsay sighed. "Is it because of Natalie Monroe?"

"It's Alvarez," he said, smiling to himself. "I guess it is about Natalie, partially, at least. But it's more about what she made me realize. I should have told you right from the beginning that it wouldn't work between us. I should have faced it, instead of pretending it didn't happen under the guise of taking the high road."

Lindsay nodded. "Can we be friends? It's going to be impossible to avoid each other."

He nodded, unbuckled his belt. "Sure. I'll see you around, Lindsay."

She tipped her head down. "Bye, Ethan."

He stepped out of the car and closed the door. Lindsay gave a half smile and a wave, then drove off down Adam's driveway and disappeared. He stood for a long time outside, staring at his truck. It was like the embodiment of all his stupid choices.

And you kept this truck?!

He smiled at Natalie's words. He hated driving around in a constant reminder that his ex-girlfriend slept with another guy, but he'd patted himself on the back for making a wise decision. He was now coming to realize that sometimes wise decisions were actually incredibly stupid.

And it wasn't just the truck. He'd avoided getting close to Natalie the whole time she was there thinking it was smart, but if he'd given his heart to her sooner, maybe she wouldn't have left so fast.

He'd probably never know, and it was better not to dwell on his missteps. As crushing as it was that she was gone, he couldn't do anything about it. But he could do something about the truck.

"What are you thinking?"

Ethan's heart stopped. His hands shot up, and he turned, ready to attack. Then came eye to eye with Adam, standing close behind him, quiet as a wolf.

After a moment, his heart drummed up a beat, and he dropped his fists. "Where the hell did you come from?!"

"I followed you back here to make sure you didn't do anything stupid."

Ethan shook his head. "I wouldn't do anything stupid."

"I don't know. You've been a mess. Three weeks pretending you don't exist has primed you to make a terrible decision."

Ethan laughed. "Actually, I believe it's brought me a lot of clarity." He stretched his arm over Adam's shoulders and squeezed. "You're a good friend, Adam."

"Yeah, just returning the favour," he said.

They exchanged a knowing look before Ethan's gaze moved back to his truck and settled there.

"Want to go in?" Adam asked. "Get a decent beer? I'll even give you back the remote."

Ethan nodded. "Yes, to the beer. But forget the remote. I need your help with something."

"Name it."

"I'm going to sell the truck."

Adam's arms shot out in victory, and he tipped his face up to the heavens. "Finally!"

Ethan laughed. "Come on."

TWENTY-TWO

Natalie made her way down the crowded Toronto street, dragging her suitcase like a dead weight behind her. She passed a homeless encampment and several questionable characters until she finally arrived at the address Speeler had given her. She pulled out her phone and checked the address—twice—then let out a sigh.

She'd never been there before, but it was a familiar sight.

The building was five-storeys high and dilapidated. It had rusty bars covering the ground-floor windows, a broken front door, and every visible window had sheets or flags for curtains. With a glance at the broken keypad on the wall, she pushed the unhinged door open and walked in.

The smell hit her first, a mix of mould and stale cigarettes that flooded her mind with memories.

She took in the brownish-gray walls, which had likely once been white, and the crusty geometric carpet and was transported back to the apartment she'd been living in across town when Elizabeth had picked her up to take her to Mapleton.

She passed the elevator, knowing better than to trust it, went to the stairwell, and climbed to the fourth floor. By the time she made it down the dark, damp hall to Chelsea's front door, she felt sick to her stomach with guilt.

This was what Elizabeth had been trying to help Chelsea out of. She probably worried that Ben would grow up the way Natalie had and wanted to do something about it. And instead of helping, Natalie had let Anne scare her off. She steadied herself and knocked.

Time to face it. Make it right.

Soft footsteps slapped the floor on the other side of the door. And disappeared. She knocked again, this time louder. But no more signs of life came from inside the apartment.

"Chelsea!" she yelled, knocking again. "Open up!"

Nothing.

She was about to pound on the door and yell when she heard a faint, "Go away."

"I'm not leaving."

When no response came, she banged harder.

"Open up. I'll stay here all night, knocking. I've got nowhere to be."

A few seconds later, footsteps were followed by the unlocking of several locks, and finally, the door swung open, and Chelsea stood there, wearing a black sports bra with high-waisted, wide-leg patchwork plaid pants.

Natalie looked her up and down, then shook her head. "How do you pull off all these outfits?"

Chelsea's eyes narrowed. "It's called being poor. I wear thrift store clothes and act confident enough to make it work. What do you want?"

Natalie cleared her throat. "You always look beautiful. I want to come in and apologize."

"I'm busy," she said. "Working late."

"Please, Chelsea. I know the way I left was really immature."

"And you just realized that now? It took you three weeks to see how ghosting your family with a fucking note was wrong? Do you know how hard it was to tell Ben you'd left? He cried."

Natalie squeezed her eyes shut. "I thought I was doing the right thing. I'm so sorry. I—"

"Hey!" someone yelled from down the hall. "Shut up!"

Natalie looked over at a middle-aged lady with two yappy little dogs barking at her feet. She cocked a brow and gave a pointed look at the dogs. "You're making a lot more noise than us, lady."

"You're not shutting up!"

Natalie's blood boiled. She'd spent so much time with cheerful people on vacation that she'd forgotten what it was like to live next door to miserable assholes. She had a lot of anger pent up, mostly at herself and Anne, but if someone was going to step in and make themselves an outlet for it, by all means.

"Fuck off back inside," she said, taking a step toward the woman and shooing her away. "And take yip and yap with you."

The lady gasped, then backed into her apartment, and slammed the door. Man, did that feel good.

Natalie turned back to Chelsea with a smile. "Maybe you should let me in before I swear at all your neighbours."

"You're in a feisty mood."

Natalie shrugged. "I've reached my breaking point. I'm sick of people and their crap."

"In that case, maybe I'll leave you out there. Ralph in 4D is bound to show up and start harassing you. He's a real slimy little turd."

"Chelsea . . ."

Chelsea rolled her eyes. "Fine," she said, stepping aside. Once Natalie pulled her suitcase in, Chelsea set about relocking all six locks on the door.

Natalie took off her sandals, pushed her suitcase against the wall, and looked around. It was a tiny one-bedroom apartment, with a galley kitchen that had a table for two, a living room that had a single bed pushed up next to the couch, and a small bathroom.

"Where's Ben?"

"Asleep in his bedroom. It's eleven at night."

"Right. I'm on Sydney time. Just landed. Do you sleep there?" she asked, pointing at the bed.

Chelsea nodded, walked over to a desk in the corner and sat down. There were three computer monitors and several other pieces of equipment that Natalie didn't know the name of in front of her. She clicked a few things until her screen saver of Ben on the beach appeared, then she spun in the chair to face Natalie.

"Why are you here?"

Natalie walked to the two-seater couch and sat. "I saw Anne's offer, and it really pissed me off. I refused to sign it."

Chelsea rolled her eyes. "Great. So now it's going to drag out even longer?"

"No. I'm back now, and I think I have a way we can all get what we want. Well . . . almost all of us. Speeler's putting it together right now, but I need you on board."

Chelsea narrowed her eyes. "You're back?"

"Yes. For good this time," she said with a nod. A smile cracked through the anger. "I'm moving to Mapleton."

"I don't believe you."

"I figured you wouldn't, and I can't blame you." She stood from the couch, paced the tiny room, which only allowed her to walk three steps in each direction. "I acted like a total asshole."

"I don't get why, though. You said you were going to stay for two weeks."

"I guess I just didn't realize that things had changed so much for me. I've never had a great home—even when my mom was alive. Being away from family isn't something I've had to face before. I thought I was doing the right thing."

She sank back down onto the couch, her shoulders slumping forward. The anger left, and she just felt sad. "I missed you and Ben. I missed Ethan," she said, dropping her head into her hands. "God, I even missed Mapleton."

Chelsea nodded. "Welp, I don't want to say I told you so, but . . ."

"Go ahead. You were so right," she said.

"Mapleton is pretty great," Chelsea said with a sigh.

Natalie looked up at her. "I'm so sorry, Chelsea. I want to make this right. Do you still want to live in the manor?"

Chelsea looked around. "Yes, I do. I never thought I'd end up in a dump like this."

"I grew up in a dump like this. I don't want that for Ben."

"Me either. You haven't even seen the school."

"It's probably just like the one I went to."

Tears sprang into Chelsea's eyes. Natalie closed the distance, pulled Chelsea into a hug.

"It's going to be okay. Elizabeth wanted to help you, and I'm going to make sure it happens. I swear, I'm not leaving again."

"What if Ethan doesn't forgive you?" she asked.

Natalie bit the inside of her cheek. She'd thought about this long and hard over the twenty-three-hour flight. She knew Ethan shouldn't forgive her. What she did to him was probably worse than what Lindsay had done. But she was going to ask for forgiveness anyway, and hope.

"If he doesn't want me, I won't blame him. But I'm not leaving. I'm trying this new thing where I ignore my flight response and let the fight happen."

"Even with Anne?"

Natalie laughed. "Especially with Anne."

Chelsea blinked her tears away and smiled. "I hope you know what you're doing. Let's hear the plan."

Natalie could feel her face break into a fiendish smile.

"Here's what we're going to do . . ."

· · • •· • • • ·

Natalie sat in a small room at Speeler's office, down the hall from the conference room where they were going to meet with Anne, Emily, and Victor Monroe. Next to her sat Chelsea, nervously chewing on her thumbnail and bouncing her knee. When they heard Anne's voice pass by their door, Chelsea stood and paced.

"You need to relax. Everything is going to be fine."

Chelsea rounded on Natalie. "I have a lot riding on this. Maybe I should have just taken the five hundred grand."

Natalie stood, took Chelsea by the shoulders. "Listen to me. You can't act like this in front of Anne. She can smell fear. If she thinks she has the upper hand, she won't yield."

Chelsea flopped down in the seat. "God, I hate her so much!"

"Me too. But don't think about that. Just . . . try to play it cool. You've seen actors in negotiations, right?"

Chelsea nodded, then sat up straight in her seat, leaned back at an angle, and narrowed her eyes. "Like this?"

Natalie smiled. Chelsea had worn her "interview outfit": a silky blue blouse tucked into a purple-and-blue tweed skirt with black polka-dot nylons and white ankle boots. She kicked a foot out, crossed her legs, and lifted a brow.

"Perfect."

A knock on the door grabbed their attention. Speeler's assistant opened the door. "They're ready for you."

Chelsea stood, looking like a completely different person. She held her purse by the handles and squared her shoulders. "Showtime."

Natalie wiped the smile off her face as they followed the assistant down the hall. The moment they walked in the room, all chatter ended, and every pair of eyes swung their way.

But one set of dark-blue eyes was notably missing.

Natalie shook off her disappointment and took in the faces around the table. Victor sat next to his lawyer, stone faced and silent with a glare that seemed to come easily to him. Anne was across from him with her own lawyer and a vicious scowl on her elegant features. And Emily sat alone, closest to the door, looking like a bunny waiting to make a run for it at the first sign of a hungry wolf.

Natalie walked directly to her first, put out her hand. "You must be Emily. I'm your sister, Natalie."

Emily's jaw dropped, and her eyes shot to Anne, who looked away. She turned back and shook Natalie's hand silently.

"And this is Chelsea, our other sister."

"Hi," Emily finally said. Her brows knitted together as she shook Chelsea's hand, then she ducked her head away.

Natalie made her way into the room, nodding at Victor as she passed by, then at Anne. She took the empty chair at the head of the table and sat. Chelsea sat next to her, then leaned back, crossed her legs, and glared, just as rehearsed.

"Are we still waiting on Ethan?" Natalie asked Speeler.

"No. I didn't invite him to attend. This seems like a family matter."

Natalie nodded as she consciously made sure her features were neutral.

"Get on with it, Speeler," Anne spat. Her lawyer rested his hand on her forearm, and she sat back.

"My clients have an offer for you," Speeler said, looking at Emily.

Emily raised a finger to point at her chest, as if to ask whether he really meant her. Speeler nodded.

"We already have an offer they all accepted," Anne said. "What the hell is this all about?"

Natalie cleared her throat. She'd been worried she'd get nervous near Anne in the meeting, but she was way too angry to care what Anne thought. "We *had* an offer that was agreeable, but that is no longer the case."

"She signed it," Anne said, jerking a thumb at Chelsea. "So did Ethan Pierce. It was a done deal."

"I didn't sign it. And I won't. Consider that entire offer void."

Anne seethed for a split second, then tried to change tactics. She drew her brows together and tipped her chin down, trying to make herself look like an abused little orphan. "You just want more money?"

Natalie shook her head, then looked to Speeler.

He opened the folder in front of him and took out four copies of a document. He stood and passed them out to Natalie, Chelsea, Victor, and Emily, then passed by Anne and sat back in his seat.

"Where's mine?" Anne asked, her victim charade faltering.

"This offer doesn't involve you. My clients are no longer interested in selling the property, and they are prepared to fight your contest in court."

"Then what is this all about?" she asked, gesturing to the paper in Emily's hand.

"We'd prefer to settle now, so we can all move on from this. Elizabeth wouldn't have wanted her family fighting."

He waited silently for everyone to read through the document. Natalie watched Victor and Emily closely. She could tell the exact moment when they had got to the point.

Victor's eyebrows rose fractionally, then he passed the document to his lawyer without a word.

Emily gasped, looking up with eyes the size of bus tires. "You're including me in the inheritance?" she asked.

"What?!" Anne reached out and snatched the paper from Emily's hands, scanned it quickly, and handed it to her lawyer.

"That's correct, Ms. Monroe. My clients are prepared to sever the land they have inherited into three lots. The lot with the manor will be Ms. Davenport's, the lot to the west of the manor with the waterfall will be Ms. Alvarez's, and the remaining lot to the east of the manor will be deeded to you."

"But why?" Emily asked.

"Because they believe it is fairer this way. You were a granddaughter of Elizabeth, so you, too, should inherit some of the property."

Emily shook her head. "I wasn't . . . I mean, I'm not . . ."

Victor's eyes narrowed in on Emily, and he leaned forward with interest.

"Is this not agreeable, Ms. Monroe?" Speeler asked

"Well, yes. I mean, it would be great to own land. But . . ." She took a breath to steady herself. "I'm not —"

"Emily!" Anne snapped, cutting her off. "Quiet." She turned to address the rest of them. "She won't accept this. You're clearly using her as a pawn to get in my way. You think I won't contest the will if Emily gets part of the inheritance. I'm not naive. I'll see you all in court."

She stood and reached for Emily, but Victor's voice stopped her in her tracks.

"You're not what, Emily?" he asked in a bitter voice.

Emily withered.

She glanced at her mother, then back at Victor, then closed her eyes, and took a deep breath. She was just about to speak when Anne grabbed her arm and started pulling her out of her chair. "We're leaving."

"I knew it," Victor said.

Anne and Victor locked into a terrifying staring match, as Emily started gibbering in panic.

"What the hell is going on?" Natalie asked. She looked at Chelsea, who shrugged and turned back to watch the drama unfold.

Emily's eyes dropped. "Elizabeth wasn't my grandmother," she said. She looked at Natalie and Chelsea. "I thought you knew."

Natalie gaped at her as the words and all their implications sank in. If Emily wasn't Elizabeth's granddaughter, then she wasn't Robert's daughter, which meant Anne cheated on Robert.

"Shut up, Emily! She's lying," Anne said.

"No, mother," Emily said, squaring her shoulders. "I won't keep doing this."

"Who?" Victor asked Anne.

She shook her head.

"Andrew?" he asked, looking between Anne and Emily.

Andrew . . .

Natalie scoured her brain for the familiar name. She'd met an Andrew at the manor one day when he came to collect his inheritance.

"The tomato seed guy?" Natalie asked.

"Tomato seed guy?" Chelsea repeated. She looked clueless.

Emily nodded. "Yes," she said, silencing them. "Andrew, the tomato seed guy, is my father. Harold is my grandfather."

Anne dropped into her seat, rubbed her eyes with her fingers as Victor stared her down with a murderous look.

They all sat in silence for a moment before Chelsea broke it.

"Who the hell is Andrew?!"

Natalie leaned over toward her. "Harold Monroe is Victor's brother, Elizabeth's brother-in-law, so that means that Anne was sleeping with her husband's cousin."

Chelsea gasped the way a person watching a daytime soap that left on a cliffhanger would. With a cringey smile, she said, "Ew."

Natalie nodded. "She's falling off a pretty high horse. Hope she doesn't break her nose."

Anne sneered at Natalie. "No one can prove any of this. I was a devoted wife to Robert."

Victor rolled his eyes. "Cut the bullshit, Anne. We all knew. You and Andrew have never been discreet. Besides, Emily looks just like him. She acts like him, too. Gentle. Not like these two," he said, tilting his head to indicate Natalie and Chelsea. "Anyone could see they are Robert's daughters."

Natalie would have been offended, but her mind was spinning.

What now?

"So," Chelsea started, looking at Emily. "That makes you our . . . cousin?"

Emily nodded.

Speeler cleared his throat. "Could we please have the room for a moment? I'd like to discuss these . . . revelations with my clients."

He waited for the door to close behind the last person before speaking.

"Would you like to continue with this offer?" he asked. "Considering this new information, Anne's play for the property would never stand up in court. You could fight her over it and keep things the way Elizabeth intended."

"I want this over with," Natalie said. She was ready, now more than ever, to call her piece of land home. She didn't want to walk out of there without things fully resolved.

Chelsea nodded. "I need a home and a school for Ben. And I have a career to get off the ground. I can't be fighting court battles with fucking Anne."

"So you still want to offer Emily a third of the property?"

"Yes. As long as she agrees to the terms."

Speeler nodded, then a grave look took over his features. "Ms. Davenport, I feel compelled to ask. Are you certain you want to take on this property? The taxes alone are quite substantial, even after a severance. Not to mention the upkeep of grounds that size and the maintenance on a house that old."

Chelsea sighed. "The timing isn't ideal, but I love that house. It's going to be a bit of a struggle right now, but I already know how to make it work."

"Okay." He walked to the door, opened it, and invited everyone back in.

To Natalie's shock, Anne was still there.

"Ms. Monroe," Speeler said. "The offer stands. If you agree to change the land zoning and not build more than one dwelling, the property is yours."

Emily's face contorted. She looked at Natalie and Chelsea. "Are you only doing this to stop my mother from contesting?"

Natalie nodded before Speeler could say something diplomatic, and it earned her a glare from him, but she didn't care. No sense in lying now. "Primarily, yes. But also because the taxes on the property are ridiculously high, and severing the land lessens our share."

Emily blinked. Then smiled. "Are you always this direct?"

Natalie laughed. "Yes. When I'm not being bullied by your mother."

"You think I'm bullying you?" Anne spat. "Your mother ruined my life. She knew Robert was married, and she didn't care!"

Natalie stared at Anne, the woman who'd caused her so much heartache and guilt. "You know, Anne, I've always hated that my mother stayed in a relationship with Robert after finding out he was married. I was on your side. I wanted to leave Mapleton because I didn't want to cause you more pain. But I'm not my mother, and my actions today can't change things that happened in the past, and I'm not to blame for any of those things. If you want to blame someone, blame Robert ."

"You don't have to be here, throwing it in my face though, do you?"

Chelsea's face reddened. "You hypocritical old bi—"

"Chelsea," Natalie said, putting a hand on Chelsea's shoulder to stop her. "It's okay. Look, Anne, you can't pretend and manipulate and coerce your way out of this. It happened. You need to deal with it. Emily," she said, getting everyone's attention. "You in or not?"

Emily looked at her cousins before sparing her mother the briefest of glances.

"Don't you dare sign any—"

"I'm in."

"Excellent, Ms. Monroe," Speeler said, handing her his pen. "Is this agreeable, Mr. Monroe?"

Victor looked at his lawyer, who nodded. "Yes."

"Good," he said, turning his focus on Anne and her lawyer, who watched in horror as Emily flipped through the pages of Speeler's document, signing each one. "Will I be hearing from you again?" he asked.

Anne spun on her heel and stomped off out of the room. Her lawyer followed.

When Emily finished signing, she passed the papers and pen to Victor , who signed off that the matter would be closed from his end as well.

"Do you live with your mom?" Chelsea asked.

Emily nodded.

"You can always stay at the manor if you need to."

"That's very nice, thanks. I may end up on your doorstep at some point," she said with a laugh.

"Anytime," Chelsea said. "But I should warn you, I have a four-year-old who is very busy and loud."

Emily smiled briefly, but it dropped. "We'll see what happens."

Victor finished up signing. He slid the papers to Natalie but didn't pass her the pen.

"You happy?"

Natalie tipped up her chin. "Almost."

"What now?"

"I don't think that's any of your business," she said.

"Do you have work here?"

"Why?"

"I value a cool-headed and tough negotiator. Perhaps you'd be interested in joining the family business? I know your grandfather wouldn't have hesitated to offer you a position in the company. He would have wanted me to do the same."

Natalie stared at him with her mouth open . "Uh, thank you, but no. I have something lined up already."

Victor nodded. "Very well. If you change your mind, call me."

He shook Speeler's hand and walked out the door with his lawyer in tow.

"Oh my God," Chelsea said. "That is the most terrifying person I have ever met."

Emily laughed. "He has a shih-tzu named Primy that he sleeps with, and he watches Hallmark Christmas movies. All year round."

Shaking her head and laughing, Natalie scrawled her signature on all the lines and passed the papers to Chelsea to do the same.

When the last signature was inked, Chelsea threw open her arms and pulled Natalie into a hug.

"Oh my God! I'm a homeowner!"

Natalie laughed. "And we're neighbours."

Chelsea jumped up and down, doing a little clap. "What now? Are you going to go find Ethan?"

Natalie let out a deep breath. "There's something I need to do first."

"What could you possibly need to do?"

Natalie picked up her purse and started for the door. "I need to go shopping."

Twenty-Three

E than lounged back in his parents' deep sectional with a bottle of Tipped Canoe stout in one hand, his phone in the other, and a smile on his face. He was listening to Amy and Jaclyn recount the adventures they'd had on their three-week island-hopping honeymoon in the Caribbean. The moment they'd mentioned petting pigs on the powdery white-sand beaches of the Bahamas, he'd pulled out his phone and, in a moment of uncharacteristic spontaneity, booked a trip to Costa Rica for the week after Thanksgiving.

It had been years since he'd gone on a vacation purely for enjoyment and relaxation, and he was determined to make his life more fun ever since Natalie had left.

Jaclyn sat on the floor in front of the coffee table where his mom had just placed a platter of butter tarts. He slipped his phone into his pocket and reached for one.

"Remember the catamaran tour to those caves in Aruba, Ames?" Jaclyn said around a mouthful of pastry.

Amy nodded. "It was so cool. Ethan, you would love it."

"I'm going to Costa Rica," he said, then took a swig of his beer.

"Really?"

"Yeah. I just decided."

"Okay. I'll text you the name of the travel agent we used," Amy said.

"No. I just booked it. Now, on my phone. While you were describing the pigs."

All eyes around the room widened and stared at him.

"Are you going alone?" his mom asked .

Ethan shrugged, took another drink. "Yeah. Why not?"

She looked at his dad, who looked at Jaclyn, who looked at Amy.

Amy squared her shoulders and zeroed her attention in on him. "You've been a little . . . erratic since we saw you last. Are you sure you're okay with everything that happened? With Lindsay and Natalie?"

Ethan nodded. "Everything with Lindsay is re-solved. And Natalie has moved on, just as she said she would. And I . . . I'm trying to live my life differ-ently than I used to. Why shouldn't I go on vacation?"

"You should," said his father. "It's just a lot of changes in a short amount of time. You sold your truck, hired a real estate agent to sell your house, now this?"

Ethan looked at his family. An equal amount of love and annoyance overcame him as he took in their worried faces. "These are things I should have done all along. Life is meant to be lived!"

"Oh God," Amy said, taken aback. "Now he's talking like Adam."

Ethan rolled his eyes. "I've just learned that you can't always make the most practical decisions. Sometimes, you just have to do what feels right. Even if it's wrong."

His father shrugged as Jaclyn and his mother nod-ded. But Amy was frowning.

"I think you were in love with Natalie, and she left, and now you've gone off the deep end—"

Ethan's phone rang in his pocket with Adam's ring-tone, and he leaped off the couch. "Sorry Ames, I gotta take this."

"No, you don't! It's just Adam."

"Hello?" Ethan said, answering and walking out of the room to the kitchen. Luckily, Amy didn't follow.

"Hey. Where are you?" he asked with an urgency that made Ethan's fists twitch.

"My parents', why? What's wrong?"

"Are you with Natalie?"

It took a moment for the question to sink in. But hearing the question correctly didn't mean he actually understood it. "Huh?"

"Natalie. Have you seen her?"

"How would I have seen her? I'm here."

"Yeah, so is she! Why the fuck haven't you got an Instagram account yet? Ninety-five percent of your problems could be solved with an Instagram account."

Ethan shook his head, trying to clear the confusion. "Start over, Adam."

"Natalie is back in Mapleton. She just posted a bunch of pictures to her Instagram Stories of her—"

"I gotta go," Ethan said, then hung up on Adam.

He stared at the phone in his hand for a minute. If she was back, why hadn't she called him, or texted him, or stopped by? Maybe she didn't want to see him. Maybe she thought he wouldn't want to see her.

He didn't know.

But he wasn't about to sit there wondering any longer.

He walked back into the living room. "Sorry, I gotta go."

"Is something wrong? Is Adam okay?" his mom asked.

"Yeah, he's fine."

"Then what is so important that you're going to miss the first viewing of my wedding video?" Amy asked.

"Natalie is back."

Without waiting for a reaction, he threw on his shoes at the front door and jogged out to his brand new hybrid Jeep parked in the driveway. He was finally getting a second chance to tell Natalie how he felt, and he was going to take it, even if she was only in town temporarily. Even if he had to scream it at her. Dithering back and forth endlessly analyzing the possibilities and outcomes of every decision was a thing of the past.

He was going to tell her he loved her.

Now.

· · · ● · ● · · ·

Ethan pulled his Jeep up to the front of Monroe Manor, turned it off, and sprinted to the front door. He knocked. Waited. Knocked again.

Chelsea's car was in the driveway, which meant she must be there. He'd been told that Chelsea had moved out when Natalie left, and his brain started drowning in questions, but he set them aside and focused on the task.

He wiggled the door handle, but it was locked, so he knocked again.

Finally, the door swung open, revealing Chelsea and Ben standing together in the foyer, clothes covered in orange paint. Mi and Mi appeared right after, following on their heels and weaving around Ben's little legs.

"Ethan!" Chelsea said, her eyes going wide. "Hey, how—"

"Hey," he said, rudely cutting her off. He didn't have time for pleasantries. "Is Natalie here?"

"No," she said, looking confused.

He stepped back as if someone had kicked him in the stomach. He knew it was too good to be true. Adam probably read the wrong—

"She went to see you," Chelsea said.

"She did?" he asked. Chelsea smiled and nodded.

"I haven't been home all day. I must have missed her. Maybe I can still catch up to her," he said, turning to go back to his Jeep.

"No," Chelsea said. "She didn't go to your house. She went to your pond."

Ethan stopped and turned, his brain refusing to absorb her words. "My pond?"

"Yeah, she said you're usually out there on Saturdays. She left about twenty minutes ago."

"To my pond? My pond?"

Chelsea nodded.

"She went to your pond!" Ben yelled. "Can't he hear us, Mama?"

Ethan turned without another word and walked off the porch. He was in a daze as he walked through the clearing of trees and into the forest toward his pond. He was still unsure whether Chelsea knew where Natalie was. She'd sworn up and down that she'd never go to the pond. It all sounded like a lie. But just in case she was there in sandals, bitten, or hitting the snakes with her stick, he kicked up his pace to a jog. When he made it to the spot where the trees opened to a clearing, the pond came into view. He scanned the area but didn't see her.

Too good to be true.

He walked closer, slower now, and that's when he finally saw her.

The tall grasses that were swaying in the light breeze shrouded her. She was sitting on the ground right at the water's edge with her back to him and her soft hair shining in the sunlight. Every thought and worry fell from his mind. He walked closer until she flinched and spun around, meeting his eyes. He froze in place, as if even a flicker of movement would scare her off like a doe. Make her run again.

But she didn't run. She smiled.

She stood from the ground, her eyes not leaving his. The setting sun streaked the sky with purple and backlit her, creating a bright glow around the edges of her hair. He wondered if he was hallucinating.

"Hi, Ethan."

It wasn't until he heard her voice that his brain allowed him to accept she was really there, standing in front of him.

"Hi."

Her smile grew, and she used her hand to gesture at the pond. "It's really beautiful here. The flowers and the grasses. I should have—"

"I love you."

Her eyes went wide, and her lips parted. But he didn't care.

"I should've told you the morning you let Mi out of his cage. I knew then."

She stood in shock for a long moment. Then she smiled.

"I don't know why you're here, or how long you're staying, but I wanted you to know that before you disappear on me again."

Her smile grew, and it gave him a glimmer of hope. "I'm sorry I left the way I did."

Ethan's shoulders relaxed. "I don't know when you plan to leave again, but I want you to know that I think you should stay here, with me, forever."

Natalie smiled. "Actually, I'm leaving on Monday."

Ethan shook his head. "Don't go."

Her smile grew, and it set his emotions spinning. He wanted to scream. He opened his mouth to say more, but she spoke, cutting him off.

"I'm going on training for my new tour on Monday. Niagara Falls to Quebec City, then back. I'll be away eight days."

"Eight . . . You're . . . Does that mean you're staying? In Canada?"

She nodded. "And I love you, too. I should have started with that."

"Are you sure? I can't watch you leave again."

She closed the distance between them, reached for him. That was when he realized she was wearing a jacket. And boots. And a scarf.

"You have thick clothes?" he asked.

She laughed. "Yup. I also own bedding, slippers, towels, and that piece of land," she said, pointing in the distance.

He glanced at where she was pointing. "Your waterfall?"

"Yes. It's mine."

Ethan pulled her close, wrapped his arms around her and kissed her. Her warm lips slid over his and took the air from his lungs. Nothing had ever felt more right. When they broke apart, she snuggled into his chest, wrapped her arms around his torso and sighed. Knowing she was staying suddenly wasn't enough. He steeled himself and went for what he really wanted.

"Let's move in together," he said.

"Okay," she said with zero hesitation.

His face split into a ridiculously gleeful grin. He was on a roll. Now that he'd said what he wanted, he couldn't stop.

"I'm going to sell my house. Let's shop for one together."

She pulled back and looked up at his eyes, and for a second, he thought he'd taken it too far. But she smiled.

"You're going to sell your house?"

"Yes. I sold my truck, bought a Jeep, and booked a trip to Costa Rica. Do you want to buy a house with me?"

He held his breath, searching her eyes, hoping.

She narrowed her eyes in thought, then nodded as if to herself. "Why don't we build one near the woods by the waterfall, with a deck and a fireplace and a bathroom?"

With a sigh, he pulled her to him as close as he could and gently kissed the top of her head. "Even better."

EPILOGUE

Natalie's boots crunched over the forest floor as she walked hand in hand with Ethan toward her waterfall. It was late summer and humid, but the sun had yet to rise, so the temperature was still a little cool.

Ethan had woken her up early that morning with coffee already in to-go cups, saying he had a surprise and wanted to visit her waterfall. They'd planned to go to the site of their new home to check where the crew had staked out the area for the foundation. Adam had called the night before and said his crew were set to dig that afternoon. They'd jumped and hugged each other when they heard the news, both beyond excited for the day when their new home would be complete and they could move out of Ethan's house and into their new home together.

"Are you cold?" Ethan asked, giving her hand a little squeeze.

"No," Natalie said with a smile. In fact, her smile hadn't left her since the night before when she'd got in from her tour and gone straight to Ethan's bed. "I'm perfect."

She stopped in front of a huge oak whose branches stretched into the sky endlessly and took a deep inhale of fresh air, then pulled out her phone, and snapped a picture. "Every time I come here, I see something I missed the last time. It's so beautiful."

"I know," he said, tugging her along. "Come on. I have a surprise." He hefted a bag he was carrying up his shoulder and pressed on.

Natalie laughed. He'd said four times that morning that he had a surprise. Did he really think she'd forget? "Why can't you just tell me what's in the bag so we can walk slower?"

"I'm sure you're familiar with the concept of a surprise."

She rolled her eyes and followed him the rest of the way to the river where they made their way along the edge toward the big willow at the base of the falls. The path was narrow, so Natalie followed directly behind Ethan. When they finally made it to a clearing, he stepped aside, and she gasped.

Right beside the enormous old weeping willow was a shiny wooden bench with two throw pillows resting on a small flagstone patio surrounded by bushes. In front of it was a little firepit, and next to that was a covered rack holding dry logs.

"Oh my God, Ethan. Did you make this?"

He took her hand and tugged her toward it. "Yes. Adam helped, though. I thought you'd like to have a place to sit off the ground when you're watching your waterfall."

She reached up on her tippy toes and kissed him before trying her new bench. "It's beautiful. I love it so much."

He smiled and set down the bag. "I'll make us a fire." He took some kindling, newspaper, and matches from the bag, pulled some logs from the stack, and knelt by the pit. In no time, they had a warm fire burning. With the waterfall in the backdrop and the last of the summer flowers brightly blooming, it made for an absolutely stunning picture.

"Thank you, Ethan. It's perfect."

"You haven't even seen the best part yet."

He stood, then came around behind her, unlatched the armrests, and folded the back of the bench down flat. "It converts to a bed. Here." He moved a pillow and helped her lean back. "Now you can look up at the leaves, and you won't get attacked by the snakes."

She lay back and stared up at the soft blue sky in wonder. The hanging green leaves were just ever so slightly showing signs of colouring up gold for the fall. This was, without a doubt, her favourite place on earth. And her favourite person on earth had made it even more perfect for her.

She hadn't imagined she could love him more than she already did, but each day was better than the last. She never wanted it to end.

"Ethan," she said, sitting up from the bench. "I love you so—"

The sight before her stopped her midsentence. Ethan was kneeling on the flagstone in front of her, holding out a blue velvet box.

"Natalie, I love you. I know it's soon, and if you want to wait awhile, that's fine. But I didn't want another day to go by without telling you that I want us to get married."

Natalie stared, shocked, at him and the box. She actually had to order herself to breathe. She'd never imagined he'd do something so . . . rash. "Ethan, are you sure? It's very sudden."

"I have never been more positive about anything in my life. And a sudden decision isn't necessarily a bad decision."

"Don't fools rush in, and all that?"

He shook his head. "Fools, in my experience, sit on the sidelines waiting for the right moment. Wise men can recognize the best thing that's ever happened to them. I'm never going to think marrying you is a bad decision. You're my home. And I'm yours. Marry me, Natalie."

Natalie looked into Ethan's determined blue eyes and felt the full depth of the love she had for him. Marrying him was something she secretly dreamed of, hoped one day would happen. She just never imagined he would ask so soon.

She almost couldn't believe how far she'd come. Only a few months ago, she didn't belong anywhere, and now, she was exactly where she was meant to be. At home. With Ethan. And she couldn't wait for whatever came next.

There wasn't a single doubt in her mind that Ethan would forever be her home. She wanted to spend the next sixty years with him, living with him, holding his hand, hearing his voice, and weathering whatever storms may come, together. And he wanted that, too. So why wait?

She flung her arms around his neck and kissed him, smiling against his lips. "Yes."

"Yes?"

She nodded and laughed. "Yes. I'll marry you right this minute, if you want."

His handsome face split into her favourite crinkly smile as he pulled the diamond ring out and slipped it onto her finger. He took her face in his hands and kissed her. Then he let out a breath and sat down next to her, stretching his long arm around her shoulders as he kissed her temple. "How do you feel about eloping? Niagara Falls?"

She laughed and kissed him again, then snuggled into the side of his warm body.

"Sounds perfect."

THANK YOU!

Thank you so much for reading Fight or Flight. If you enjoyed the book (or even if you didn't) please visit the site where you purchased it and write a brief review. Your feedback is extremely valuable to me.

Also, I'm super excited to share that I am currently working on Adam and Chelsea's story. For updates and sneak peaks, visit dianadeehan.com and subscribe to my newsletter. You can also follow me on Instagram @dianadeehanwrites. (See if you can spot Easter eggs in some of my posts!)

Thanks again,
Diana

ACKNOWLEDGMENTS

The first thank you has to go to my husband who HATES romance novels but feigned interest in mine for years. I'm forever grateful for your love, support, and exceptional feedback. Without you, who knows how many dreadful pumpkin-dirt scenarios might have slipped in?

Thank you to my sons who are super excited that their mom wrote a book, but are too young to understand that it's full of sex. One day, you will be horribly embarrassed by it. I'd say we're even, after all the times I cleaned up your puke in restaurants, friends houses, airplanes...

A huge thank you to my amazing editor Maggie Morris (The Indie Editor) for fixing up my writing and making me look way smarter than I am. I still don't know how to use a semi-colon; Sorry!

Another huge thank you to Ashley Santoro for designing the beautiful cover. I'm a pain in the ass, but you never made me feel that way.

Lastly, thank you to my mom, my sisters, family, friends, and acquaintances who have been so encouraging when I told them I was writing a book. I'm so lucky to have you all in my life.

Manufactured by Amazon.ca
Bolton, ON

32568789R00208